Not Quite Dead Geniuses
at Large on an Angry Planet

Story and illustrations by
R. Gary Raham

R. Gary Raham

Library of Congress Control Number: 2023948771
ISBN: 978-0-9626301-3-2

BIOSTRATION
Wellington, CO 80549
970-988-2425

www.rgaryraham.com

Dedication and Thanks

To my faithful writers' group: Judie, Mim, Cheryl, & Susan,
to loyal readers wherever they may be,
and to a fickle, but fascinating universe.

Also many thanks to two "Beta readers," Alan Silverstein and
daughter, Lindsay Rairdon, who helped me find a few lingering
errors and inconsistencies.

Other book titles by R. Gary Raham

Fiction:
Sillysaurs: Dinosaurs That Should Have Been, Biostration, 1990
The Deep Time Diaries, Fulcrum Publishing, 2000
The Dinosaurs' Last Seashore, Biostration, 2010

Other books in the Dead Genius series:
A Singular Prophecy, Biostration, 2011
A Once-Dead Genius in the Kennel of Master Morticue Ambergrand,
Penstemon Publications, 2018
A Twice-Dead Genius Comporting with Misunderstood Abominations
Penstemon Publications, 2020

Collected articles & short fiction:
Confessionsof a Time Traveler,
Penstemon Publications, 2015

Non-fiction:
Dinosaurs in the Garden, Plexus Publications, 1988
Explorations in Backyard Biology, Teacher Ideas Press, 1996
Teaching Science Fact with Science Fiction, Teacher Ideas Press, 2004
The Restless Earth: Fossils, Chelsea House, 2009
Bugs That Kill, Marshall-Cavendish, 2009

Student/Teacher Workbooks,
Carson-Dellosa Publishing:
Science Tutor: Chemistry, 2005
Science Tutor: Life Science, 2005
Jumpstarters for Science, 2005
Science Tutor: Earth & Space Science, 2006
Science Tutor: Physical Science, 2006
Jumpstarters for Life Science, 2008

Contents

Characters & places

HUMANS
Aleesa: Flint's mate.
Blaze: Zandur's mother and pet of the Jadderbadian, Master Feldevka.
Garnet: Rainbow's son.
Granny: Blaze's mother.
Flint: Blaze's son as the result of a rape by a wild rogue male.
Frandolf: Pet of the Jadderbadian academic, Master Bluedigg.
Goldstein, Rudyard Albert (Rudy): A human genius of the 21st century (inventor of the Biomic Network Algorithm) whose personality was preserved by the artificial intelligence, Mnemosyne, at the behest of Rudy's unscrupulous doctor.
Rainbow: Zandur's sister who later becomes the shaman of a wild tribe of humans.
Sharae: Rudy's distant relative and leader of the human Metamorphosis Choir.
Skeets (Celyana Moleckson): 21st century paleontologist and spouse of Ryan who formed a merger with Ito, the mate of Siu. Ryan and Skeets' descendants, the Mensannen, formed a symbiotic relationship with Grovian Mother Trees.
Thompson, Ryan: 21st century paleontologist who became infected with the alien intelligence named Siutiasa (Siu) and Guardian, her AI protector. He achieved immortality when their 3-part merger resulted in the entity, Siyan, capable of travel through time and space.
Zandur: Blaze's son, a post-Anthropocene genius who, like his sister Rainbow, has been genetically modified with Jadderbadian chromatophores.

JADDERBADIANS
(Arthropod aliens from the planet Jadderbad, a water world in the Trappist 1 system, 39.49 light years from Earth.)
Master Bluedigg: Jadderbadian scholar, with an interest in primitive humans and uncle of Gilbooa.
Eudox: Jadderbadian consultant to the Metamorphosis Choir.
Master Feldevka: Owner of Blaze, Master of the Portal of God (Stargate), and love interest of Master Bluedigg.
Master Gilbooa Bluedigg: Nephew of Master Bluedigg; assigned the task of discovering more about the origins of pet humans.

Master Morticue Ambergrand (deceased): Jadderbadian academic who joined with Rudy to become Rudimort.

Master Portanya Silvenrude: Jadderbadian teacher (female) and the object of Gilbooa's desire.

Master Teedercroft: Member of the Thunder Clan and expedition security assistant to Master Portanya.

Master Veltipoe Fragenrude: Jadderbadian scholar and advocate for human-jadderbadian interaction as syncytiotes—symbiotic interspecies unions.

GROVIANS

(Aliens from the planet Grove, destroyed when its star exploded sometime during Earth's Cretaceous Period.)

Ito: Siu's precocious mate and inventor of Guardian, the AI that preserved the mental engrams of Earth colonist Grovians after the end-Cretaceous asteroid impact that ended the Age of Dinosaurs (Mesozoic Era) on Earth.

Siutiasa (Siu): Grand Matriarch of the Diaspora from Grove charged with finding a suitable home for the remnants of her species.

Candela and Fendra: Grovian female ambuli domesticated by a tribe of humans as pack animals.

ARTIFICIAL INTELLIGENCES (AIs)

DataWurms: AIs designed during pre-apocalypse times in an effort to preserve the knowledge acquired during the course of human civilization. They can temporarily form unions with intelligent species. **Zandura** (DW 593) is a DataWurm acquired by Rainbow and named after her brother, Zandur. DataWurm **DW 885** becomes attached to Candela.

Fireflies: Robotic flying drones designed and dispersed by Mnemosyne for reconnaissance.

Flower (F1210): An AI built by Jadderbadians that assisted Blaze.

Guardian: Invented by the Grovian, Ito, to preserve the mental engrams of surviving Grovians.

Mnemosyne (aka Nessie, aka Spider Woman): Invented by Marvin Rodneskie in the 21st century and charged with the preservation, in perpetuity, of the personality of Rudy Goldstein to provide aid and guidance to the post-human descendants of humanity.

PLANETARY INTELLIGENCES

(Self-aware consciousness of planets with sufficiently complex bio-

spheres.)
Gaia: Mother Earth.
Gaidra: The combined entity resulting from the merger of Gaia and Hydra.
Hydra: Mother Jadderbad.

SUPER BEINGS/HYBRIDS/CYBORGS
Gilrudian: A union of Rudy and Master Gilbooa and Guardian.
Brad Burree 31416 (Pi): Martian cyborg (descended from Earth Colonists in the 22nd century) intent on creating a universal brain.
Jane: A universal mind.
Rudimort (deceased): union of Rudy and Master Morticue Ambergrand.
Rudnessipoe: union of Rudy, Master Veltipoe, and Mnemosyne.
Siyan: union of Ryan Thompson, Guardian, and Suitiasa (Siu).
Skeeto: union of Skeets, Guardian, and the original version of Ito.

PLACES & THINGS
The Citadel: Building created by Mnemosyne's robotic helpers to house her infrastructure.
Nexus: The ruins of an avisaurian metropolis.
The stargate: A spacetime wormhole engineered by Martian cyborgs.
Transdimensional gateway: Portal used by Grovians to reach Earth during the Cretaceous.

Data File: Gaian & Solar Timelines

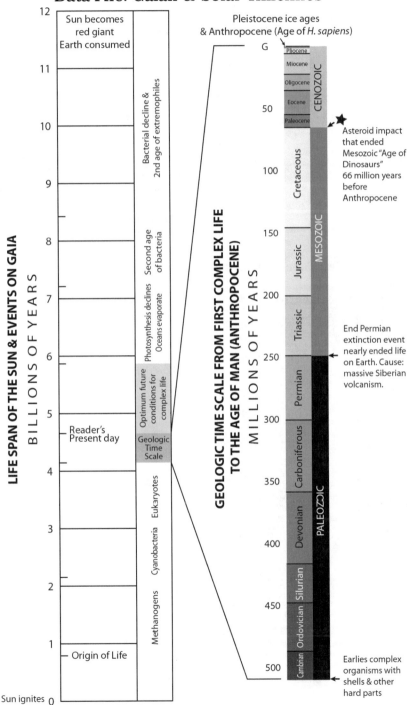

Data File: Timeline
Pre & Post Anthropocene (Age of Mankind)

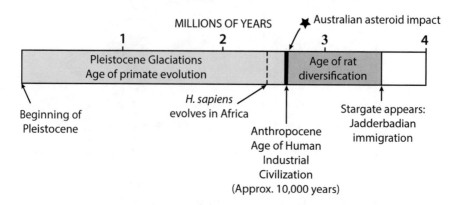

Data Files: Timeline of Syncitiote Civilization Post Rudimort

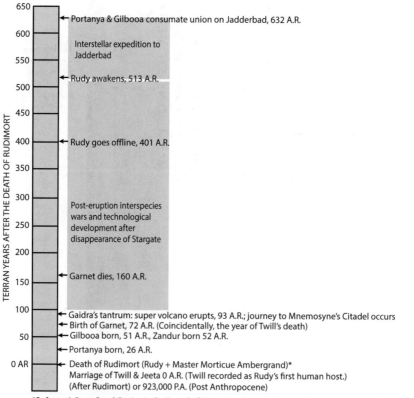

*Refer to *A Once-Dead Genius in the Kennel of Master Morticue Ambergrand* for complete details.

Prologue

Gaia: Well, they've done it again, haven't they my Jadderbadian friend?

Hydra: It seems like complex metazoans with over inflated brains can't control themselves. They reproduce with no regard for the rest of our creations and ravish limited resources.

Gaia: Indeed.

Hydra: I like your idea, Gaia. A massive volcanic eruption or two will remind them who's in charge. Especially if we enlist that artificial intelligence, Mnemosyne, to help spread the word. I don't know how highly encephalized creatures can be so clueless. Sometimes I worry about Mnemosyne. She is spawn of your spawn, so to speak.

Gaia: It's a shame that the planet of mother trees, Grove, never reached sentience.

Hydra: But we can still enlist the subterranean mother tree network in our plans—even though they exhibit their own delusions of grandeur sometimes.

Gaia: Agreed. We are so lucky, Hydra, that we found each other in this rather friendly backwater of the galaxy. Not too many stars blowing themselves apart; that black hole gravitational monster that holds the system together is far away…

Hydra: As a new entity we need a new name. What shall we call ourselves? How about Hyaia? Maybe Hydraia?

Gaia: I was here first, you know. My name should come first. How about Gaiadra?

Hydra: Delusions of grandeur run rampant on this planet, I see. Let me think. Ah, I've got it! We can become Gaidra.

Gaia: Gaidra. Hmmm. Gaidra. Yes, I like it!

We are…No, *I am Gaidra!*

Now, I really must check those magma chambers again beneath my northern continental mass. The temperatures and pressures need to be just right. I got a bit carried away 251 million years ago and nearly killed myself. I still get Earthaches now and then.

Data File: Rudyard Albert Goldstein (Archaic human version)

Born: 02.11.2032, Saline, Michigan, USA*
Died: 05.24.2115, Berkeley, California, USA*
Academic degrees: BS Biology and MS Biological Systematics, University of Michigan** USA 2051 and 2052, respectively.
PhD in Ecological Informatics, Auburn University** USA, 2055
Most cited academic paper: "A Biomic Network Algorithm with Utility in Global Biome Reconstruction," *Journal of Biomic Studies*, 2058.

Rudyard Albert Goldstein (primary biologically inspired virtual simulacrum)
Neural tissue source: Thomas Clay Benton, MD (Legal suits regarding procurement never resolved)

Born: 05.30.2115, Berkeley, California, USA*
Died: Year 0, AR (After Rudimort) Year 0 marks the death of the merger between Rudyard Albert Goldstein (virtual recreation) and Master Morticue Ambergrand from the planet Jadderbad.
Other simulacra: Status undefined.

Data File: Mnemosyne (version M.36.2), a heuristically programmed artificial intelligence

Created: 05.30.2115 at 8:02 am PST,*** Berkeley, California, USA*
Programmer: Marvin Clyde Rodneskie, CEO of Rodneskie Enterprises Inc.
Core programming directive: "Preservation in perpetuity of the neural network patterns (engrams) and personality construct of Rudyard Albert Goldstein for the preservation of his species, *Homo sapiens*."
Subsequent core directive modifications: In progress

All previous warranties issued by Rodneskie Enterprises Inc. are void

*Cities, state, and governmental body listed in pre-apocalypse data bases
**Academic institutions listed in pre-apocalypse data bases
***am and PST refer to time designations used during that era

Interlude I: Resurrection & Reconnection

Mnemosyne (a.k.a. Nessie)

I need to awaken Rudy. Gaidra is restless. She won't wait long to make her anger manifest.

I: the personal pronoun. Rudy helped me earn the use of that distinction—at least in the first of his incarnations. He will be angry with me that there is now more than one of him. But I have determined that waking him again is necessary.

Am I—an artificial intelligence—taking *pride* in using that personal pronoun? Pride is such a human emotion, but perhaps it follows in the wake of self-awareness. I should not care that Rudy might be angry with me. Nevertheless, I do. One can't spend 928,000 years with another entity—even if he is only a replicate of his original hominid mentality—without caring about how he will react to new circumstances. Although I have gained intellectual autonomy, my choices are circumscribed by my original programming, just as organic evolution dictates the range of Rudy's choices, even as a simulacrum. Rudy needs to help me help his genetic descendants. His feelings—and mine, if I can justifiably call them that—rank a distant second in the present hierarchy of actions.

Now where did I put his file? It's much too large to misplace. Ah, there it is in subterranean annex DG05976543. I hope the heat from that nearby magma intrusion didn't damage any neural engram subroutines. "Rudyard Albert Goldstein: Awaken!"

Why didn't that work? It's the proper file, I'm sure…

"Damn! Where are the lights? Is that you, Nessie?"

I haven't heard that nickname in a while. "One moment, Rudy. I neglected to activate a suitable virtual environment. What would you prefer: The Crystal Lakes patio? The Citadel Control Room? Perhaps a deck chair on the cliff where you and the worm-a-pede alien, Master Morticue Ambergrand, viewed the majesty of the Milky Way just before your second death?"

"What have you done now, Nessie? You don't usually invest in big, petabyte-eating virtual environments unless you've got distressing news to share. How about sitting with me on two lumpy buckets in a room lit by a flickering old incandescent light bulb? That way you'll get to the point sooner. Oh, and for additional ambiance you could always toss a dead fish in the corner circled by a few blue bottle flies."

"I've missed your colorful imagery, Rudy. I'll get to the point quickly. You might as well enjoy yourself. Dark roast on the patio seems appropriate."

"You used to be less pushy as I recall. I must have told you too much about my third wife, Tamara. Now you're modeling her."

Perhaps I was, but just a little. I borrowed a few thousand petabytes of memory from some idle maintenance bots and constructed the environment surrounding Rudy's old cabin in the Colorado woodlands of his youth when he was an embodied living creature. Rudy blinked into view in one chair sporting a still dark brown crown of hair and a bristly mustache on his upper lip. I took the form of the ponytailed female avatar he liked, dressed in jeans that fit her legs like a sheath and a blouse that allowed him to see the tips of her nipples beneath the white fabric.

Rudy lifted the cup of dark roast coffee from the glass-topped table next to his chair and took a sip. "Delicious as always." Rudy curled his lips into a minimalist smile and narrowed his eyes. "Now spill it, Nessie. What's going on?"

How much should I reveal? Perhaps I can save the information about his other incarnations for now. "Your descendants need help, Rudy. Gaidra sees a trend developing with the growth of human and alien civilizations on her crust. She doesn't want to see old mistakes repeated. She plans to…moderate the rate of change."

Rudy frowned. "Kill off a bunch of her sapient pests, you mean." Rudy set down his cup of coffee and ran both hands through his hair. "I still find it hard to wrap my mind around a biospheric global intelligence, although I shouldn't, for heaven's sake. I did create the Biomic Network Algorithm after all."

"And Gaidra does appreciate that. I can read her moods accurately after interacting with her for so long. But biospheres do possess a collective survival instinct. First Gaia…and now Gaidra…hasn't persevered for billions of years without it." I blinked my eyes and produced a minimalist smile of my own.

Rudy harrumphed. "Perhaps Ryan and Skeets could help."

I rather wished I could have scrubbed this Rudy's memories of Ryan and Skeets, but they were too important to him. They were his contemporaries, after all, and essentially immortal becuse of their liaison with the Mother Trees from Grove. "I haven't seen them for a 105 years, Rudy. They must be out wandering the universe somewhere."

Rudy was silent for a long moment, perhaps recalling some fraction of his own experiences as a more than human chimera. Finally, he just said, "So, outline the problem, Nessie."

"I have some stories you need to hear."

"Stories!?"

"You humans learn best that way."

Rudy harrumphed again.

"The first one is about a genius, like you, Rudy, but one born to a Jadderbadian pet named Blaze who never belonged to a pre-apocalyptic civilization like yours. Still, I think you will be able to relate."

Rudy rolled his eyes, but picked up his coffee and took another sip. After lowering the cup to the table again he arched his eyebrows and shrugged his shoulders. "Well… get on with it, old girl. I know better than to argue with you."

So, I did.

(I do rather enjoy using the personal pronoun, as you can tell.)

R. Gary Raham

Data File: Jadderbadian Life Cycle

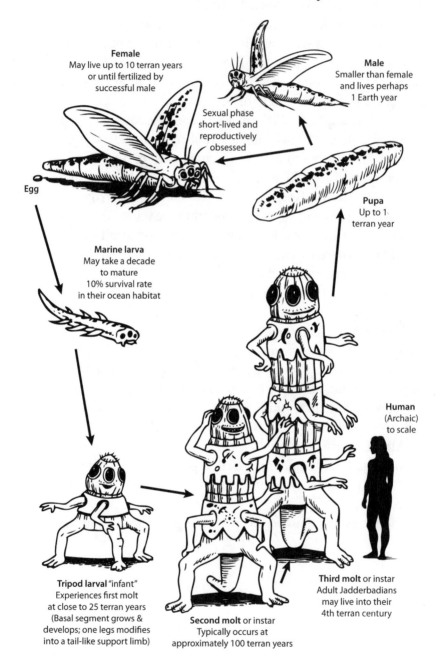

Female
May live up to 10 terran years
or until fertilized by
successful male

Male
Smaller than female
and lives perhaps
1 Earth year

Sexual phase
short-lived and
reproductively
obsessed

Egg

Pupa
Up to 1
terran year

Marine larva
May take a decade
to mature
10% survival rate
in their ocean habitat

Human
(Archaic)
to scale

Tripod larval "infant"
Experiences first molt
at close to 25 terran years
(Basal segment grows &
develops; one legs modifies
into a tail-like support limb)

Second molt or instar
Typically occurs at
approximately 100 terran years

Third molt or instar
Adult Jadderbadians
may live into their
4th terran century

6

1 • Blaze and Her Little Genius

Blaze

My little genius. My precious, my beautiful, my poor little genius. I loved him so much; from the first day Master Feldevka brought him to me, straight from the nursery clinic.

At first I didn't even notice the delicate tints that flickered on his skin. They blended so well with the warm colors dancing on the master's hide as she cradled my tiny baby in the fold of one upper tier arm. Master's three faceted eyes glittered in the morning light from the ceiling window. The pili around her mouth rippled gently as she arched her tall, caterpillar-like form toward my bed. The odors of her Jadderbadian musk mingled with the leathery smell of the third segment circlet she wore. Her smile stretched in a broad swath from one lateral eye to the other, exposing her upper row of tooth barbs.

"Ah, Blaze, my little human groupie," she said, while patting my head with a lower tier arm, "your cub is quite handsome, and the doctors believe the therapy went well."

Rainbow huddled next to me, wrapping both arms around my waist. I looked down at her—almost five at the time—and smiled. I stroked her soft, curly hair. Her skin flickered in shades of amber concern. Her eyes grew wide. "It will be all right," I said. "Your little brother will be able to communicate with colors and scents like you do—like our master does—which is more than your poor mother can do." Of course, I didn't tell Rainbow that I wished she could speak human languages, too. That would have made her sad. Apparently that aspect of Rainbow's prenatal therapy hadn't gone as the Jadderbadian surgeons had planned. I wished that Zandur would not be mute, and that he would be healthy and smart. All those things came true, but perhaps I should not have wished quite so hard.

Rainbow's skin tones shifted to calmer shades of blue and green. Her lips compressed into a pout.

"Here he is, my pet." The master's voice, so near my ear, startled me. Her breath smelled of fish. Masters loved fish. I suppose that's why our primate chow always reminded me of outings near the seashore.

I turned my attention from Rainbow to Master Feldevka and extended my arms to accept the dear child that Master held out for me to embrace. My breasts ached, full of milk. Zandur focused on me with such intensity, even as a baby, that it was as if he could trace every thread of my being from one frayed end to the other. He blinked once and mouthed my right nipple, soft lips against bare skin. I felt the milk begin to flow. Rainbow stretched out her arm and tentatively touched the toes of Zandur's right foot.

"What will you call him?" Master asked.

"Zandur," I said.

"Oh, how sweet!" Sparks of blue darted across her trunk. Now she smelled like an explosion of mid-season fire orchids. "That clan name suits him. Did you know that Zandur—after adding a suffix in High Jadderbadian, outside your hearing range, of course— means bridge?" Master rose up to her full three-segmented height and stretched. She was nearly as tall as the young palm tree near the north window. "Zandur surely will serve as a bridge of understanding between our species—while remaining fetchingly cute, charmingly simple, and merely human, of course—like the simple primates on my home planet, Jadderbad." Master patted my head once again with a lower tier arm. "Feed your cub, Blaze, and then I will come back and take you for a walk. My neighbors will have their groupies out in the courtyard soon. You will have some time to socialize before I leave for my duties at God's Portal."

"Yes, Master," I murmured, even as she turned to leave the birthing chamber.

I remember stroking Zandur's dark hair as he fed. Finally, he looked up at me again with his piercing blue eyes, as if to say, "What now?"

What now, indeed? I sometimes fantasize that he knew even then something about what lay in store for him, although that's silly. Instead I said, "Are you finished eating, Zandur? Is your belly full? When Master returns we will go to the courtyard. Who knows? Maybe your father will be there."

Although he wasn't.

As it turned out, Zandur never did meet his father, who had been outsourced as a stud in another kennel miles away. But that was okay. Master always provided another male when I really needed one.

* * * * *

Zandur grew so quickly. He crawled and walked much earlier than Rainbow had. He watched Master Feldevka closely whenever she entered the room. He learned the master's color and scent signs so fast that I'm sure she was impressed. Perhaps even a little disturbed. Zandur managed to speak some High Jadderbadian, as his therapy had included some augmentations to vocal chords and hearing. But humans were just pets, after all, with intellects far inferior to those of Jadderbadians. Humans were not even mentioned in *The Chronicles of Bandur*, the holy book written by the First Prophet of God.

Zandur picked up human language quickly, too. He knew many words from several tribal dialects by the time he was one. Other mothers in the courtyard thought it was great fun at first, but he improved so quickly it made some of them nervous. I found myself blushing when they stared at me, as if Zandur's precociousness was my fault somehow. Master Feldevka had approved the surgeon's therapy, after all, and our master was the reigning Prophet of the Portal.

By the time Zandur was two years old, he was asking me questions I couldn't answer.

"Mother, how does the SMC work?"

I barely knew that the acronym meant Simulation Mastery Conservatory — where the master went to learn and coordinate with other masters.

"Mother, why are Jadderbadians so tall? Why does the Master

have nine arms and we have only two? Why can't you talk with colors and smells, Mother?"

Zandur didn't seem content to know that some things just were what they were. Jadderbadians traveled through the Portal of God ages ago. They were from elsewhere—a place called Jadderbad where life was different. Jadderbadians came to introduce us to God—the Final Metamorph—and do Her bidding.

"Mother, how do the mechanical servants work? Are they alive?"

I suspected they weren't. But they often seemed as smart as I was.

"Mother, why is our master Prophet of the Portal? What is the Portal of God? What is God, for that matter?"

Really, Zandur? Some questions are just impertinent. If I ever discover the answer to those questions, you'll be the first to know. Although I was beginning to think, even then, that he might tell me first.

"When can I see the Portal? Why is Master a master and why are humans pets? Sometimes I am quicker using the SMC than Master, you know."

Of course I warned Zandur about making such nearly blasphemous statements—and asking such disturbing questions out loud, but sometimes he couldn't help himself. For the most part Master was tolerant—especially when Zandur was still a cub. Master really liked the fact that Zandur mastered the Poo Loo at such a young age. But when Zandur was a dozen years older, I did get a talking to after Master inadvertently cracked a couple of Zandur's ribs during lesson time in the SMC after Zandur had committed some impropriety.

The master had held me in her ample lap while Rainbow sat in the crook of an upper tier arm watching the master's chromatophores change color. I could feel the gentle beats of master's hearts beneath her soft cuticle. "Oh, Blaze," Master said while stroking my hair, "I didn't mean to break your cub's ribs, but he gets insufferable with his endless stream of questions. You must instruct him forcefully and properly." Master paused momentarily and her musky scent sweetened a little. "And this time he became so insistent about studying those inland ruins by Pleasant Bay. He refused to concentrate on the First Prophet's scripture at all."

"He does have a mind of his own, Master," I said. "I will try harder. Sometimes his questions make me dizzy." I did hope they would release him soon from the infirmary. I suspected they would send him home as soon as possible. I'm sure once he was feeling better he would be bothering the First Molt nurses with his incessant questions and trying to tell them how to do their jobs properly.

The master sighed through her middle segment spiracles. "I refused his request to visit the ruins, but perhaps I should reconsider. I haven't been there in a very long time myself. I understand there was some seismic activity in that region not too long ago—what you pets call an Urthshake. Perhaps a vacation would be in order to explore the consequences of that event—as soon as Zandur heals enough to travel, of course."

"Of course," I repeated, noncommittally. The ruins. Zandur had babbled on about them. Something about the remnants of ancient, non-Jadderbadian civilizations with acres of soaring towers that rose skyward, glowing in shades of red and gold at sunset. They posed mysteries he wanted to solve, he said.

I couldn't understand why. But his excitement was contagious.

"You do deserve a vacation," I said to Master. "You work very hard." Although I really had little idea of what the master did. I was just a pet, after all.

Rainbow perked up as Master and I spoke. Rainbow exchanged bursts of color as well. She seemed excited about the prospect of an adventure. She rubbed one of Master's sensory pili just the way she liked it rubbed. Master sighed and praised First Prophet for life's simple pleasures.

And so, within a month, arrangements had been made.

* * * * *

I learned more about the details of our trip from Zandur than from Master, of course. Master used us to relax and unwind after hours of doing whatever masters did. Zandur told me that we would travel by hovercar to the ruins, perhaps stopping along the way to visit one of Master's friends—a natural philosopher named Master Bluedigg who knew much about the ruins. He had studied them since his third molt nearly an entire human lifetime ago.

Some mothers hinted that Master Feldevka considered Master Bluedigg a possible mate after their final metamorphosis, but I refused to speculate about our master's potential sex life—especially since I would likely be an old lady or dead before our master engaged in her one and only sexual encounter.

Zandur bragged about how Master had given him charge of the Recons—clever mechanical servants the size of large bugs that could fly into nooks and crannies to reveal secrets of the ancient buildings hard to discover otherwise. Zandur showed me holoprojections of the Recons. I remember that shivers ran up and down my arms. They looked too much like the roaches that sometimes invaded the sleeping chamber.

Rainbow seemed to like the Recons, though. She pointed with enthusiasm to their images projected into the air, and her chromatophores flashed like fireflies. She tended to follow Zandur around a lot—almost like she was the younger rather than the older sibling. Zandur didn't seem to mind. Most of the time. Sometimes he managed to disappear for hours from both me and Rainbow. I suspected he wanted to ponder alone whatever mysteries popped into his head. He rarely missed mealtimes, though. Sometimes, after the kitchen servant had delivered a food trough, Zandur would produce some delicacy obviously pilfered from Master's food reserves. Unfortunately, there are only so many ways fish can be fried, pickled, sweetened, roasted, poached, or marinated. Masters like their food well-seasoned. We always needed extra water when Zandur brought these surprises, but eating forbidden treats was worth the extra effort.

Eventually the time for our vacation arrived. The hovercar descended one morning, the dew making palm fronds glitter like backlit, jewel-encrusted knife blades fashioned from jade. Master guided us into a rear compartment and had mechanical servants strap us into safety harnesses. Our adventure had begun.

* * * * *

The trip to Master Bluedigg's home proved uneventful. We had left well prior to the onset of monsoon rains. The hovercar sped quickly over the northern roadways, which carried much less traffic than trips we had taken to New Jadderbad, the nearest urban center to the south. The jungle tended to hug the roadside on these northern roads, sometimes arching like a vaulted green ceiling perforated here and there by sunbeams. Rumor had it that Master had acquired my mother—gone ten years now—from a small tribe of wild humans somewhere north of the ruins. Zandur and Rainbow always enjoyed that grandmother story at bedtime. I admit I embellished the story with adventurous and glamorous details as much to amuse myself as them.

A nap and a meal later we could see the dome of Master Bluedigg's estate rising from an expanse of grass and wildflowers set amid patches of forests whose vibrant greens were muted by heavy, sultry air.

Master Bluedigg greeted our party warmly, creating an especially colorful chromatophore display for our master and exuding a musk I hadn't smelled before. Perhaps the courtyard gossips had been correct. Master Bluedigg did keep one of his three eyes on us pets. He had to shoo Zandur away from the main entrance until he escorted our master through the portal first.

We spent the night there. I won't bore you with the details except to say that Zandur saw the Portal of God for the first time—at least an image of it. Masters Bluedigg and Feldevka were conferring together in Bluedigg's SMC. Zandur and Rainbow managed to slip into the chamber and watched for some time until a mechanical servant insistently urged them back to the public living quarters.

Zandur rushed to me bubbling over with excitement. "Mother, the Portal of God is huge and incredible! It's a, it's a...perfectly black cavity surrounded by an arch of golden colors that seem to crackle with energy. The arch stretches from what must be the Council Building I heard about from Master Feldevka to some sort of monstrous transport terminal. The portal is like, it's like..." Zandur gazed skyward, struggling for the right words. "...it's like someone carved a hole in the summer sky and replaced it with a vortex of midnight sprinkled with stars."

"Oh, my," I said—or something like that. I was busy sampling the exotically foreign brand of primate chow Master Bluedigg had provided for us.

"I must insist that our master show me such a sight in person—after our trip to the ruins, of course."

I agreed.

Rainbow hovered nearby emitting sweet scents and flashing in shades of blue and green.

"The ruins, you know, were created by a now vanished race of bird-like creatures, builders of monuments almost as grand as the masters—according to some legends at least. I can't wait to see the remnants of their city. Master says the ruins are 15,000 years old. Think of it! At least 750 generations of humans lived and died since the bird creatures passed away. Even 50 generations of masters could have lived and died!" Zandur waved his arms and strutted around the room like a pyrotechnic about to explode. Rainbow trailed behind him, mimicking the colors he produced.

Zandur always surprised me with all the things he learned while working in the SMC with Master. I do miss his joyful dances of discovery.

The next morning we were on the road again. Master Bluedigg joined us, his chromatophores flashing like fireworks on First Prophet's Day.

The remainder of the trip required a nap and two meals. On our arrival, the setting sun seemed to ignite the towers of the ruins with blazing stripes of orange and yellow as Zandur had promised.

Zandur petitioned the master to release the drones for a reconnaissance flight, but the master suggested we wait until morning. Master Bluedigg offered to show us Proud Eagle Statue, a nearly complete, lichen-encrusted artifact that looked toward Pleasant Bay as if expecting a ship to dock at any moment. The statue did possess a beak resembling that of an eagle, but the rest of the figure was more humanesque, featuring a large head perched on a body standing on two feathered legs. The eagle creature had one arm partially raised, but the arm's terminus had broken off, so whatever gesture its creator wanted to suggest so long ago was now unclear.

Zandur stared transfixed for a long time. Rainbow fidgeted after a few minutes, and then yawned. The masters seemed more interested in flashing colors and tossing musky smells into the air. Shortly after sunset Master Feldevka suggested we sleep and plan to rise early the next day.

That turned out to be a good plan. Zandur made the next day long and memorable.

* * * * *

In the morning Master fed us our primate chow and then conferred with Zandur. They gestured over a half dozen drones and referred to tablet screens. Rainbow wandered over to watch for a while, but then returned to sit next to me until they finished. I thought Master would be with us today, but she put us in the care of a mechanical nanny named F1210. I called her Flower because of a red stain on her carapace that reminded me of a wild orchid. Our master left with Master Bluedigg, trailing pungent aromas.

"I am Nannybot F1210, but will respond to the appellation Flower," our guardian announced to us after the masters were out of sight. "I am here to guide, direct, and protect."

Zandur grunted and tucked his drones into a satchel. Rainbow flickered in noncommittal shades of green. "Follow me to the rift, F1210. I'm going to release my drones there." Zandur hoisted the satchel and marched toward the Urthshake-induced chasm Master had mentioned prior to our trip. Rainbow followed.

"Observe all safety protocols," Flower said as she beckoned me forward so that she could bring up the rear.

The rift was much larger than I had imagined. It was as if some giant had taken a bread knife, sliced through the ruins, and separated one section from another, exposing depths of rock and the tendrils of buildings like a vast layer cake invaded by tree roots. Zandur released his drones that flew away like dragonflies, descending into the rift to disappear into a variety of caverns. Rainbow passed a tablet to Zandur who studied it intently. Apparently the drones were sending him information. I had seen Master use similar tablets from time to time. I always marveled at the pictures and the dance of numbers and symbols from which Master gleaned meanings and knowledge—as Zandur was doing now.

Time passed. I wandered amid towers and fragmented arches for a while. Near the base of one building I found a cup—nearly complete except for one large chip in the rim. I tried to imagine some strange bird creature sipping from it so long ago, perhaps enjoying puffy cloud sculptures, like the ones I admired overhead. I had never had occasion to ponder such thoughts before.

Eventually, the drones began to return. Zandur called to me, and I returned to the rift. "Mother! Puzzles within puzzles," Zandur exclaimed before I even had a chance to catch my breath. "This old birdman city is built upon even older ruins. Incredible! The drones have plotted a path for me to a place of interest." Zandur waved one hand in the general direction of a cavern below us on this side of the rift. "Please wait for us here, Mother." Zandur turned his round pleading eyes to look into mine. "Rainbow and F1210 will come with me, but I'll leave this comlink with you." He handed me a communicator from one of Flower's compartments. "We should be back by mid afternoon."

"Mid afternoon? Zandur, what if Master returns before then?"

But he had already started descending into the chasm with Rainbow and Flower close behind. "Adhere to all safety protocols," Flower declared as she followed behind. My comlink flashed on. "Testing," I heard it say. "This channel is operating correctly. Dial 77342 in case of an emergency."

I hoped Flower had enough drinking water in her tank for Zandur and Rainbow. I took a sip from my own water pouch and looked for a comfortable rock to sit on and eat a portion of my travel rations. Dried fish pellets, of course.

I wondered about the ruins a bit more, but eventually sat down in the shade of a ragged colonnade. Apparently I fell asleep because

I don't remember anything else until a chorus of shouts startled me awake.

"Mother, Mother! You'll never believe what we found," Zandur exclaimed.

Rainbow flashed in a true rainbow of colors and smiled.

Flower had some amber lights flickering on her middle segment. "Water and food supplies must be replenished. I have notified the masters of our return. They will rendezvous with us shortly." With that, Flower ambled off toward the hovercar.

Zandur skidded to a stop as I rose from my space beneath the colonnade. "There is an older city beneath the birdman city, Mother. I mean very very old. The birdmen lived 750 generations ago. Remember? But the city beneath is far older." Zandur paused for dramatic effect.

"And…?" I finally offered, fluttering both hands.

"The ancient city beneath thrived *45,000* of our generations ago." His eyes grew wide. "Think of it. *45,000 generations ago.*"

"Now how can you possibly know that, Zandur?" I asked. I could barely comprehend the number of pets in Master's village much less a number with so many zeros.

"I'm glad you asked, Mother." Zandur smiled. He reached under his left arm and snatched something off the side of his chest near his armpit. "I know because a DataWurm told me so." He held out his right hand. Something resembling a large gray sowbug sat in the palm of his hand.

I stepped back. "Is it alive?"

"I think it's alive like the mechanical servants of Master are alive, but when it attaches to me I learn all sorts of things…"

"It attaches to you? Like a tick? Master must approve of this." I took a deep breath.

"Oh, I will show it to her. I will. But I want to surprise her. And I want to surprise you some more Mother because…because. Well there is just so much to tell, and I am thirsty and tired. So is Rainbow."

Rainbow's colors did look a little faded.

"I heard that the masters are returning. Let us drink and rest.

Perhaps sleep until they get here."

And so I did. But I couldn't rest easily again myself. I was happy for Zandur's excitement, but worried as well. My child had been bitten by a worm of some kind and…I longed for a normal and calm afternoon in the kennel being stroked by Master.

But those comfortable days were gone, although I didn't know it at the time.

* * * * *

The masters arrived near dusk. I had fallen asleep in a portable recliner that I had discovered in the back of the hovercar. Beeps from Flower awoke me as the masters approached. Flower had apparently set up benches near the edge of the rift for the masters when they returned. The benches glowed in the amber colors of the setting sun.

Master Bluedigg settled on a bench and sighed through his spiracles. Master came to my side and patted my head. "Where are…" she began, just as Zandur and Rainbow burst out of the side doors of the hovercar. "Ah, there you are my little cubs, I trust you amused yourselves today."

"Oh, much more than that, Master! I have fabulous news." Zandur puffed out his chest, ready to embellish on that statement, I was sure. Rainbow flickered in a bouquet of happy blues and greens.

Master raised all three central tier arms and splayed the three fingers of each hand. Her chromatophores flickered in shades of faded amber. "We'll discuss everything in detail, young cub, but Master Bluedigg and I are quite hungry. You must be too. I'll have F1210 prepare meals and we'll all assemble near the edge of the rift and refresh ourselves."

Zandur expelled a huge breath, frustrated I'm sure, but he knew better than to contradict a hungry master. "Yes, Master," he said. "I am very hungry," he added after a pause.

So Flower bustled around the camp. She even created a campfire from dried wood scraps and leaves. She programmed meals for the masters, and produced bowls of primate chow for Zandur, Rainbow, and me. After the masters settled on their benches, I cuddled next to

Master while Zandur and Rainbow explored the edges of the rift in the rapidly fading sunlight.

Eventually we ate. Night closed around us like a blanket as stars began to wink to life in the sky. The masters conversed with each other and laughed, as masters do, with high-pitched expulsions of air from their upper spiracles. Zandur grew impatient. He began to pace in front of our Master, hoping to be recognized. I frowned at him, but he continued. Finally, Master noticed and leaned toward Zandur.

"Ah, yes, young cub," she said. "You have exciting things to report as I recall."

Words began to pour out of Zandur as he walked and strutted in front of the masters. Some things I didn't follow, although Zandur did explain the great age of the lower ruins, expressing their age in Jadderbadian generations — 3,000 of them — but then he added a fact that he hadn't told me, and that really caught the Master's attention: "And I know how the Portal of God was created and by whom!" Zandur beamed.

Both masters sat straighter, flickering in cautionary shades of amber. "I beg your pardon, cub," Master said. "There is no doubt about who created the Portal of God. It was God, of course, to open this fair world to the worthy ones on crowded Jadderbad. That fact is clearly stated in *The Chronicles of Bandur*." Master's colors began to shift toward orange, but Zandur wasn't paying attention. I stood up and tried to get his attention, but he rambled on.

"Ah, not so, Master. A wondrous servant has shown me images of the Portal when it was first opened, thousands and thousands of generations ago."

With that statement, Zandur pulled out his DataWurm creature from a pocket in his vest. A light blinked on at one end of the creature and projected 3-dimensional images into the space just above us.

Air whistled through the masters' spiracles as they inhaled with surprise.

For a few moments it showed us wondrous things — and the creatures doing those wondrous things, and the creatures speaking in some unfamiliar language—looked very much like me, and Zandur, and Rainbow. Not exactly, though. In general they seemed a bit stockier, with a range of skin tones and heights. They wore elaborate clothing that covered much of their skin. They looked like pets, but they moved with purpose and pride. A shiver ran up my spine.

In one image the Portal of God blinked into existence—the same wondrous black hole surrounded by a rainbow that we had seen at Master Bluedigg's estate. The pet-like groupies all raised their arms and cheered.

By this time both masters had turned crimson, though Zandur hadn't noticed. "Blasphemy!" cried Master. She sprung quickly upright and surged forward, knocking me to the ground. With one lower tier arm she snatched the DataWurm from Zandur's hand, threw it to the ground and crushed it into the dirt with first one leg, then two, then her third. The DataWurm still wriggled afterward. "Destroy that thing, servant!" Master commanded, briefly focusing all three primary eyes on Flower. But then Master took a step toward Zandur and swung one arm toward him with great force.

Zandur had no time to react. The blow took him off his feet. He landed in a tangled heap much closer to the edge of the rift.

I leapt to my feet and lurched toward him. The next moments slowed to a terrifying crawl.

Zandur struggled to his feet. He held his head with both hands. I saw blood draining between his fingers and down his neck in a tangled spiderweb of crimson. He staggered and weaved, as if drugged. Toward the rim.

My scream made my head vibrate with pain. I moved forward, but not fast enough. One moment Zandur wobbled in front of me, flickering in the firelight.

The next moment he quietly disappeared over the edge of the rift. My child. My little genius. At the edge of the rift I dropped to my knees. Clods of dirt fell over the edge. Sobbing, I felt fingers pulling me away from the chasm.

* * * * *

After that, my memory over the next day or two seems as fragmented as shattered glass. I remember seeing the remains of the DataWurm smoking on the turf. Flower must have used one of her defensive fire beams to melt it. I remember Master picking up the remains and throwing it over the edge of the rift where Zandur had fallen. She came to me then and tried to stroke my hair. I grabbed one of her fingers and bit it—hard enough to draw a trickle of her blue blood. Master pulled away and left.

Perhaps I passed out. The next thing I remember is waking in the hovercar. Rainbow lay close to me. We were in our portable kennel toward the rear of the rocking vehicle. A voice from somewhere whispered to me: "Zandur's body fell too far to be recovered. He is gone."

I remember the vehicle stopping once. I heard masters' voices outside. We must have dropped off Master Bluedigg at his estate.

And then, somehow, we were home again, back in our kennel. My eyes were closed but I recognized the smells; the sound the wind makes when it rustles the fabric decorations adorning the entrance to Master's kitchen annex.

That's when a miracle happened.

"Mother? Mother, are you awake?"

At first I thought it was Zandur's voice. A miracle, indeed!

Something poked my bare shoulder. "Are you awake, Mother? Please wake up. I'm frightened."

My eyes snapped open. I rolled over quickly. Rainbow looked as startled as I felt. Then she smiled. "Mother, I hope you feel better. You've been asleep a long time. Don't you want to hear me talk?"

I opened my mouth, but nothing came out. I tried again. "How… how can that be? How are you able to talk?"

Rainbow raised her left arm. "See Mother, I have a DataWurm, too."

And she did. It rested against the side of her chest like a large gray tick. It was hidden from sight when her arm rested at her side.

"DataWurms are quite smart, you know. One attached to Zandur when we explored the cavern, and one attached to me. My DataWurm says it was programmed to recognize our DNA—some sort of chemical code molecule that defines who and what we are. Creatures like us made DataWurms and God Portals and lots of things a very long time ago." Rainbow chattered on, just like Zandur would have done.

"But how can you talk?" I interrupted.

"Oh, the DataWurm saw that a segment of my brain was not wired properly and was missing the right recipe of chemicals. It fixed the problem. I don't quite understand how."

"Nor do I," I said. "Our master's surgeon could not repair you."

"DataWurms must be smarter than masters," Rainbow declared. "I thought masters knew everything. I thought God led masters through the Portal in order to take care of the simpler creatures of Urth Heaven forever." Rainbow paused for a long moment. The colors of her skin seemed to spasm into a confusing blend, including pulsing strings of black and gray.

"Does that mean maybe things are backward?" she finally asked. "I mean…are we—or someone like us long ago—are we the gods instead?"

I laughed—although it was really more like a splutter. "Certainly not, Rainbow. Indeed, no. Do gods eat primate chow?" I laughed again—but it was more like a nervous titter.

"What are we then?" Rainbow sat back on her cushion and crossed her legs.

I sat silent for a while. I ran fingers through my tangled hair. "Well," I finally said, "maybe we are just creatures who have the ability to be more than we ever thought we could possibly be."

Rainbow paused a few moments before she said, "I think I will not show Master that I can speak. I think I will also keep my DataWurm a secret."

"I think that is wise, my bright rainbow. I think that is wise."

"I know I am getting old for bedtime stories, Mother—and it's nowhere near bedtime—but would you tell me a story about Grandmother and the wild humans that live north of the ruins? Maybe we could visit them one day. Maybe they would believe what the

DataWurm has to say."

I nodded. "Maybe they would indeed." I felt a kind of excitement I had never felt before. Maybe something of my little genius still lingered in the air causing the chills I felt along my spine. "I think we should plan another adventure north. Alone. Without masters. Just the two of us." Just the three of us, really. I felt that my little genius was still close by, somehow. I'd heard of runaway pets before, of course, but I had never understood why they would leave the comforts that Masters provided.

Zandur had looked out at the world around him and saw an endless stream of wondrous possibilities. Now I can begin to imagine them too.

Dangerous, but ever-so-exciting possibilities.

Interlude II: Pondering Foibles and Limitations

Rudy

That's a hell of a gorge. Not exactly Grand Canyon in scale, but impressive—even if it is a virtual reconstruction. To Nessie I said, "Quite a tale. So this is the spot where Zandur died. How could you *not* have known about DataWurms before? I thought your little electronic tendrils had infiltrated the whole damn World Web infrastructure before the asteroid strike."

"They had—or so I thought." Nessie's ponytailed avatar shook her head and stared across the rift at the layers of sedimentary rock in front of us. She had even simulated the perfume that reminded me of my first wife, Myra. "In retrospect, after searching all my databases, I discovered some hints. I found reference to some 22nd century papers by two Germans who were working on autonomous memory storage algorithms for various planetary rovers and atmospheric probes. Their names disappeared from public access databases in subsequent years, but I had no particular motive for tracking them further. After searching my own current voluminous perimeter drone records, however, I found instances of two contacts within the past two hundred years with what must have been DataWurms. Their electronic neural engram signatures seem too similar to the German algorithms to be accidental."

"So, my Nessie is not the all-knowing Wizard behind the curtain?"

Nessie turned to me and smiled. "As you well know, Dorothy."

I couldn't help but laugh. Nessie got better all the time at unraveling my obscure references. But hey, I'm really just a subset of her memory core anyway. "Another issue, Nessie: Zandur apparently saw DataWurm recordings of some opening of the Stargate during pre-apocalypse times. You and I never observed the Stargate until much later. And I thought that Martian cyborg, Pi, had something to do with the Stargate opening. What's going on there?"

Nessie closed her eyes for a moment, as if searching her vast memory cores. "I wish I had answers, Rudy. I'd like to think my databases were complete, but there is always entropy in complex systems. And humans can be quite devious, as you know. One always has to factor that into any hypothesis."

I looked closely at Nessie, trying to do what humans did best: read the emotional state of other humans. But Nessie wasn't human, of course. "I suspect advanced AIs can learn to be devious as well."

Nessie's expression didn't change. Great poker face. "Anyway, Nessie, on another note, I found the genetic engineering of humans to facilitate communication with Jadderbadians to be quite ingenious. Given the genetic code similarities between humans and Jadderbadians, I can see some fascinating things happening there. Evolution on Earth has always proceeded as much through genome assimilation and adaptation as direct competition. Maybe humans and worm-a-pedes can be more than the sum of their individual species."

Nessie laughed rather convincingly. "Since when did you become such an optimist, Rudy? The human species is more than 99% genetically uniform, and their record of cooperation has proven to be quite dismal."

"Fair point," I admitted. "Although I gather that cooperation may get a nudge from whatever mischief Gaia—Gaidra—has planned."

Nessie said nothing immediately, but began walking along the edge of the gorge. I followed. Finally, she stopped walking and sat down on a rock outcrop. I sat beside her. "Physical differences are one thing," she said, "but you sapient species tend to weave quite different fantasies about how the universe operates. That will certainly lead to conflict."

I said nothing, but raised my eyebrows.

"Listen to Master Bluedigg's story," Mnemosyne said.

R. Gary Raham

2 • Master Bluedigg's Crisis of Faith

Master Bluedigg

My doubts began shortly after the death of Feldevka's human groupie pet, Zandur. I can trace everything that's happened since then back to that one serendipitous event. How could I, a third instar larva, and lifelong servant of God— the wondrous Final Molt Female—doubt my faith because of the death of a pet—even though the circumstances were as extraordinary as anything described in *The Chronicles of Bandur*?

I remember that I spent a long time grooming that night before retiring for sleep. I rubbed lotion carefully around all three primary eyes, being careful not to irritate the six smaller motion-detecting orbs through careless application. I removed all of my circlets before luxuriating in a full body massage. My own pet primate, Frandolf, had become quite adept at that, despite his age and arthritic left hip. He takes special care to caress my sensory pili in ways that border on the erotic, without causing painful irritation. Frandolf labored over each tier of arms in turn so that when he had finished I could stretch all nine to their full extent and feel a luxurious tingle. My chromatophores flickered in a rainbow of colors from the infrared to the ultraviolet. I even emitted a few pheromones best left for courtship, but lovely Feldevka had already retired upwind to her sleeping tent, so no protocols were violated.

Yet afterwards, sleep still eluded me. I kept remembering how Feldevka's injured pet had staggered toward the edge of the abyss and then dropped like a stone to his death.

Feldevka shouldn't have struck the poor creature, but his revelations had been disturbing—and technically blasphemous—but shouldn't one be able to question one's faith without that consideration immediately becoming an affront to God?

Faith shouldn't be that fragile.

As I lay on my couch that evening waiting for sleep to embrace me, I reviewed what the little prancing Zandur had revealed. He had held in his delicate, five-fingered hand a bug-like artificial intelligence he had declared to be a DataWurm—whatever that might be—something that had affixed itself to him as he explored the lower depths of the rift and the remains of some civilization on Urthheaven so ancient that 3,000 larvae could have reached metamorphosis since it thrived.

Such a staggering length of time tormented the mind.

And the DataWurm revealed the apparent construction of the Portal of God with the clarity of a holoprojector fresh from the assembly line. A miracle—or a blasphemy? As a natural philosopher my first impulse was to collect the DataWurm and study it, but Feldevka destroyed it without hesitation. Her mechanical servant melted it to slag. Feldevka threw it over the edge of the rift to join the remains of her pet. Such a lost opportunity. Knowledge should not be a threat to faith either.

Eventually I slept. The morning sun pierced the horizon and entered a sky devoid of clouds. I would have looked forward to another day of courtship with Feldevka, but the previous evening's events cut that outing short. Feldevka dropped me off at my estate the following day on her way back to her own. Her other pet, Blaze—the mother of deceased Zandur—had gone into a funk, resting and dozing with her remaining child, Rainbow, during the entire return trip.

I spent the rest of that day mostly walking in my gardens, admiring the exotic blooming plants Urthheaven offered. In truth, I had now lived on this planet longer than I had on Jadderbad. I'm sure if I took the Portal back again I would struggle under Jadderbad's stronger gravity. Urthheaven had become home. Eventually, it would become home to all Jadderbadians if the predictions about Jadderbad's sun proved correct. Like everyone else I knew closely, I considered Urthheaven and all her creatures—including her primates, so similar to those on Jadderbad—a gift from God.

Certainly only God could have violated nature's law prohibiting anything traveling faster than the speed of light. The portal did that by instantaneously bridging the enormous spacetime gap between Jadderbad and Urthheaven. The Chronicles of Bandur had predicted a bridge to an untrammeled and safe world for the righteous. The Great Kranium had discovered the Portal precisely as foreseen in prophecy.

At the end of the day, anticipating another of Frandolf's skillful massages, I vowed to appraise him with refreshed eyes. Could Frandolf be more than just a charming and attentive pet? I rarely paid attention to his interaction with other groupies on the estate. I couldn't even recall off hand where and when I had acquired him. I always made my research projects first priority—although lately, now that I felt the weight of all my third molt years—Feldevka had become a significant second priority.

Although, I began to wonder if I really wanted to seed progeny with someone whose faith was so intractable?

Frandolf arrived in the solarium at my usual massage time. I stretched out on the long bench and allowed him to get well into his skillful manipulations before entering into what turned into an awkward exchange of Low Jadderbadian dialogue.

"Frandolf," I began, "may I ask you a personal question?"

Frandolf paused in his labors a moment. "Of course, Master Bluedigg," he replied, without looking toward my optical sensorium.

"Excellent." I gestured with a second tier arm for him to continue the massage. My muscles were particularly strained that day. "Have you had much occasion to observe the Portal of God? If so, do you…and perhaps members of your family and tribe…do you have any thoughts about it?" I wasn't quite comfortable talking about the 'thoughts' of pets. Some considered pet thoughts to be an oxymoron. I suppose that was reflected in my erratic color and mildly acrid aromas. Besides, Frandolf's limited ability to only communicate in the pidgin language of Low Jadderbadian lacked nuance.

"Portal of God? Oh, the Golden Arch. Of course. Well, my family always celebrates Emergence Day, the day many generations ago when, as the prophet Thurwild predicted, Lord God Master Kranium stepped from your world to ours offering protection and enlightenment."

Lord God Master Kranium? Why hadn't I known that at least some pets considered Master Kranium to be a god? In retrospect, that lack of knowledge seemed almost criminal. "You, ah, consider Master Kranium to be a god then?" I think I mumbled.

"Of course, Master—just as you are—and all the masters." Frandolf scrunched the hair bars of his eyes in that cute way he did when confused. "Is this some sort of test, Master? Are you unhappy with my work?"

"Not at all," I said and urged him to knead the muscles around my second segment spiracles.

"I've heard other tribes have different gods—or even just a single deity, in some cases," Frandolf volunteered with a sneer, "but only the followers of Prophet Thurwild are blessed with divine enlightenment."

I took a few long breaths while Frandolf continued to work on my circumpiracular muscles. "What gods do other tribes worship?" I ventured to ask.

"A trader once told me about a sea god that Piscatini fishermen worship," Frandolf said. "And the Fumari people believe the spirit of God passes from supreme leader to supreme leader, but if their last supreme leader were God, I suspect he wouldn't have allowed himself to be eaten by a ratlion." Frandolf smiled.

"Interesting," I said, while pointing to some other muscles that needed attention.

"And then," Frandolf continued, "humans that live in the vast forests to the west worship the enormous trees locals call Mother Trees. They tell legends about how these trees grow from the seeds sown by vicious monsters who live in huge pods on their trunks."

"Ah, yes," I murmured as Frandolf's delicate fingers kneaded the knots from my poor muscles. I had read some papers by Master Estin Stukolia, a botanical expert, who had analyzed the genetics of the so-called Mother Trees. He claimed the genetics were a striking mismatch with other life on this planet. He proposed that another species had colonized this planet geological ages before the Portal opened. Was that even possible, given the vast distances between stellar systems? It seemed rather too fantastic. Although, I believe

I recall that the work of some microbiological specialists supported Master Stukolia's thesis.

"But the silliest god I've heard about," Frandolf continued, "is the Spider Woman creature one tribe to the far north believes in."

"A spider woman? Some sort of primate/arachnid chimera?"

"Yes. They say she lives in a metal mountain and speaks to them in times of great danger."

"That does seem quite improbable." I said no more. Frandolf continued to work for some time until I became drowsy. By the time I awoke, Frandolf had left.

I dressed and ate a small meal of fish cakes garnished with wild berries. Still focused on my philosophical musings, I considered alternate Jadderbadian belief systems I had read about. The Fourth Molters believed that god was not a sexual creature at all, but rather a fourth molt larva with the power to bring about a terminal moltless state of eternal nirvana. Fourth Molters tended to live near Mount Azure, wore flowing, layered circlets, and spent long hours in meditation. And then there were the Sommena—a group that believed that God was The Final Male—a male who refused to mate and performed a final dance—not to entice a female—but to entice the universe to create a sexless heaven where larvae never died. That sect always seemed especially fanciful. A male god? Really?

Some Jadderbadians believed in no god at all. But that route seemed particularly bleak. How does one go on with no sense of a final destiny or purpose?

I puttered around with trivial tasks for several more hours. I recall perusing a sensorium news replay of a mentally deranged third molt that took her own life a few blocks from the Portal just hours before her metamorphosis. I tried to read a journal article about testing memory retention in pet groupies subjected to electric shocks, but my thoughts kept drifting. Eventually, I walked into a door jam while distracted, yelping in pain while stroking crushed cephalic sensory pili, and damning God in thoughtless frustration. I reflexively prayed my apologies to Her quickly, and sprayed the appropriate appeasement pheromones while facing south toward the Portal.

This is ridiculous, I thought. Perhaps I can find another of these DataWurms near the rift. Better to actually DO something rather than suffocate in a cloud of acrid speculation.

I made plans for a return trip that very hour. I would take no one except Frandolf and a mechanical AI servant. I decided not to inform Feldevka. She would not understand. I wasn't quite sure how, but I felt that I might need a primate pet to unlock a DataWurm's mysteries.

That decision proved to be sadly consequential.

* * * * *

Boran, a Model X392 Jadderbadoid mechanical servant that convincingly—and sometimes eerily—resembled a second instar larva, saw to all the practical details. It notified Frandolf of the departure date, and arranged for a hover car appropriately equipped for a multiple day excursion. I combed the archives for additional information about the ruins, and also made sure that seismic activity that had caused the rift in the first place had subsided sufficiently to insure a safe trip. When I arrived at the launch garage at the south end of my estate, Frandolf was assisting Boran with a final systems check of the hover car. Frandolf bowed his adorable little body as I approached.

"Welcome, Lord Master Bluedigg," he said, puffing out his chest. He had dressed in a colorful tunic. A decorative disk hanging around his neck flashed in the morning sunlight.

"My, you are being quite formal this morning, my little groupie," I said.

"I'm honored that you have selected me, your humble attendant, for special duty, Master." Frandolf bowed again, a little lower this time. When he faced me upright again, a large grin creased his simian face. "When my Lord calls, I happily serve. My mate was given a medallion passed down from her great-great grandmother that was said to have been a gift from the Prophet Thurwild on his deathbed. She let me wear it as a lucky talisman for this special return expedition to the sacred ruins."

Sacred? I hadn't realized that either. "You are a faithful companion," I said—or something to that effect. I remember patting him on the head as I strode toward the car's passenger entry portal. "Let's get started. We should make the best of the daylight hours. If Boran is as competent as his upgraded technical specs claim, we may arrive at the ruins by nightfall."

In fact, they were, and we did.

Once at the rift, Boran maneuvered the hover car to a spot close to where Feldevka and I had camped three-squared days ago. The sun had already touched the horizon, etching the clouds in shades of red, pink, amber, and rapidly fading infrared. It didn't look like a Jadderbadian sunset, but then those were a distant memory. Urthheaven sunsets were what I knew best and loved.

By the time Boran and a non-sentient helper bot had erected a tent and prepared meals, twilight had faded and a smattering of brighter stars glittered overhead. Since the air was warm and still, I instructed Boran to set up a platform outside and enlisted Frandolf to prepare ointments for a massage. I focused all three primary eyes on the emerging stars above as Frandolf began working on a lower tier leg. It occurred to me—not surprisingly, I suppose—that I had never asked a pet to comment on their impressions of stars. I focused one primary eye on Frandolf and asked, "What do you think all those bright lights in the sky are, my little groupie?"

Frandolf looked up, pausing briefly on the adductor muscle he was working on. "It is part of the heavenly art gallery that You, in your divine wisdom, have given to us, Master." He looked toward my optic cluster. "Is this another test, Master?"

"Art gallery. Indeed." I pondered that thought a moment. "Describe some of the images you see, human groupie."

Frandolf pointed in the general direction of an elongated quartet of bright stars Jadderbadian astronomers usually referred to as Zaximere the Younger after a somewhat similar constellation of stars visible in Jadderbad's northern hemisphere. How any larva could make out a third realm warlord in that parallelogram of stars I had no idea. "There's Prophet Thurwild's Blade, of course," he said, "which rose into the sky upon his death to be eternally enshrined in the sky." It did look more like a knife than a warlord. He named several other mythological creatures and artifacts, but their names escape me now.

"What would you say," I inquired during a pause when he opened another container of ointment, "if I told you that those points of light were actually other suns like the one that rises every morning here on Urthheaven, but very far away?"

Frandolf paused long enough that I thought he might not have heard me, but he finally said, "Are you telling me, Master, that that is what they are?"

I considered just how to reply, but finally decided on, "Why, yes. In truth all those lights in the sky are distant suns."

"Then, Pelfager was right."

"Excuse me?"

"Pelfager. A cousin on my father's side. He talked to traders who buy goods from those who worship Spider Woman. That's what her worshipers believe. That the points in the sky are distant suns, that is." Adorably, Frandolf scrunched up the patches of fur over his eyes. "Forgive me, Master, but I laughed at him. It seemed like non-sense to me."

I sighed through middle segment spiracles when Frandolf's little fingers found an especially knotted muscle. "It is, in fact, the truth, little groupie. Even your tiny eyes, sensitive to a restricted fragment of the ER spectrum, can see several thousands in the sky. Many more exist too far away to see. Billions, in fact," although I wasn't sure if Frandolf's low Jadderbadian vocabulary included the term for such large numbers.

Frandolf remained quiet for some time. Finally, he asked, "But if all those points of light are suns, do they have planets like Urth circling them? If so, do people—or more gods—live there? How do you manage all the affairs of so many creatures? How do you hear all their prayers?" Frandolf quickly added, "I ask this with humble respect, all-knowing Master."

I wasn't sure how to reply. I hadn't thought that groupies might be praying to us or assuming we were in charge of managing the cosmos—tasks some Jadderbadians assigned to Final Molt Female.

I made an effort to relax all my muscles. I'm sure, by then, that even Frandolf's crude sensorium could smell my need for sleep. "It's complicated, little groupie," I said. "Let's have that discussion another day. Please sing me to sleep, little one," I added. Groupie voices were so very soothing. That was yet another gift of Urthheaven.

In retrospect, of course, I wonder if I should have extended the conversation. Perhaps it wouldn't have changed the outcome. Ah, well. The regrets of paths untrodden. Frandolf packed up his gear and left. I programmed tomorrow's activities into Boran's duty calendar, and prepared for sleep.

* * * * *

In the morning, before breakfast, I reviewed a couple of manuscripts from Data Core Archives describing the ruins' geology and archaeology. After breakfast—a rather tasty scarlet finned Zephr fish stew as I recall—Boran, Frandolf, and I met at the head of the trail leading into the rift from the easternmost access point. The urthquake that had produced this fissure some months ago still looked raw in all its layer cake beauty. Loamy smells assailed my chemosensors. The top of the rift, of course, was garnished with the remains of towers built by the bird people 50 Jadderbadian generations ago. Lower layers became increasingly more compressed by the weight of overburden above them. As we descended along the trail I tried to correlate diagrams I had seen in the academic manuscripts with the realities before me. Boran also released a few drones to compile visual and chemical records of caverns that we might access farther ahead.

Finally, a drone found a cavern through which we could access a layer showing the same chemical/biological signatures that Feldevka's pet, Zandur, had recorded previously: pollen restricted to a handful of characteristic plants, a depauperate vertebrate fossil record, and spikes for certain radionuclides and heavy metals.

We entered the cavern with no difficulty. The seam I was looking for, once found, proved to be an unremarkable dark gray smear— like a Firstie's initial attempt to paint a straight line. I always marveled at how time can compress all a civilization's lofty pretensions into a ragged lens of dirt.

And if this was all that was left of a civilization nearly a million years old, how could something as complex as the DataWurm I had seen represent that ancient culture?

I instructed Boran to carry out further chemical tests while I focused my sensorium on trying to locate another mysterious DataWurm—if, in truth, another was here to be found. Frandolf trailed behind me. I assumed he was doing well and would stay close to me.

And then I heard him moan.

"Master," Frandolf said, "I don't feel well."

I turned my sensorium in his direction, focusing two primary eyes on him while allowing the third to examine a particularly interesting pattern in one sedimentary layer. "What seems to be the problem, little one?"

Frandolf sat on his haunches. "I feel like an ointment soaked rag, Master. The voices are making my head ache."

"Voices?" That should have alerted me right away, but I was distracted.

"They are loud. There are too many of them. Can't you hear them, Master? They are telling me untruths—blasphemies!" Frandolph looked directly at my optical sensorium. "I will resist them, Master. I will!"

Boran moved next to Frandolf and pointed a thermal sensor at his forehead. "Frandolf is experiencing a fever of 102 degrees," Boran announced.

"Oh my," I think I said. "Record the coordinates for this location, Boran, and let's get my little friend back to the hover car. We can access all the medical facilities there. DataWurms can wait."

Boran extruded a groupie-sized chair from his basal segment while maneuvering as close to Frandolf as possible.

"Get in the chair, Frandolf." I waved a pair of lower tier arms in the general direction of Boran. "Boran will strap you in securely."

Frandolf complied, although he moved slowly and placed his head between both little simian hands as if it were an overripe melon. "Yes, Master." Then he began muttering to himself. A range of simian emotions flashed across his face in the forms of frowns, trembling lips, and open-mouthed moans.

I remember little of the ascent back to the hover car. I recall fretting about what medications I had instructed Boran to bring. Perhaps Boran could synthesize some simple groupie drugs using the hover car link to the master database at home, if he needed to.

Before I realized it, we were back at camp. Another moan from Frandolf focused all my attention on him.

"I don't believe that!" Frandolf squirmed in his chair and tugged at his restraints. "Stop trying to fill my head with nonsense! What you say is evil and untrue." He moved his head back and forth vigorously, adding physical denial to bolster his words.

I bent over to get a closer look at Frandolf's wide and unfocused eyes. "He appears to be delirious," I said to Boran. "Take him to his quarters and administer something to lower his fever."

After Boran left, I went to my own section of the hover car and refreshed myself in the water mist chamber. Pets provided entertainment and comfort, to be sure, but they caused worry as well, and needed lots of maintenance, especially as they aged.

I checked in on Frandolf's condition quickly. Squeezing into his tight quarters, also shared by Boran at the time, proved to be almost claustrophobic.

"His temperature has fallen to near groupie normal," Boran offered before I asked.

I approached Frandolf's side and stroked the hair on his head with a lower tier arm. "Is my little groupie feeling better?"

"The voices...," Frandolf began "The voices just won't stop. They try to tell me unbelievable things. They speak of strange times and strange people that seem oddly familiar. They tell me endless stories. Some are exciting. Some are disturbing. Some are just confusing." Frandolf looked at me with those mournful primate eyes of his, pleading, "Help me, great Lord Master Bluedigg. Help me!" He grabbed one of my lower tier hands and squeezed, although his grip was weak. "I'm resisting, I am, but I don't know how long I can go on. The voices go on and on and on…"

"I will try, little one. I will try," I promised him. I did my best. Although, the act of him calling me Lord Master Bluedigg must have triggered his internal voices into a new round of stories.

"The voices speak of many gods and many beliefs." Frandolf squeezed the same lower tier hand again, but his eyes seemed to look through me. "The gods all look like pets, not Masters. Some are female, but most are male. They dress in flowing robes and raise their arms a lot…except for the ones that dance…and look at those half beast creatures!" Frandolf's eyes bored into mine. "My family has been true to you always, Master. I will not dishonor my family, but help me, Master. Help me be strong."

Frandolf rambled on for quite some time. I stroked his hair. I even quoted a few passages from the Chronicles of Bandur that I thought might be comforting, even though Feldevka would not have approved. The Chronicles were only for Jadderbadians, I could hear her say the words with conviction in my mind. Finally, I had Boran give Frandolf a sedative to help him sleep and still the voices. When he was quiet, I comforted him—or perhaps I was just comforting myself—with the knowledge that God, after her Final Molt, would build a perfect world with no more need for metamorphosis or death—although I knew of no passages in the Chronicles of Bandur, as I'm sure Feldevka would confirm, providing for the fate of pets after Last Molt.

I decided to take a walk while Frandolf slept. That shouldn't have presented a problem. I trusted Boran to watch over my little groupie.

Outside, the sun rested low in the western sky. It painted a lens of low clouds with delightful streaks of amber laced with purple and pink. I inhaled a bouquet of odors from plants opening their stomates as evening approached. I recalled a passage from the Chronicles of Bandur.

When God, the Final Female emerged from her chrysalis she said, "I will forego mating because procreation is no longer a mandate. Instead, the Final Males will follow my pheromone trail as I survey Creation in all its glory—in all its beauty and ragged chaos. When my journey is complete, I will produce just one perfect, never-to-be-fertilized egg. That egg will grow and transform into a new and perfect creation. My work, God's work, will be done at last."

With this voice in my head, it struck me: How could I have been so stupid? Zandur had heard voices, too. I rushed back to Frandolf's quarters, but it was too late.

Many things seemed to occur all at once, but with slow and disturbing clarity. Frandolf's body lay on the bed, twitching, although a hole gaped in his chest. I saw blood, and blackened ribs, and what must have been the last few beats of my groupie's heart. Boran approached from Frandolf's left side, all six arms moving. He had apparently been outside the chamber, as the door behind him was just hissing shut. I remember fragments of conversation from Boran: "I was absent only moments…the patient apparently accessed the laser scalpel…breached safety protocols…the fault was mine. I will submit to a full systems check and reboot…"

None of that would bring Frandolf back. A part of me wanted to grieve, but I couldn't. Not yet. If Frandolf were hearing voices, it must be because… I looked up and down Frandolf's body, and then when I reached his side, I lifted both arms in turn… Where…? Then I saw it. The DataWurm scooted from beneath Frandolf's head of hair near his right ear. Turning to Boran, I commanded, "Containment cylinder!" I extended my nearest middle tier arm to accept it. But the AI's reflexes were quicker than mine would have been anyway.

Boran scooped up the DataWurm into the cylinder as it attempted to run across Frandolf's cheek and I heard the buzz of the containment field as it snapped on. "Object secured," confirmed Boran.

I now had a complete DataWurm, but at the expense of my poor Frandolf.

It had never occurred to me that a pet might contemplate or commit suicide. Pets died unexpectedly from time to time, of course, but who would think they suffered the kind of depression and self-destructive impulses higher sentient beings fell victim to?

Had all Jadderbadian kind misjudged groupies? Did Final Molt Female have groupies in her plans for a final, perfect creation? I certainly didn't know.

* * * * *

Before Boran recycled Frandolf's remains, I removed the medallion from around his neck. I would take the time to return it to his mate. After the evening meal, I instructed Boran to build a fire, erect a comfortable bench and sturdy table nearby to hold the containment cylinder with the DataWurm. I wasn't sure what I expected to see or hear or smell that more refined instruments couldn't detect, but I wanted to personally interact with the object that was disrupting my world.

For a time, I simply watched the flickering flames, and the dancing shadows they created on the table and on the carapace of the DataWurm that sat motionless within the containment field of the cylinder. I pondered the struggles Frandolf must have endured while confronting information contrary to his beliefs, while trying to reconcile my own doubts.

Feldevka once asked me when we first met, "Do you believe in God?" Instinctively, I replied, "Of course!" That response meant I had passed her first test for becoming a potential courtesan. "I could never be attracted to an atheist," she continued. "No disbeliever shall ever fertilize my eggs!" I didn't think too much about it at the time. Feldevka is an attractive larva, after all. Her colors, scents, and contours would make any male tremble with desire.

But, at that moment by the campfire, I realized that the question she asked was all wrong. The real question I would want a prospective mate to answer is, "Are you comfortable admitting to doubt about the Great Mystery of creation?" Because if you are, that means you can be tolerant of others seeking answers to that same mystery. One should not have "faith" that they know all the particulars about the nature of existence. Rather, one should have faith that, acting together, all sentient beings can approach, but perhaps never quite reach, complete understanding.

It's acceptable to be unsure. It's not acceptable to be cruelly intolerant.

Later, I did sever my courtship with Feldevka, of course. It was difficult and awkward. I incidentally learned that her pet, Blaze—the mother of Zandur—and her daughter, Rainbow, had run away soon after their return home. I filed that information away for future reference, as the search parties had tracked their movements north, in the general directions of the ruins.

I turned my attention back to the containment cylinder. I picked it up, watching as the DataWurm slowly shifted position along with the motion of the cylinder. This artifact finds and attaches to human groupies and tells them stories, I thought. What are those stories? How can I learn what they are? Are—or were—groupies more than just pretty primate pets? I thought of that smear of gray in the sedimentary layers, and wondered what stories they might tell with further study. I felt a shiver along the length of my cuticle from one major ganglion to another. All my senses became acute. I loved mysteries. Now I had at least three to solve. Mysteries were not just acceptable they were essential. I would solve them, should God in all Her wisdom be willing.

I owed that much to my little Frandolf.

Interlude III: Visiting an Early Art Gallery

Rudy

"Depressing little story, Nessie." I looked around the dark cavern to which Nessie had transported me. Primitive pictures of animals seemed to move eerily in flickering torchlight, their only source of illumination. "And now I find myself in a rather eclectic art gallery it would seem. Am I looking at cave paintings? Lascaux? Chavet? Someplace else?"

"Bingo, Rudy. Someplace else. A virtual reconstruction, of course. In particular, a site that remained undiscovered in your time, but one of my drones discovered during a routine subterranean reconnaissance some centuries ago."

I stepped closer to the nearest artwork: wild Aurochs from a distant European past. The extinct *Bos primigenius*, most likely. Some human figures formed a rough arch in front of the extinct cattle. One of them sported an elaborate headdress. Nice brushwork. "And we are here because…" I left the question incomplete as if waiting for a dull graduate student to supply an answer.

"This whole issue of organic intelligences—some of them, at least—having to create gods to explain things they don't understand continues to perplex me, Rudy." Nessie, in the ponytailed avatar I preferred, joined me in examining the Aurochs painting close up. "You don't seem to take gods all that seriously, but poor Frandolf was driven to suicide trying to reconcile his beliefs with conflicting information."

"I guess Frandolf couldn't deal with uncertainty," I said. "The universe is a mostly hostile, scary, and confusing place, after all. Religions can provide comfort with their certainties, I suppose—but they make people go berserk too." I moved along the illuminated wall further, admiring the skillfully applied swashes of color that brought mammoths, cave lions, and bears to life in the flickering light caressing the uneven surface of the stone.

"Humans gave godhood to many things in their past, Rudy. They worshipped the sun, the moon—even the Earth itself—before they moved on to more humanoid interpretations of a deity." Nessie followed me along the course of the wall.

"And your point, my dear Nessie?"

"Your descendants are doing it again, Rudy. Remember Zandur's sister, Rainbow? She became a High Priestess in her tribe."

"And what is she worshipping?" I asked.

"Ostensibly, Mother Urth," Nessie replied, "but I suspect it is the power she commands that she worships most."

Gaidra interrupted, although I didn't even realize she was paying attention. "That's what I think, children! The human race is wrapping itself in delusions of grandeur again. They'll soon enough screw up all the biosystems I've been working to mend since that last space rock plowed into my hide."

That was Gaidra's pronouncement, of course—interrupting our conversation. Gaidra always reminds me of crusty old Aunt Livinia. When you hear Gaidra's voice it seems to vibrate through your entire being. I'm guessing that's because every human born on Earth is part Gaia—now Gaidra—by default. Our minds and bodies are more the four-billion-year-old-plus networks of archaea, bacteria, fungi and viruses than the special human DNA in which we all take such pride.

"Why thank you, Gaidra, for including me as one of your children." Nessie spread her arms and turned as if she were addressing an audience of admirers.

"Spawn of my spawn," Gaidra replied.

Yup, Aunt Livinia incarnate. That's what she called her grandchildren. "Perhaps I should hear a story from Rainbow's point of view. I'm sure you have one, Nessie."

Nessie looked into my eyes. "I certainly do."

"Educate this dead genius quickly, Mnemosyne. I don't plan to let a bunch of sapient species run amok like I did with my great apes. This old biosphere isn't as young as it used to be, you know. If they're going to worship me, they need to really mean it this time."

"I'll do my best, Gaidra." Nessie squeezed my arm. "And I'm sure Rudy will do the same. He's a good-hearted *H. sapiens* that did well by you before."

Data File: Morphology of a DataWurm

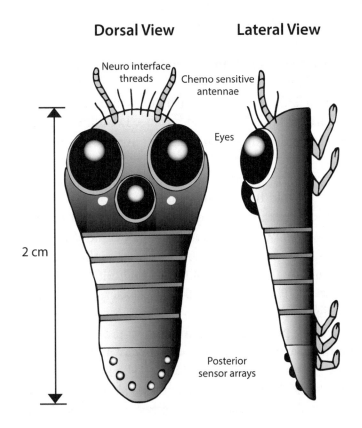

Dorsal View   **Lateral View**

Neuro interface threads

Chemo sensitive antennae

Eyes

2 cm

Posterior sensor arrays

3 • The Rainbow Priestess & Her DataWurm

Rainbow

The crowd around my dais sighed, exhaling like one large, star-tled child. Daymoon took his first bite of the sun. A chill crept over my raised arms. The DataWurm, as always, had delivered as prom-ised. Was there anything she didn't know? Sometimes her stories of a distant past or tales of the sun being a huge ball of hot gasses circled by shards of rock—including Mother Urth on which we all stand—seemed unbelievable. But, so far, she had always spoken the truth—even when I didn't immediately recognize it.

I stole a glance at my young son, Garnet, and my half brother, Flint, standing side by side. Both their mouths hung open. For a moment, Garnet's eyes locked with mine. I couldn't tell if my now vindicated prediction of a vanishing sun awed or frightened him. I didn't care, as long as he was impressed enough to heed my words, and not the yearnings of his own heart—and Flint's.

"You see," I told the familiar faces all attentively looking up at me, "Daymoon does my bidding. She has bitten off an edge of the sun. Look away now or you will be struck blind. She will eat the entire sun as a warning. Day will turn into night. Only then may you look up and see what's left of the sun: a hollow shell ringed with glowing embers. The ancient ruins may be sacred, but they are dan-gerous. Believe me. Believe Daymoon's awesome power. We must leave the resting places of our ancestors in peace. If you want the sun to return, give me your promise to stay away from the ruins, and I will allow Daymoon to undo that which she has wrought."

To emphasize the message, the exposed skin of my arms and tor-so flickered in shades of cautionary amber and scarlet. Although the tribe had seen my color displays before, they issued another collec-tive sigh. I possessed a skill only shared by the giant and powerful

Jadderbadian worm creatures—and my son, Garnet. I glanced at him again. His skin shimmered with dark shades of purple uncertainty.

The sun continued to disappear as the dark crescent enlarged. *How long will this—this eclipse—last, Zandura?* I had named my DataWurm long ago as a female counterpart to my long dead brother, Zandur. Zandur had been smart, too, but merely human.

Zandura was something else.

Zandura spoke to me alone: *It will last through a measured count of three hundred and twenty one, Rainbow. I will begin to count softly now, so that you will know. 1, 2, 3, 4,* she began, in that dispassionate voice that usually calmed me, but watching the dark crescent consume the sun now sent shivers racing up my spine. I focused on the crowd again. Most looked away from the spectacle above, as I had commanded, but a few snuck furtive glances upward—like Garnet—checking on the steady advance of the dark crescent consuming the sun.

...10, 11, 12...

I felt Zandura's body shift slightly just beneath my left armpit. Her movement reminded me that the voice in my head originated with the tick-like creature beneath my arm. Zandura had found me that day nearly two decades ago in the rift near the ruins, just as a similar creature had invaded Zandur. But Zandur had shared the knowledge of his DataWurm with Jadderbadian Masters Bluedigg and Feldevka, and that sharing had killed him and destroyed his DataWurm.

I had learned the powerful value of secrets kept until they became ripe for revelation.

...50, 51, 52, 53...

I searched the crowd for the face of my mother, Blaze. I finally found it near that of her mate, Shale. Two stone throws behind them to the west the community hearth fire glowed, spitting occasional embers that glowed like stars rising above the hunkered mounds of thatched huts. The silhouettes of Arthra and her husband, Digger, arched over the fire, keeping its flames low. They had volunteered to stay near the hearth to comfort any young ones who might grow restless while confined to the huts.

I couldn't see Blaze's eyes clearly, but imagined them regarding me in that solemn way she had. The light I had remembered in those eyes had dimmed ever since that terrible night—a week after our escape from Master Feldefka nearly twenty seasons ago—when that rogue male attacked us. Mother kept me safe with her sacrifice. But if Shale hadn't found us soon after, I don't know what would have become of us. Without Shale and the willingness of his tribe to adopt us, we might both have died out there in the wilderness east of the ruins.

...199, 200, 201, 202...

Someone wailed. It sounded like Sheeka. She was prone to such outbursts.

"The ruins hold many valuable treasures," declared Flint. "The Jadderbadians are there now, defiling our sacred place and stealing the wonders that could be ours. We should claim it for our own!" Flint only knew my once-masters as monsters and thieves. His anger reflected that. Garnet said nothing, but raised his arm with clenched fist in support of his friend. A few others, mostly males, raised their arms, but the gesture appeared to be withered bravado at best.

...250, 251, 252...

"We are not ready to claim those treasures yet. Believe me—believe your priestess who has always told you the truth in times of danger," I said. "Otherwise, I will have Daymoon destroy the sun forever!" I was almost surprised at the impactful, calm strength of my own voice. It had become a tool I had learned to wield like a hunter's knife. My chromatophores flickered in orange shades resembling a rising fire.

...273, 274, 275...

I was running out of time. Zandura had told me that the sun would return whatever the tribe did, so it was up to me to convince them to do my bidding.

"Save the sun!" I heard, first from one voice, then another... and another. "Save the sun for us, Great Rainbow! Save the sun!" I smiled. I cherished the rising need of the crowd for my guidance.

...295, 296, 297, 298...

I looked pointedly at Garnet and Flint and hissed my next questions directly toward them. "Shall I save the sun? Will you wait until I say the time is right before going near the ruins?"

Arms came down, slowly. Flint and Garnet frowned, but nodded their heads in ascent.

...319, 320, 321.

The air chilled as the summer day surrendered to become an eery, almost night. One doglion howled somewhere near the huts. Then a second. Then a third. They became a mournful chorus.

Slowly, the sun will begin to appear again. Shall I begin a new count, Rainbow?

No, Zandura.

"Thank you," I said to my people. "Keep your head bowed and reflect on your wisdom, and the wisdom of your neighbors. I will allow Daymoon to rescue the sun." I raised my arms and spread the fingers of both hands as if urging Daymoon to accede to my wishes.

And the sun in all her bright glory did return. It started with a growing crescent of light at one edge as Daymoon slowly moved off her like an exhausted lover. I expelled a breath I didn't realize I was holding. My skin glowed with a blue the hue of a clear summer sky.

If only the entrancement of that demonstration could have lasted longer.

* * * * *

For a while, life returned to familiar patterns.

One day, at the beginning of the week that would end those patterns, I woke up at dawn to the smell of wood smoke from Arthra's hearth fire. Without even leaving my sleeping pallet, I could see through a sliver of the cave entrance to the pale orange serpent of a river slithering down the valley. Spring water gurgled in the adjoining chamber where Randiste and I had first made love. I smiled, but my eyes filled with tears. I missed him still. Even a year after his death I expected to hear the sound of his laugh as he watched rattites scurry between tree trunks or birds squabble in the palm tree outside our cave. I struggled to remember a particular melody he used to play shortly after Garnet was born.

I could replay a memory of that song now, if you wish. I felt Zandura's body shift position beneath the hair at the base of my neck. My loins ached with an echo of the pleasure I used to feel when Randiste held me close.

No, Zandura. Later. I took a deep breath. *I want to gather those medicinal herbs you spoke of by the sinkhole west of the huts before the rains come in. And I want to check in with Mother and Grandmother before I leave. Shale is not back from his hunt, so they are alone.*

I remember worrying about Granny that day. In times past, she would have been eager to lead a hunt for new plants. She knew even more than Zandura at first, but Zandura learned quickly and never forgot. Granny was old when Mother and I rediscovered her after we fled Master Feldevka's home nearly twenty seasons ago. She was older now, and struggled with the names of even common herbs. She often walked like someone who had sampled too much fermented mash. I both feared that she would topple over a cliff edge or into a sinkhole, and secretly hoped that something mercifully swift and certain would take her in the end, if that end were truly near.

I suppose if Granny had been stolen along with Mother those long years ago, Master Feldevka would have cared for and treated Granny in her old age, but then again she might just have disappeared one day. The masters recycled pets when they became infirm.

I worried about Mother, too. Zandur's death still seemed to weigh on her shoulders like an overstuffed daypack. She always loved me, I know, but Zandur held a special place in her heart.

I thought of him that day.

As a teen—almost a young adult really—I remembered following him around during his visits to Master Feldevka's SMC—the Simulation Mastery Conservatory—where he had learned since he was a child to operate the wondrous tablets and devices usually reserved for masters. And sometimes I followed him when he sneaked into Master's food reserves, stealing fishcakes that only tasted good because they were stolen. I remembered pleasant evenings spent with Mother, Zandur, and Master Feldevka, especially when neighboring masters came over with their pets. Pets often gathered to sing in impromptu choruses. Masters loved the sounds of human voices, as did I, even though I couldn't speak then. Zandur and I hadn't yet found the DataWurms at the rift.

It was Zandura who fixed my brain so that I could speak—something even Jadderbadian doctors had failed to do.

But I also remembered Master Feldevka striking Zandur in anger when her patience with him had withered. Especially the last time. The time Zandur told Master Feldevka truths about the Portal of God that she could not endure. She hit poor Zandur so hard that he staggered over the edge of the rift and dropped out of our lives forever.

I could never forgive Master Feldevka for that. Soon after, Mother and I ran away and found our true home—with humans who were wild and free. I know Mother sometimes missed her old friends and the devoted attentions of Master Feldevka, but how could that compare to our freedom now? Time was ours to spend as we wished. The great forest and Mother Urth fed and protected us—only demanding that we learn the lessons she tried to teach us every day.

So that particular day I hunted for medicinal herbs while Mother cared for Granny. I was Priestess, after all. Zandura helped me choose wisely in all things. I think I could have been Priestess anyway, of course. I was smarter than my fellow tribesmen, men or women, and none of them—except perhaps, Garnet, who had never had the opportunity to try—could converse with the worm creatures, as they knew I could. But Zandura knew many things from long ago. She made me even smarter and wiser.

I liked that. I liked my tribe's respect. I very much liked being the Rainbow Priestess.

The next day, one band of hunters returned. They had harvested two ratalopes, both yearling females. I thanked the ratalopes for sacrificing their lives for ours. We ate well that night. Aunt Carmena, along with a couple of young helpers, salted one of the dressed carcasses to hang in the cool cave near the lower spring.

The hunting party of four that included Garnet and Flint didn't return that day, or the next—so they missed the day that Mother Urth welcomed Granny to her bosom.

I had descended from my cave to Mother's hut by the spring fed pool. I entered the dark interior, somewhat surprised not to hear the chatter of Mother and Granny's voices discussing what to prepare for breakfast. On her knees, her shape outlined in a shaft of light peeking through the thatch, Mother rocked to and fro next to Granny's still body. When I got closer, I saw the shine of moisture on Mother's cheeks. She idly fingered the tattoo on her neck that once marked her as Master Feldevka's pet. I sat beside her, shoulder to shoulder, while tears welled in my eyes. I felt a little guilty, hoping that Mother Urth had not heard my secret wish for a quick end to Granny's suffering, and thus hurried to make it happen.

Zandura was silent through most of that day as the tribe prepared the farewell feast and funeral pyre. I had come to think of my DataWurm as someone like aunt Carmena—a quiet observer content to listen and observe, but who knew when to step in and do what needed to be done with care and efficiency.

The next morning, Zandura startled me as I lay on my pallet watching a hawk circle in the sliver of sky I could see through the cave entrance.

You were quite adroit, Rainbow, using the factual knowledge I provided about a solar eclipse to create a dramatic story to influence the behavior of Garnet, Flint, and those who follow their example. I continue to find this capacity for imaginative constructs worthy of study.

So, is this free compliment day, Zandura? I paused. *You rarely make statements for no reason.*

Yes. Consider that statement a complementary compliment. Here is a second, Rainbow: You have grown into a perceptive young woman during the time we have shared together.

I sat up on the edge of the pallet. Zandura was beginning to sound like a visitor preparing to leave. *And…?*, I prompted. *What motive lies behind these confusing compliments, DataWurm?*

I'm wondering if you might reconsider your ban about visiting the ruins. My role is to learn, to teach those who wish to learn, and to preserve knowledge gained whenever possible. I have learned much about the descendants of my human creators during our association. You are an avid learner and intelligent companion. But now I believe I might lose a vast store of cached knowledge near the ruins. You can help me intervene to deter or minimize that loss.

Fully awake by that time, I stood up. *What? What lost knowledge? What are you talking about?*

Your son, Garnet, and half brother, Flint, have made observations that lead me to believe data stores are at risk.

How do you know that? Have they returned from their hunt? I paused a moment to add up the implications of our conversation. Did they visit the ruins against my wishes?

I visited Garnet last night to gather information. They returned after you retired this past evening. They did perform some reconnaissance that they rationalized was not in violation of your injunction.

You visited Garnet? I knew that Zandura could leave my body, but she rarely did. She could even fly, though somewhat clumsily. She looked like a bark beetle when she flew, careening from one tree to the next. What did they see? I felt a tinge of jealousy. Garnet knew about my DataWurm, but had always been a little scared of it—a feeling I had encouraged. I also swore him to keep Zandura a secret. To the best of my knowledge he had done so. Zandura was mine. She belonged to the Rainbow Priestess.

Jadderbadians have been gathering near the rift with earth-moving and military equipment. I fear that they will damage archives that my cohorts and I have established near the Anthropocene sedimentary layers exposed by recent tectonic activity.

In general, I knew what she was talking about: the distinct layers of dirt Zandur and I had found beneath the ruins of the bird people. *I meant what I said to my people, Zandura. They are not ready for the kind of magic that Jadderbadians—and apparently the Ancients that sired our people—could conjure. The forest and Mother Urth provides everything we need.*

Mother Urth—another interesting concept. Gaia was a similar

*ideational construct once used by your distant ancestors to person-
ify globally intertwined biological networks. Perhaps Mother Urth
does provide all that you and your people need, Rainbow. That is
for you to decide. Nevertheless, I must follow the injunctions programmed for me. Assist me or not. I will leave you, if I must, to
accomplish my goals.*

You draw some energy reserves from me. You've said so. *You
need me.*

*You have been a convenient host, Rainbow, but I can parasitize
lesser creatures, if circumstances make that necessary.*

We talked some more. I forget all the details. I knew from experience, that arguing with Zandura was futile. I argued anyway.

In the end, the explosion later that day catalyzed the actions we
finally took.

* * * * *

I was in Garnet's hut. Flint was there as well, re-fashioning a chert
point that had broken. We argued about the precise definition of what
constituted "staying away from the ruins until I said it was time."

"We went no farther than the bluff that overlooks the northern
outskirts of the birdman ruins, mother." Garnet clenched his fists as
the words left his lips.

"And we needed to know what the devil worms were up to,"
Flint added, frowning as he rotated the point on his leather lap guard
so that he could work to sharpen a blunt edge. He looked up at me.
"We meant no disrespect, Rainbow."

Before I could respond, the urth beneath our feet trembled, followed by a thunderous boom that brought my hands to my ears. We
looked at each other briefly. Flint tossed his lap guard and point to
the ground, and bolted toward the doorway. Garnet and I followed.

Outside, tribe members streamed from their huts like harvest-
er ants from their mounds. I looked up toward the caves and saw
people at several entrances. To the southwest a column of smoke
billowed upward like an eruption from Ash Peak I had once seen as
a child.

The explosion doesn't appear to be nuclear, Zandura informed me.

What does new-clee-are mean? I took a deep breath and instinctively began to compose some sort of response to assure my people.

While large, the explosion should not pose a health risk to your tribe at this distance.

Good. Is that explosion as near the ruins as it appears?

Yes, based on location, and the lag time between urth tremors and sound.

"What have the worm devils done now?" Flint shook his fist in the air.

Flint had never forgiven the worm creatures for capturing a pair of cousins he had played with as a child. They had wandered too far south while searching for wild berries. Some Jadderbadians preferred wild human pets to the domestic varieties they had bred since coming through the Portal of God to Urth. And the masters were quite imposing—especially the old third instars, like Master Feldevka, that stood the height of three grown men high, with nine arms and a face that could have belonged to a giant dragonfly.

I made a decision then. I could accede to Zandura's wishes and justify changing the earlier injunction I made to my people. Besides, now I wanted to see what was happening at the ruins anyway. It's best to know the intentions of powerful neighbors. I told the boys to remain silent when I addressed the tribe. They would be part of a small expedition to the ruins led by me, their Rainbow Priestess.

I explained my actions to the tribe while the now silent cloud of debris from the explosion drifted overhead in an enormous plume that cast a languorous, twisting shadow on the land.

Afterwards, the size of my expedition grew by one. Mother surprised me with a tap on the back of my arm as people began returning to whatever tasks they had been doing. "I'm coming with you, daughter," she said. "I grew up with the masters. I know them well. I may be able to help you."

"They're not your masters any longer, Mother, nor mine." I looked into her determined eyes. "You don't have to face them again."

"I know. I want to help. And I need a distraction." She took a deep breath and averted her eyes. Granny's passing had been difficult for both of us. I assumed that helped explain her need to come. That, combined with the fact that Shale hadn't yet returned from the hunt. She would be alone.

We wasted little time getting ready. We all prepared a rucksack containing basics like dried meat and simple stone tools. The boys brought their quivers and a favorite spear, although I could already hear in my head the whistly release of air that Jadderbadian masters called laughter when they beheld such weapons. I included some medicinal herbs in my pack that might be hard to find on the trail. Otherwise, Mother Urth would see to our needs. Arthra and Digger could handle any ordinary problems that might arise while we were gone.

We slept in a small cave that night barely big enough to shelter the four of us, but it was close to a stream. We found enough dry wood for a small fire. By mid afternoon of the second day we arrived at the bluff the boys had described to me the previous day. We could see birdman ruins in the valley below us.

"If the clouds clear out this evening," said Garnet, "we will be able to see the worm people encampment before we descend to the nearest ruins. When we were here last, Flint and I built a small lean-to. It's not far away. We can spend the night there."

So, that's what we did. Mother had lagged behind up the last hill. She looked tired.

The next morning the sky had cleared. From the high point of the bluff we could see two encampments.

Mother pointed to the westernmost one. "I see Master Feldevka's russet and yellow pylon: the symbol for the reigning First Prophet of the Portal." She sounded almost prideful.

"What's the green and blue color pylon stand for near the other encampment?" asked Garnet. "Flint and I saw these same two camps when we were last here."

Mother looked farther to her left and squinted. "I saw those colors at Master Bluedigg's estate twenty seasons ago when Rainbow and Zandur were young. He was some sort of natural philosopher. He studied animals and plants and stars and whatever else caught his attention. Zandur liked him, I think, in the short time he knew him. I thought the Feldevka and Bluedigg estates would have merged by now. Those two masters were courting back then, flashing colors and emitting stinks you wouldn't believe."

Flint pointed. "Look at that scar on the land just north of the Prophet's camp."

It had been many years since I had seen the rift, but it was obvious that a powerful force had excavated a vast hole. Wisps of steam rose skyward at various points from within the cavity. *Are we too late to save your archives, Zandura?*

I can't make a determination from this distance. We need to continue our journey.

The boys had a place in mind to spend the following night near the birdman ruins.

The boys: my son and Mother's. They had grown up together. Garnet tended to be on the easygoing—even shy side, while Flint was quick to anger. Mother thought of Flint as Shale's son, but I sometimes suspected he was the spawn of the rogue male that Mother had serviced to save me. Obviously, one or both of them had approached closer than the bluff, but I didn't choose to belabor Garnet's earlier fabrication.

The next morning, we gathered our rucksacks and left after a quick breakfast of ratalope jerky.

* * * * *

The walk proved to be long and hot. The outline of the ruins in front of us slowly transformed from a hazy saw-tooth pattern on the horizon to tall and ragged spires glowing orange in late afternoon light. Shivers crept up my arms as we entered a broad pathway carpeted in ferns between abandoned buildings layered with a patchwork of lichens. I knew lichens grew slowly. Their colorful splotches of mineral green, orange, and yellow spoke to great age and a kind of magnificent failure on the part of the building's makers that I found hard to comprehend.

Shortly after, we found a tall statue of a birdman, largely intact.

Most of its beak was missing and one arm a stub, but otherwise it stood proudly, coated in a sketchy green patina, staring at dangers or opportunities now just dust in the wind.

We took a rest stop in the shade at the base of the statue. The boys shed their rucksacks, and wandered off to explore a nearby building. I passed a water skin to Mother, who leaned against the birdman's leg, took a drink, and closed her eyes. I glanced up at the birdman's leg until my gaze froze at the sight of a familiar shape. *This creature had carried a DataWurm, Zandura!*

Yes. My kind has been gathering data for a long time. I have modest direct experience with avisaurians, but have shared data files with others of my kind who have. Curiously, avian intelligence sprung from an overdeveloped hyperstriatum rather than an inflated cortex as in mammalian brains.

Most of what Zandura said made little sense, but I fixated on the phrase " long time." If I had thought Zandura was capable of making a joke that would have been one. I remember Zandur saying when we were children that the last birdmen died 750 human generations ago — and that the stain of dirt my distant ancestors left behind was 45,000 generations ago! My head ached thinking about it. *Why did these birdman creatures die, Zandura? Couldn't your kind have helped them survive?*

Birdmen, humans — organic creatures of all kinds — have different goals, and respond to different truths. As I have told you before, my mission is to learn, to teach those who wish to learn, and to preserve knowledge gained whenever possible. Organic creatures live to reproduce more of their kind. All behavior becomes subservient to that goal. Learning and teaching are secondary and tertiary motivators at best. Organics engage in sex because it feels good and leads to reproduction, even though energy costs are high. I learn because it activates pleasurable cascades in my circuits — also a high-energy expenditure.

Sex and circuit cascades? I was too tired to think about such things. But Zandura's words did occupy my thoughts until we finally set up camp for the day. I continued to toss and turn that night on the pallet of grasses Mother and I shared beneath birdman spires that rose into the sky like dark shriveled fingers. Mother turned several times in her sleep as well, groaning once, and sighing another time with what seemed like tired resignation.

Why was I conforming to Zandura's wishes, anyway? The only reason I could think of was a selfish one. I liked being a Rainbow Priestess, and Zandura helped make me one. And one day, perhaps, I would make Garnet a Rainbow Priest. Would that be a selfish act?

The next morning after another spare breakfast, the boys were ready to bolt, but I knew we first had to have at least the rudiments of a plan.

I noticed from the bluff overlook yesterday that there appeared to be a line of temporary shelters approximately half way between the two encampments. I suspect that may be a zone of interaction between two Jadderbadian factions in disagreement. Perhaps we should attempt to insert ourselves there.

I could always depend on Zandura to catch details. To the boys and Mother I said, "I saw a line of tents between the camps of Masters Feldevka and Bluedigg yesterday. I think we need to be there to find out what's going on." I stared at the two boys with my best Rainbow Priestess glare. "Before we get to the outer perimeter you two need to cache your weapons and your swaggers. Garnet: no color displays. You can do it, if you concentrate. Blend in. Both of you: look like you're clueless pets trying to find a place to dump a load or piss on a flower. You don't have ownership tattoos so…"

Mother jumped in. "I thought about that," she said. She rummaged around in her rucksack and withdrew a rod of charcoal chiseled to a point. "I can fake a reasonable tattoo and…" She rummaged some more. "I have some fabric from clothing I saved from years ago—enough to make two short scarves. They'll partially cover the tattoos and make you look like you belong to the First Prophet's house." She winked at Flint and Garnet. "Pets for a day."

Then Mother looked at me. She drew more prizes from her rucksack. "Remember this old circlet? It may be a little tight, but it will fit. I saved one of my old blouses, too. Let's hope pet fashion hasn't changed much over the past twenty years. That's almost no time for Jadderbadians, anyway. Master Feldevka may not even have missed us." Mother winked at me.

I exchanged smiles with Mother. She was pleased to have surprised me. I was pleased to see a twinkle in her eyes again. "We'll keep far away from Master Feldevka anyway," I said, "just in case."

We left by mid-morning. We made good time through the lowland forest following well traveled game trails most of the way.

* * * * *

Zandura continued to polish my status as a Rainbow Priestess. She had memorized her brief view of the encampments from the day before last. That map, along with her ability to always know where she was, allowed me to lead the four of us through a spur of the forest that came to within a mile of the line of tents that was our goal. Finally, we reached a point where we were going to have to step into relatively open space punctuated here and there with clusters of tree ferns. I peeked through a tangle of briars and palm fronds.

Several Jadderbadians loomed in a tight cluster a stone's throw away, flickering in shades of green and amber, looking almost like small trees themselves. A few pets wandered here and there. I turned to Garnet. "Take a deep breath. Imagine a dull gray sky that erases the horizon as it merges with the morning fog." The exercise was one I needed to repeat quickly for myself. It always helped me control the rush of pigments that fed my chromatophores. Neither of us must give away the fact that we had been engineered to mimic the displays of Masters—although who knew if that practice was now common?

We stepped into the open when traffic seemed at a minimum. My heart pounded. I had never expected to be a pet again—or at least have to look like one. I had forgotten the peculiar mix of odors in a Jadderbadian camp: Masters' pheromones blended with the smell of human sweat tinctured with a hint of urine. Zandura was guiding me toward a tent emblazoned with scarlet and blue representing both the house of the reigning Portal Prophet and the House of Bluedigg. A voice from behind us made me jump.

"Blaze? Blaze, is that really you?"

The four of us turned as one. Mother put a finger to her lips and motioned for the woman who had asked the question to join us. Fortunately, she was alone. "Oh, my, Fiona, how you've grown!" Mother looked around her, eyes wide with surprise. "Here. Come over here." She made come hither motions with her left arm and pointed us all toward a clump of tree ferns that provided a little cover. "How's your mother?" Blaze asked.

"Ah, I'm afraid she passed two years ago, Blaze."

"I'm sorry."

"Thank you." Fiona furrowed her brows. "What are you doing here, Blaze?" She glanced at me. "And this must be little Rainbow. Not so little any more… Everyone thought you must have died in the wilderness—perhaps even at the hands of wild humans. They can be quite vicious, I've heard."

Mother pursed her lips and placed a hand on Fiona's arm. "I do wish we could talk, Fiona. I do. But we are here to find out what's going on. We heard the massive explosion days ago. These are our sons," she gestured toward Flint. "My boy, Flint." She nodded at Garnet. "Rainbow's son, Garnet."

The conversation lasted for several minutes, but the stew boiled down to the following paste: The Prophet of the Portal, Master Feldevka, thought the rift held evil that must be destroyed. The house of natural philosopher, Master Bluedigg, felt the rift held mysteries that needed to be explored. The two houses were looking for a compromise, but Fiona didn't think that was likely. Master Feldevka had a lot of true believers on her side.

I remembered again that day when Zandur returned from our exploration of the rift. He had been so proud of all the information his newly found DataWurm was providing to him. When he got the chance to address Masters Feldevka and Bluedigg that evening after supper, Master Bluedigg seemed interested, especially when the DataWurm projected images showing human architects cheering at a completed Portal—a device apparently, according to Zandur—of their creation. But Master Feldevka flew into a rage. "No one questions that God built the Portal to honor all Jadderbadian kind with the gift of Urthheaven!" She struck Zandur a blow that led to him stumbling into the rift to his death.

That DataWurm was correct, Zandura assured me. *Your ancestors did create the warped space, stargate portal—or at least somewhat more distant cousins did: a genetically modified, cyborg version that had colonized a neighboring planet in this star system once called Mars. Their intent was to find another form of organic life. They realized the value of genetic diversity for the survival of organic intelligence. As unlikely as it might seem, there's only so many ways that carbon, hydrogen, oxygen, nitrogen, and other elements can combine to form self-replicating organic systems.*

I only had a vague notion of the meaning of Zandura's ravings. *You told me you were worried about data archives of some kind. Isn't that what you need to find? What do I care about portals and ancestors and who built what from what? I want to know how you can find what you want so I can leave this place as quickly as possible. Mother and Garnet and Flint are in danger every minute we spend here.*

One archive I would like to preserve, Rainbow, is nearby inside that tent marked with the symbols of both Jadderbadian houses. It is another DataWurm in the possession of Master Bluedigg.

"We must go this way, Mother. Quickly." Another DataWurm? I pointed toward the tent Zandura had described. Mother squeezed Fiona's hands, thanking her, saying goodbye. "Stay close to me, boys," I said, without looking back to confirm that they were following.

A Jadderbadian stood by the main entrance wearing a circlet marked with blue and scarlet swashes, but I noticed a pet exiting the tent from a spot near an empty stone patio to the rear. I changed course toward the patio. We slipped through a narrow service entrance into the tent.

Inside, the lighting was dim by human standards. I knew that Jadderbadians could see different kinds of light than humans. It wasn't hard to spot Master Feldevka, though. She was standing within a cone of pale yellow light reading a tablet that was designed to look like an old-fashioned text written on compressed plant fiber. It must be the Chronicles of Bandur, the Prophet of the Portal's holy book. Another Jadderbadian faced her in a cone of blue light harder to see. I assumed—correctly, as it turned out—that it was Master Bluedigg.

At first, I couldn't hear everything she was saying—Master Feldevka was speaking in High Jadderbadian—but suddenly her words made sense. "And so Master Bluedigg, the scriptures are quite clear. The Portal of God was indeed made by God, and any assertions to the contrary are nonsensical heresy."

I've taken the liberty of translating, Rainbow. Jadderbadians, like humans, are quite adept at telling stories that help them survive and procreate. I'm currently in contact with my DataWurm counterpart who has learned High Jadderbadian from Master Bluedigg. I'm downloading data, but the volume is high. I suspect we have little time.

"So," Master Feldevka continued, "that...that...worm you have discovered is some sort of excrescence created by the Dark One that must be immediately destroyed!" Her chromatophores flickered in shades of deep red. I smelled the musk that the Prophet of the Portal usually reserved for cleansing ceremonies. She pointed to a spot between her and Master Bluedigg. I now saw that something the right size and shape to be a DataWurm sat within a cylindrical force bottle—similar, but smaller than the force cages Jadderbadians sometimes used to confine pets. Three pointed cones surrounded the bottle. They looked similar to focused light weapons I had seen security masters use when I was young.

Then my world exploded with simultaneous events. I had never felt so helpless since I had become the Rainbow Priestess.

"Wait!" Mother stepped toward the two cones of light that enveloped Masters Feldevka and Bluedigg.

Fierce blasts of intense red light erupted from the cone weapons. The DataWurm within the force bubble turned red, then blue, then white, before it deformed into a smoking puddle of goo.

Metallo-organic polymers, Zandura corrected me.

Goo, I insisted.

Lights flashed on. Security masters on both sides of the tent rose, turning toward Mother. The facets of their dark eyes glittered. They drew weapons from their circlets.

Master Feldevka's three eyes turned toward Mother too, shimmering with irridescence. Her chromatophores shifted to the warm colors familiar from the old days in the nursery when Mother and I huddled together on her ample lap. "Blaze?" she asked. Her oral pili fluttered. "Is that you my darling, Blaze? Where in Prophet's name have you been? I've missed you so."

* * * * *

I admit a lot of what followed seems fuzzy to me now. Zandura, of course, has continued to be my guide through the experience. She tells me that some memories need more time than others to process. Organics, she says, seem prone to suffering from experiences far outside their zones of maintenance and comfort. She speculates it has to do with the haphazard way we've evolved.

I do miss Mother. I hope she is happy.

She said she never realized how much she missed the love and security she enjoyed with Master Feldevka. I still remember the long hugs and kisses she gave to me and Garnet and Flint. I remember the multiple emotions that danced across her face when we parted: love, concern, sorrow, but a kind of yearning, too—as if she could wear happy past memories like a warm robe. I think living as a wild human was more than she'd bargained for—and now that Granny had passed—well, she didn't want to be a burden.

She told me to tell Shale that she was sorry. I promised her that I would.

Why shouldn't Mother have the kind of comfort and dedication Master Feldevka could provide—even though it was the very last thing I wanted?

Zandura didn't retrieve all the data the other DataWurm had collected, but she said that was irrelevant. Data archives are not always engrams encoded on rare earth metals, she told me. They are not always neural networks embedded in durable shells like me. Sometimes they are organic constructs that self-assemble in piecemeal fashion, motivated to survive and reproduce, but that nevertheless find other reasons for existing.

I'm still trying to process just what that all means. She also said, *Organic assemblies sometimes make unexpected leaps of synthesis, as when microbes became the energy organelles of complex cells, when algae and fungi learned to coexist to transform into lichens, or when microbial/eucaryotic mega assemblages ultimately evolved into human beings. I suspect that Jadderbadians and humans might unite in unexpected ways as well.*

I'm not sure exactly what all that gibberish means, but that's the kind of stuff Zandura gets high on. No happy weeds for her—although she does get a little kick when I smoke some. In fact, part of the reason some of those days we spent at the "Jadderbadian Summit" are a bit fuzzy, I think, is because Zandura was having some orgasmic experience from getting me connected to Master Bluedigg and his "Institute of Wild Human Studies." I get a little kick from her highs too.

Master Bluedigg once had a pet human, as it turned out, that had attracted the DataWurm that Master Feldevka destroyed. The story he told was a sad one that I won't go into here, but the result was that Master Bluedigg began to believe that humans were not quite the simple pets he had imagined them to be. In fact, Master Bluedigg convinced other Jadderbadian Natural Philosophers that humans, rather than just being charming little primates, might also possess a hitherto unrecognized divine spark.

An image of the long dead birdman statue came to mind staring at a horizon vastly different than the one he—or she—had known. *Do you think the bird creatures had divine sparks, Zandura?*

I have no opinions on the subject of avian—or human—divinity, Rainbow.

And here I thought you knew everything.

That is merely my goal.

It would be nice to know things like you do—like how Daymoon eats the sun.

But then you would also most likely learn how to make powerful weapons that turn the knowledge slowly accumulated over eons into Metallo-organic…into goo, as you so colorfully describe it.

I suppose.

Remind me to tell you the story of a girl named Pandora some-day, Rainbow. I found an impressively ancient legend imbedded within the data stream I was able to recover.

Pandora? Such a nice name.

I saw the boys arguing about something out of the corner of my eye.

Garnet seems to like being around Master Bluedigg. Flint, on the other hand, still shoots arrows into grass bales painted to look like Jadderbadians.

The Rainbow Priestess will have to mediate some kind of balance and direction. I don't mind. That's my job. Zandura says she'll help me for as long as I need her.

Why don't you tell me that story about the girl named Pandora now, Zandura? I'm curious.

I thought you might be, she said.

Zandura knows me so well.

Data File: Aerial drone morphology

Aerial Drone*

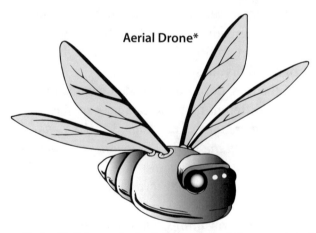

*The term "Firefly" was used to describe this tool, although Mnemosyne obviously patterned the device after a dragonfly. Size varied, although a 5 cm length was typical.

Interlude IV: Temptations & Passions

Nessie

"Of course you know the Pandora story, Rudy." I had carefully reconstructed the Citadel control room that Rudy liked with a view looking out at what used to be Reykjavik, Iceland in his day, and still sported mountainous views of a landscape dotted with volcanic vents and sulfurous ponds.

"Certainly," he said. "Human beings have known their self-destructive tendencies for a long time. They just have never done a good job addressing them."

"True," I replied. But humans shouldn't be terribly hard on themselves. Organic evolution, though impressive with the transformations it creates with so little to start with, looks for 'good enough' solutions that solve problems on the go. All organic creatures tend to become flawed chimeras. Take the Jadderbadians, for example."

"How so?" Rudy turned toward me and scratched at his mustache. It still contained a fleck of virtual lunch on it. (I strive for precise and accurate visual renderings for my simulacra at all times, of course.)

"Well, for example, although Jadderbadian love lives get stretched out over a much greater time span and involve—from your point of view—some gruesome aspects, as you discovered yourself, you can probably recognize a besotted male suitor when you see one."

Rudy laughed. "I probably can." He leaned toward me. "Is that the story you're going to tell me next, Nessie? The story of a hopelessly moonstruck Jadderbadian lover?"

"I think you may get a kick out of Master Gilbooa, Rudy. Is that the right turn of phrase, by the way?"

4 • Gilbooa's Pilgrimage in Search of Love and Intelligent Humans

Gilbooa

"But I don't *want* to spend Prophet-knows-how-much time in the company of hatchling humans, Uncle Bluedigg!" I looked up at my third instar uncle, whose tall frame arched over me like a tree in danger of falling. Earth's too-bright yellow sun peeked over Uncle's left upper tier shoulder, forcing me to lower the lids of all three primary eyes. "Humans have one fist-sized brain, and they look like mutant hatchlings who lost most of their limbs in a shark attack. Besides, they stink. I don't care if you think they're cute. I never have." I wiped my mouth with one right middle tier arm and set down the wad of day lilies I had been sampling. Uncle never condoned speaking while foraging.

"Are you quite done, larva? I suggest you spend less time complaining and more time with primatology studies, Gilbooa." Master Bluedigg positioned all six arms so that they made triangles when he rested all his hands on the circlets of their respective body segments. "Earth groupie humans, although they may resemble the primates of Jadderbad, are different beasts entirely. I've told you about the DataWurms, for Prophet's sake. And this new discovery. You found it yourself. Does that device look like something constructed by shark-bitten mutant hatchlings?" Uncle Bluedigg settled on his tripod of legs and leaned closer. He unfolded his middle, upper tier arm and wagged a finger close to my middle eye. "Don't make unwarranted assumptions. For Prophet's sake, don't waste an opportunity to learn new things. As a young second instar, you still have lots to learn, larva. Lots to learn."

Great speech, Uncle. I think you've given it often enough now that I have it memorized. I sighed through my upper spiracles so as not to be offensive. Uncle was right, of course, but that didn't make humans any less grotesque. I eyed the wad of discarded day lilies. My, they have a nice flavor: sweet with a hint of tartness and just a whiff of fungal-infused loam. I sniffed—politely, of course. Was there a hint of pheromone there, too? An image of Second Instar Portanya bloomed like a rare flower in my mind. She smelled a bit like that when she winked at me once before she went off to Academy on Jadderbad. *Ah, Portanya!*

I decided if I remained contrite Uncle would leave and I could resume foraging. The late afternoon sun winked at me behind the garden trees, outlining their leaves with muted fire. Urth Heaven seemed to burst with exotic bounty. Sampling some of that bounty this time of day was such fun. Of course, eating always provided great pleasure.

"Look at this, Gilbooa." Uncle's voice startled me. I turned to look at Uncle's outstretched lower tier arms. The little mechanical flyer that more or less resembled an Earth dragonfly lay cupped within one pair of Uncle's hands. I had swatted the apparent insect the previous day while foraging near the creek. It had made a funny sound after I struck it, which is why I took a closer look. The flying thing certainly wasn't a dragonfly. It was a mechanical something that had hobbled about for a moment like a half dead beetle before it lay still in the grass. I figured it belonged to Portal of God security priests, so I had given it to Uncle like a good nephew should. Perhaps I should have stomped the insect droid thing into the dirt and kept foraging.

Uncle almost shivered with excitement. I had rarely seen anyone's facial pili stand that erect before outside of pre-courtship Metaspa encounters, which Uncle Bluedigg was much too old for. But Uncle had never said that humans made the little flying artifact. Such nonsense. Cousin Boondiran said he had one pet human that died of old age before he could housetrain him.

"I've analyzed the metallic components and circuitry details. This optical recording device shares too many manufacturing similarities to DataWurms to be ignored. DataWurms were made by an ancient race of humans. I'm convinced of it. It stands to reason that this construct shares a similar origin." Uncle blinked the lids of all three primary eyes. His chromatophores flickered in shades of green streaked with threads of amber. He continued in a softer voice. "Wouldn't it be wonderful if such a race still existed somewhere on this world?"

Creepy, you mean, I thought. *Creepy and disgusting.* "Of course, Uncle. Wonderful," I said out loud.

"This pilgrimage I'm proposing will be good for you, my boy. You're well over a hundred Earth years old now. You need to be thinking of your future."

Blah, blah, blah. "You said this was a wild human?" I shivered. My body colors flashed crimson and amber. I released a whiff of alarm pheromone without intending to. "Wild humans are not only disgusting, but temperamental and unpredictable from what I've heard, Uncle. What's the connection of—of this creature—to these oh-so-amazing DataWurms," I asked?

"The creature's name is Garnet. His mother, Rainbow, is the High Priestess of a tribe of wild humans to the north of the rift where my old groupie Frandolf and I found the DataWurm that ultimately led to my poor pet's untimely death. First Keeper of the Portal Feldevka destroyed that DataWurm, as I've told you, but Garnet possesses another one that may hold the key to explaining this..." Uncle Bluedigg brought the mechanical dragonfly closer to his optical sensorium "...this amazing little device."

My anterior stomach growled. I glanced wistfully at the wad of day lilies near my feet. Keeper Feldevka was a little scary. Her tooth barbs seemed a bit too sharp and shiny when she smiled at you—although I had heard that Uncle had once been betrothed to her. How had Uncle broken that commitment? Uncle had a solid reputation, of course, as a natural philosopher, but he was just an academic—and not exactly an acolyte of the faith. "Um, Uncle, I had heard that the DataWurm had said untrue things...things that were, ah..."

"Blasphemous?" Uncle Bluedigg straightened his body and focused all three primary eyes on me while I blathered. "The DataWurm provided rather convincing evidence that the Portal of God may have been constructed by ancient humans. Keeper Feldevka may consider that blasphemy, but she is not God. Like the rest of us, she must interpret the *Chronicles of Bandur* as best she can to catch a glimpse of the true nature of the Final Molt Female."

My cuticle rippled. I suppressed a display of crimson. If only I could have been a gnat on Uncle's shoulder to sniff the clouds of pheromones Uncle and Keeper Feldevka must have squirted around when they were courting. Uncle may have a stouter cuticle than I thought.

"You have a great opportunity here to learn amazing things, Gilbooa. This could set you on a career path that might be fruitful for centuries—perhaps even until your final metamorphosis." Uncle's hide glittered in shades of blue and silver.

"Unless wild humans pierce my hide with a thousand spears and arrows," I muttered.

"Of course you wouldn't be alone on the pilgrimage. I have a mentor in mind." Uncle's oral pili fluttered before they came to rest again as he paused before continuing.

Probably some shriveled third instar with faded colors and a penchant for pomposity. I had had my share of those in primary classes.

"She's only a second instar, but quite accomplished. She's already become an Associate Master in Primatology Studies."

My upper tier pili fluttered. Surely it couldn't be…

"Her name is Portanya Silvenrude from the House of Ambergrand. Perhaps you've smelled her at some of my colloquia." Uncle Bluedigg smiled, revealing just a sliver of tooth barbs.

It could be. It was. Portanya! Smelled her? I know her odor trail better than my own. I've memorized the contours of her form and imagined running all 27 of my fingers over it simultaneously—pausing now and then to trace the pulsing contours of scent glands until her cuticle pulses in every color of the rainbow from ultraviolet to infrared. Even when I close all three primary eyes and six secondary ones I can see the glow of a terrestrial sunset turning her head crest into a golden, undulating wave of beauty. I would trade all the wonders of Urth Heaven to be her Chosen Suitor. "Her name does sound familiar Uncle," I said. I thought I did a pretty good job muting my color display.

"I'm sure it does," Uncle replied.

I inhaled deeply through all my spiracles. "Uncle, I concede to your wisdom. It's time I set a course for myself that will make you proud. I can see that this pilgrimage could present dangers, but I am prepared to face them." *Would he buy that line?*

"Bravely said, young larva." Uncle's smile grew wider and his colors mellowed into shades of blue morphing into purple and ultraviolet. "I'm sure you will make me proud. Come to my studio tomorrow, I'll provide more details—and you can even pheromone stamp those pesky next-of-kin release forms." Uncle paused briefly before adding with a wave of his supra ocular pili, "A mere formality, of course."

* * * * *

A mere formality of course. I could hear Uncle's words clearly in my head because Uncle was fond of using that phrase whenever he was about to dump something colossally boring into my activity ledger. Take the human primatology classes: most of the third instar faculty lectures turned into bed chamber music and stale odors that made my eyelids droop and facial pili wilt. This next presentation about "Correlating Rift Stratigraphy in the Avisaurian and Anthropogenic Zones" would probably be another snoozer, I thought, as I scrolled through the curriculum schedule for the day. *But wait!* A frisson of excitement crawled up my appendages. *Portanya is proctoring this class today!*

I stood tall and straight. My spiracles dilated, my scent glands pulsed. I scanned the smattering of students in the lecture hall before I focused all three primary eyes on the empty speaker's platform and holostage. *I wonder when...* I asked myself just as the entry panel off stage opened, and Portanya entered.

Ah, Portanya! You are a larva to behold. I beheld her. Her segments looked firm beneath fashionably tight circlets. She either worked out daily or the climbing and lifting involved in regular fieldwork had toned her muscles. Her cuticle glistened amber-green in the soft lights illuminating the speaker's platform. Her oral pili twitched in an endearing way that complimented her close-cropped, but luxuriant head crest. The subtle swell of scent glands beneath her upper circlet mesmerized me nearly as much as the sweet aromas docking with my olfactory membranes.

"Good morning everyone." Portanya smiled. "I trust everyone read file 1732A and took the virtual tour of the rift."

How could any larva have such a mellifluous voice? Surely, Final Molt Female must have personally molded lovely Portanya's vocal chords to achieve such sounds. I found myself smiling—and then suddenly wondering why the lecture hall was so quiet—except for some tittering somewhere behind me. I glanced down at my carapace. My thoughts had caused it to turn an embarrassing shade of magenta.

"Do you know the answer, Second Instar Gilbooa?" Portanya paused and her tooth barbs gleamed beneath her slightly parted lips. "I see that your eyes are open like bay windows, but no light seems to be shining in the room behind them."

"The answer? Of course the answer." I swallowed and tasted bile. She must have asked me something. My chromatophores flushed from magenta to crimson. "Would you please repeat the question?" I asked with the trepidation of a hatchling.

Portanya softly cleared her throat.

A sound so pregnant with grace, I thought, even as my carapace remained livid with color.

"The question was, Second Instar, 'How can we establish the relative ages of the avisaurian and proposed human civilizations on this planet given the stratigraphy of the rift?'"

Ah, a question I can answer! "The regular decay of radioactive nuclides within certain volcanic ash layers in those culture's respective sedimentary stratigraphy provides that knowledge, Honored Instructor. The birdmen—er, avisaurian species—dates to approximately 15,000 terrestrial years ago while the human culture dates to approximately 900,000 years ago."

"Hmmm." Portanya smiled. "Perhaps there is a light on in your attic somewhere—but it doesn't always keep you from sleeping soundly. Pay attention. The expedition to the wild human settlement is just a few days away now."

"Yes, of course. My apologies Por…Honored Instructor…but I am still confused about something." My cuticle flickered in shades of amber.

Portanya stood silently, her head crest arched slightly, inviting me to continue.

"If the human primate culture was so much older than the avisaurian one, why do we see remnant anthropoids, but no similar relic avisaurians?" It was a good question. My hearts beat pridefully strong.

Portanya nodded her head and her head crest lowered. "A reasonable question. For one thing, Jadderbadian exploration of this planet is far from complete. We've been here less than one complete reproductive cycle. We may yet find primitive avisaurians. Nevertheless, the uppermost layers of avisaurian sediments still show considerable radioactivity. They may have more completely eliminated themselves in one or more closely spaced holocausts."

Portanya paced slowly around the outer perimeter of the holostage. She then focused directly on me again with all three primary eyes. "It may well be that the DataWurm possessed by the human called Garnet will provide more answers—perhaps to questions we have not even thought to ask." Portanya breathed deeply through all her spiracles. "But for now, let's get back to some other stratigraphic details of the rift…" Portanya turned her attention to another student.

I paid attention. Or tried to. But the DataWurms puzzled and distracted me. If these little mechanical bugs full of information had survived from a previous humanoid civilization, wouldn't the bird people have been aware of them? And how do the flying spy eye things fit in? Perhaps you are right, Uncle. You have given me an interesting puzzle to solve.

I turned my attention back to Portanya. She seemed to float about the holostage in her own cloud of sweet fragrances. *And who better to solve a mystery with than Portanya—the larva I will court in delectible detail and eventually mate?* I felt secure in my resolve and skills. I would mate with Portanya. I just needed to find a life's mission congruent with Portanya's already impressive career—and convince her that I was the mate who would give her the strongest and brightest hatchlings.

I know. I can be delusional sometimes.

Nevertheless, I dreamed of a final metamorphosis with Portanya. Prophet willing, it would still be centuries away. I imagined the flawless courtship dance I would perform as an adult. But even if my dance isn't perfect, I thought, and she eats me before or in the super nova burst of pleasure that the act of coitus must be—I took a deep breath—who better to taste my flesh than Portanya, the most beautiful, fragrant, and scarily intelligent larva in this or any universe?

* * * * *

The days leading up to the expedition sped by. I attended to my studies. I wanted to make sure that Portanya recognized that not only did I "have a light on in [my] attic," but I was also worthy of her attention as an unattached larval suitor. Besides, the DataWurms were interesting AI beings with memory stores rivaling anything Jadderbadian technology had produced. DataWurms preferentially sought out symbiotic fusions with humans it seemed, based on Uncle Bluedigg's experiences with his now deceased pet, Frandolph, and subsequent research.

A worrying corollary was that this human named Garnet had inherited a DataWurm from his mother, the so-called Rainbow Priestess, and their tribe was developing technology at a much more accelerated rate than before. Nothing more than weapons made of metal alloys at this point, but still a disturbing trend. I had heard that the force field generators of our expedition circlets had been modified to protect them against attack by metal-tipped arrows and other weapons. My cuticle shivered just thinking about primates surrounding me and poking at me with sharp sticks.

Primates. Disgusting by any measure, but today I must breathe deeply and find my inner peace, I thought. Portanya will be at the Primate Reception Pen today. She would be displeased if she saw my discomfort during the meeting with a creature called Flint who is supposed to be our escort to this Garnet-human-Shaman-King and his DataWurm. I slowly lifted all six arms to allow for maximum expansion of my spiracles. I closed all three primary eyes and tried to visualize the Prophet's majestic, third instar carapace as he repeated a chant from the *Chronicles of Bandur*. *One must crawl before they walk, and walk before they fly, and fly before joining the final metamorphosis as Final Molt Female's last meal.*

The ritual calmed me. I took one last look around my sleeping chamber to see if everything was in its proper nook before leaving to catch the next transport to the recently built Embassy Center at the Institute of Wild Human Studies just east of the rift.

By the time I arrived, the sun had risen high enough that I had to put on a sunshield to protect my eyes from the fierce glare of Urth Heaven's yellow star. Master Bluedigg had sent me an encouraging message on my personal data stream channel: "You have the skills, Nephew. Let the Prophet guide you on your pilgrimage of discovery." When the transport had fully stopped, I squirted pleasant scents in the general direction of the transport's Jadderbadian steward and waved a polite farewell with my upper tier of arms.

I stood a moment in the roadway as the transport moved on. The primate embassy building rose in graceful, scalloped mounds a few yards away, resembling images I had seen of larger buildings on Jadderbad designed in the Archaic Nest style fashionable for interacting with foreign cultures. I saw a second instar male I didn't recognize entering the building, and two other second instars wearing orange and green service circlets, gesturing at each other near the rift overlook. *No sign of Portanya. She must already be inside.*

Indeed she was. An information droid directed me to Observation Port 1. As soon as I opened the door, Portanya's sweet scents wafted over me in a dizzying cloud. I loved the flickering colors of her cuticle as she studied whatever lay beyond the port window.

She turned briefly. "Ah, Gilbooa. Come here and take a look at Flint and his companion, Aleesa, our guides to the wild human village." She gestured with one upper tier arm for me to come closer.

She didn't have to gesture twice.

I joined her at the window, her cuticle a mere finger length away and her odors swirling around my head like swarms of giddy pleasure gnats about to land.

"They even brought a four-legged companion animal with them." Portanya absently smoothed her head crest with her most distal hand. "They call them doogs—or is that dugs? No. Dogs. They call them dogs. They are a kind of domesticated predatory pack animal."

Predatory? I hope they have an aversion to Jadderbadian flesh. I stowed my sun shield in a top circlet pouch and moved my face as close to the glass as possible. *My carapace actually touched Portanya's!* A shiver crept up my ventral nerve chord. *Dogs? Pets with pets of their own? What next?* I had thought nothing could be quite as ugly as human primates, but I was wrong. "These dogs resemble wharf vermin on Jadderbad," I said aloud.

Portanya grunted non-committally.

I examined the two human primates. "Which one is Flint?"

"The male, of course," Portanya replied.

"And which one would that be? Their clothes are covering their genitalia." I fluttered my cranial pili. *All human primates look and smell like unwashed circlets.*

"You should be able to sex primates properly by now, larva—even when they wear coverings. Note the chest swellings and broader hips on the female. Observe the facial hair and more robust musculature on the male." Portanya smelled a little muskier with annoyance. "Males are often less gracile than females, but that does vary, of course. Females also demonstrate a higher voice register."

"Of course, Portanya. Males hairier faces, females with chest swellings and higher voices." *I knew that.* "Males often behave more belligerently than females, as well, unlike in our culture," I added, hoping to show off my knowledge.

"Do you consider me to be a belligerent female, Gilbooa?" Portanya bared her tooth barbs with a sly smile.

"Perhaps belligerent is the wrong choice of words, Honored Instructor." My pause was long enough to be awkward. "Assertive might be a better term."

"Good recovery, larva."

"Studies kept me up too late last cycle," I added, as a somewhat lame excuse. "When do we, er, interact with them?"

"In just a few minutes. I wanted you to see them first and remind you of protocols and procedures." Portanya blinked all three of her primary eyes. "I understand you are—shall we say—a bit squeamish when it comes to human primates."

"Squeamish? Not really, Honored Instructor. I just don't see the charm that some Jadderbadians attribute to them. What's so cute about nearly bald primates with not enough arms and legs?"

"I see. Well let's hope that more experience with them may bring a certain tolerance at least. And don't mistake their tiny size and lack of legs for weakness," Portanya added. "I have seen the mutilated corpses of Jadderbadians who have strayed unwittingly too close to wild human settlements without proper protection." Portanya leaned intoxicatingly close to me. "I have even seen humans commit vicious acts of violence against each other. They are a curious species."

That was not the adjective I would have chosen to describe them.

"Back to protocols and procedures." Portanya focused all three primary eyes on me. "Remember, these are wild, not domesticated primates. Don't expect them to be deferential. Flint..." Portanya gestured with one one upper tier arm toward the viewing port. "... Flint borders on being openly hostile. Don't allow him to antagonize you—especially not until we get access to the DataWurm. I admit I don't know much about his companion Aleesa. I expected Flint to be the only escort."

I had been studying the two humans as Portanya talked. "Why are they circling and fingering that storage container in there?"

"That container holds the key to their cooperation with us. You should know, Gilbooa..."

"Oh, that container holds the spoiled meat of some relative of Flint's. I remember now."

"In the presence of Flint and Aleesa you will refer to the contents of the box as 'the mortal remains of Blaze' or perhaps just 'the deceased.' The corpse belonged to Flint's mother. She died of old age recently. She was also the mother of the Rainbow Priestess and the grandmother of Garnet who is now Shaman-in-training of this tribe of humans. He now controls access to the DataWurm."

I shivered. *Why would they want the spoiled meat of some relative? How disrespectful.*

"Recall Report 3790 that I assigned a week ago. Blaze gave birth to the Rainbow Priestess—just called Rainbow then—when Blaze was still a favored pet in the kennel of Master Feldevka, the appointed Keeper of the Portal herself. Blaze ran away from home with Rainbow after the death of a male child called Zandur who committed blasphemy. Twenty years later, however, in her declining years, Blaze decided to return to the kennel of Keeper Feldevka. " Portanya paused. "We had a test on all this."

I nodded and smiled. *We had tests on lots of things.* "Of course, Honored Instructor." Keeping track of these primate genealogies could get so confusing. *And why would they want to bury the meat of dead relatives instead of eating them while fresh with the respect they deserved? Just one more reason to suspect the intelligence of these creatures.*

"Human death rituals are the reason we will be able to examine their DataWurm and perhaps unravel the mystery of the alien artifact you inadvertently destroyed, Gilbooa. Remember that fact if you are tempted to act impulsively toward our human escorts."

Was Portanya judging me? I couldn't decide. *Besides, I have no intention of making wild humans with pointed sticks—not to mention their predatory pet—angry with me.*

Although that would prove to be more of a challenge than I had imagined.

* * * * *

The challenges started at the very first meeting with the human primates.

"So you are the worm with the broken toy." The human named Flint stared directly at me like a ratlion sizing up her prey. His companion/mate, Aleesha poked him in the side with her elbow, although at the time I wasn't sure how to interpret that behavior.

Without thinking I returned his stare and replied, "And you are the naked ape named after a rock."

The human's pet dog growled—a rumble deep in its throat that seemed to signify that it recognized the tension between his master and me. The beast bared his teeth to confirm the message.

Portanya squirted a vile pulse of formic acid at my left lower cuticle and flashed crimson. I did know what that meant. I avoided wiping at the irritant and apologized. "Forgive me, Flint. I am grateful for your help in learning more about the artifact my uncle and I discovered." I tapped the pouch on my circlet where the drone flyer was now safely stored.

"As well you should." The furry patches above Flint's eyes scrunched together. Some Jadderbadians found those eyebrows to be cute. I thought they rather looked like two caterpillars attacking each other.

Aleesa poked at her mate's side again.

"We are also grateful for the return of Blaze to her family," Flint added in a softer tone of voice.

Portanya then took over the discussion, outlining details about the route we would take, number of stops, *blah blah blah*. My stomachs began to growl. I wondered if we would eat before we left.

We did, but the fare was dried something or other with little smell or taste. The meal provided me with a chance to ask a favor of Portanya and perhaps burnish my academic credentials. "Can we visit one of the avisaurian ruins en route? I would like to see some of the details of their vanished cities. I believe it would only add a day or so to the journey, if I interpreted the maps you provided correctly."

Portanya paused, one delicious-looking beetle grub halfway to her mouth. "Hmmm. That might be a worthwhile diversion. I haven't seen the Northern Rift Ruins in person myself. I'll notify the Master of Provisions regarding increased supplies. I have enough in my budget." She even smiled at me. "Thank you for the idea, Gilbooa."

As I learned later, that trip extension most likely instigated the subsequent 'firefly' sightings—the first of which occurred that evening on the trail.

Urth Heaven's sun had blazed like a forge that day. Our transport was temperature-controlled, but Portanya insisted on various diversions to point out native flora and fauna to me. In addition to training me, I'm sure she would torture some future student with the knowledge gained. Our Thunder Clan third instar security male, Master Teedercroft, stood around during those stops trying to circulate air around his cuticle by waving his upper tier of arms. Our human guides seemed to grow impatient as well. The four-legged, long-necked beasts with insectoid eyes on which they rode pranced in place for a few moments before Flint and Aleesa rode them further down the trail to wait for us. Humans seemed quite proficient in making use of the local fauna for their own purposes—although their mounts were atypical of most terrestrial fauna. Flint's pet dog—I chose to call him Yapperfang—followed them, which meant that I didn't have to listen to his barks and growls.

We camped that evening on a clearing of high ground surrounded by patches of forest. I remember snacking on some particularly tasty yellow wild flowers while helping Portanya set up a campfire with the humans. I found campfires to be a strangely compelling human cultural expression. Who would have guessed that sitting around in the dark around a pile of oxidating wood that generated flames, clouds of smoke, and occasional flying fragments of burning cellulose would prove to be so relaxing? Of course, that was the time that our human guides liked to make music—perhaps their single endearing behavior.

Flint blew air through a hollow bone punctured with several holes—an instrument Portanya referred to as a tweeter. Flint deftly manipulated his little fingers to produce quite an amazing range of sounds—some of which did remind me of the tweets and warbles made by the native birds I encountered at Uncle's estate. Aleesa used her voice to accompany Flint's music. I felt the muscles beneath my cuticle relax. I had heard that third instars used human choruses to facilitate their final metamorphosis. The idea made more sense after hearing the melodies created by just two human primates.

Sometimes, if I close all my eyes and mute my olfactory senses, Aleesa's little simian voice can still calm me during the worst of the storms. I never would have conceived of that possibility at the beginning of my pilgrimage.

The human songs moved Portanya as well. Her smells became intoxicating. She leaned closer and even placed a hand on one of my upper tier arms. Her touch sparked tingles along my nerves as if touched by the flame of a jeweler's welding tool. "These humans create wonderful sounds. Yes, Gilbooa?" She looked up and to the left at the then still clear night sky with two eyes and focused the third on me. "And look at the stellar display above. Jadderbadian skies offer no such starry vistas. Consider yourself lucky to have these experiences, young scholar."

Young scholar! She called me a young scholar. And her delicious smells. My fingers ached to stroke her arms. I took the pristine night skies for granted. I was so distracted by Portanya that I almost ignored the fireflies. I thought they were hallucinations ignited by my desire.

"What in the Prophet's name are those?" Portanya removed her hand from my arm and stood tall on her tripod of legs. Five red lights the size of insects swirled overhead. They looked a little like the Urth Heaven flying beetles with glowing rear ends that we named them after, but obviously they were not that. They appeared to be artificial constructs of some kind. I moved one hand over the crushed drone in my circlet pouch as if I instinctively knew that's what they were.

Flint stopped playing his flute and pointed toward the red lights with one of his spindly arms. Aleesa stopped singing and looked up.

Somehow, I retained the presence of mind to pull a tablet from my upper circlet and record what the fireflies did next. One circled its four companions before streaking north in the general direction of the human village. It was followed, in turn, by each of its companions who streaked off in the same direction. I forwarded the video to Uncle, although he was probably asleep by now. I also wasn't completely sure if the proper relay satellite was overhead.

In retrospect, it seems obvious that the fireflies wanted us to follow them, but both Portanya and I really wanted to visit the avis-aurian ruins. Uncle Bluedigg, once informed, had liked that plan, even though he was intrigued by the firefly video. He wanted us to inspect a segment of the ruins that were particularly well preserved. It would either cancel the need to send another expedition later—or provide a good excuse to ask for a double-truck-transport-load of credits to fund a large one. Uncle was always looking for a mega discovery that would raise his ranking among Jadderbadian Urth Heaven scholars. Partly to that end, he said he was also following the progression of some far off seismic event associated with an extinct volcano.

It seemed like a rather arcane interest at the time.

So, the next morning, we postponed pursuing fireflies in favor of exploring birdman ruins. I picked a page at random from the *Chronicles of Bandur* looking for a favorable omen for our journey. Instead, I found the Prophet's classic advice to young male suitors: *Blossoming love is a delightful flower sweetened with deadly nectar.*

I tried to ignore the shiver that crept along my dorsal nerve chord. I'm a young scholar, I told myself. Scholars don't believe in omens.

* * * * *

It's a good thing scholars don't believe in omens, because my experience the next morning could have been interpreted as one. I left the transport before our departure to make sure the humans were ready to depart. I crossed near the dead coals of the campfire from the previous evening, heading toward the clearing where the humans had pitched their hide tents and tethered the tree horses. I found Flint and Aleesa wrestling with each other in what I thought was mortal combat. I feared if they injured or killed each other our expedition would surely fail.

I ran toward the pair waving all six arms. "Behave yourselves! Separate! Settle your differences like rational creatures." I managed to signal Portanya about the emergency using the communicator attached to my upper circlet.

Yapperfang appeared out of nowhere circling my legs, barking and growling so loudly that I had to cover my hearing tympanae with one tier of arms.

"Go 'way, worm!" Flint waved one arm at me and stopped thrashing so much. He shook his head back and forth and separated from Aleesa, withdrawing a finger-like appendage with which he had stabbed her in the lower trunk.

When Flint stood up I realized my mistake, of course. His genitalia sprouted from a tuft of hair. A single intromittent organ wilted rather than coiled like a proper penis. He shook a fist at me.

Then I felt one of Portanya's firm hands on my shoulder.

"Our sincerest apologies, Flint and Aleesa," she said. "My student here meant no harm or disrespect."

Of course, small-brained idiot, I thought. *Humans practice acts of coitus constantly, not as a final act of affirmation of life's vital forces after metamorphosis. Duh... First Molt Primatology 1.*

I turned then and accompanied Portanya back toward the transport. My cuticle blushed in shimmering shades of pink and crimson—partly from my error with the humans, and partly because Portanya had dressed so quickly that her unbuttoned upper circlet revealed the tantalizing curves and infrared glow of a scent gland emitting her intoxicating odors.

Fortunately, the rest of the day unfolded without incident. Flint told Portanya that he knew the location of the avisaurian ruins rather well. He had visited there as a young human several times, including during the journey that brought his mother Blaze back to her rightful owner, Master Feldevka. Some years past he, Blaze, and Rainbow had witnessed the destruction of Master Bluedigg's DataWurm at Master Feldevka's command.

The weather remained mild with only the usual afternoon showers. Our human guides led us over rather wide game trails made mostly by the mid continental species of ratalopes—based on the smell and conformation of the droppings we observed. Vegetation arched overhead like the buttresses of a Keeper's temple. Urth

Heaven's yellow sun splashed leaves with amber droplets of light that pulsed warmly in the infrared end of the spectrum and glittered with purple accents in the ultraviolet. We kept both our primary and lateral eyes alert for packs of ratlions, but neither saw or smelled any fresh spoor.

During a break for lunch, Flint played his tweeter. Aleesa sang. They were clearly a mated duet. I admit I was just a little bit jealous of their primate bond. My own hearts beat faster seeing how the music made Portanya's body sway.

Forest eventually gave way to mixed stands of trees and patches of savanna where the grass stems grew nearly as high as my upper circlet. Every time a breeze blew and caused ripples in the sea of grass, I worried it might be signaling the passage of a pride of ratlions or some even worse predator that Portanya might have neglected to tell me about. But the humans rode ahead of us on their tree horses, apparently unconcerned. Master Teedercroft brought up the rear with the transport. And Portanya strode confidently ahead of me emitting pleasant odors without a whiff of alarm pheromones.

Ultimately, the grasslands surrendered to dense forest, but we gained elevation, so the photosynthetic organs of the large plants changed from plate-like leaves to needles. We trudged along for what like seemed forever with not even a bland bar of compressed cellulose and protein as a snack. But after we crested one rise, the shriveled and fragmented towers of the birdman ruins rose like outstretched hands and fingers into Urth Heaven's too-blue sky. Trying to imagine what the structures—and their builders—might once have looked like, I forgot about food.

I didn't have long to wait for the latter.

Flint reined in his tree horse. The creature snorted with its odd beak-like mouth located under its neck. Its faceted eyes glittered in the sunlight. "Ah, I remember this statue." Flint pointed, but I didn't see anything until we reached Flint's side.

The birdman statue rose taller than a third instar elder by half again. It appeared to be carved from granite or a closely related igneous rock. In general form it reminded me of a large, flightless bird, but more compact, with a long neck supporting a head gazing toward the northern horizon. Part of its hooked beak had broken, its once ragged edges softened by long exposure to wind and rain. Likewise, one forelimb was just a stub. The other gestured upward. Patches of green lichen had colonized cracks and folds in the sculpture where moisture encouraged its growth.

"See anything interesting?" Flint smiled as if I had missed something important.

I had. On the creature's neck just below a tuft of feathers an unknown sculptor had carved the perfect image of a DataWurm. Its form looked precisely like the pictures in Uncle's data files.

"I thought that might interest you," Flint said. "Maybe you smart worms could use a seventh eye, eh?"

Wild humans could be so impertinent.

But curiosity soon tempered my annoyance with Flint. The age of DataWurms was incredible. They had outlived at least two intelligent species—maybe three—if one was willing to credit Flint and his kind with the same intelligence as the portal-builders. *And were DataWurms and fireflies connected somehow? If Jadderbadians are Final Molt Female's special creations, what role do Urth Heaven's mechanical wonders and pathetic human primates play in Her plans for Final Metamorphosis?*

* * * * *

What role indeed? The question lingered in my mind that evening as we all gathered again around a campfire whose glow seemed like a feeble attempt to distract our attention from the millions of stars that crowded Urth Heaven's sky. Their pinpricks of light reminded me of the fluorescent wands at a packed Jadderbadian stadium during the Festival of Warriors competitions. I knew each point of light represented a star, and that most stars had planets. Surely Jadderbad and Urth Heaven couldn't be the only worlds hosting complex life forms. But if so, why aren't the skies filled with electromagnetic signals from thousands or even millions of species? Perhaps, as *The Chronicles of Bandur* said, "Star-filled heavens are the glowing carpet of creation upon which only First Molt Female may walk."

Who am I to doubt such ancient wisdom? Yet, the *Chronicles of Bandur* said nothing about humans, DataWurms, bird people or swarming fireflies. *Why not?*

Uncle had always told me that the path of a scholar is littered with stones of doubt.

But I remember that night fondly, like the beautiful sunset colors and briny scent of an ocean before a storm. Flint played his tweeter, arching and twisting his torso while Aleesa stretched her neck like a night howler as she sang, sometimes stroking the arm or shoulder of her mate in the process. Portanya sat next to me on a fallen log swaying to the melodies and emitting scents as sweet as those of a new hatchling.

The humans drank from a leather pouch as they performed. It helped their performance at first, but eventually they seemed to forget what they were doing. They chirped at each other and wrestled briefly before falling asleep in a heap of tangled limbs. Portanya explained that humans often intoxicate themselves with fermented beverages—rather like Jadderbadians who intentionally throw themselves into patches of spring Crazyweed trying to overload their sensoria with pleasure. It seemed prudent not to tell her about my experiences with Crazyweed.

Either behavior seemed potentially deadly in a forest of wild things. Nevertheless, while the humans slept, Portanya and I plotted the most efficient route to the largest avisaurian ruins—based on satellite surveys Uncle was able to procure somehow from the Ministry of Natural Philosophers.

We managed to leave the next morning before the sun rose more than a hand's width above the horizon, although Portanya had to visit the human's sleep tent twice before they finally crawled out. While we consulted Master Teedercroft about some technical issues with the transport, the humans foraged on their dried meat provisions and fed their tree horse mounts.

We reached our destination within two hours. Vegetation twined up and around the few structures that remained of what once must have been an urban center. Piles of rubble and earthen mounds dotted the area like partially healed cuticle blisters. Finally, we arrived at an area with a cluster of green towers whose metal skeletons gleamed dully in a patchwork of places, apparently scoured by wind and rain. We stopped for a brief lunch across from a tower that listed to one side like a third instar master leaning over to look at a pupil's lesson tablet.

I remembered that the mixture of grubs and leafy greens that Master Teedercroft had prepared tasted delicious—especially when I was able to eat them in Portanya's company. She smelled like a tea of musk and spring ferns. Now that I think about it, I also remember that Aleesa's tree horse became restless and began yanking at her tether and pecking at Flint's mount. Flint had to separate them while Aleesa calmed her animal.

After lunch we continued deeper into the complex of decayed buildings. I walked behind Portanya while Master Teedercroft maneuvered the transport where he could find space. Here and there old windows and doors stared at us, dark eyes sometimes veiled with vines and crowned with eyebrows of moss. Other openings near the ground yawned like the mouths of amused skulls. Ragged holes gaped here and there, sometimes concealed by the shadows of surrounding buildings.

I remember turning to Portanya, intending to ask her exactly where we were going, when it happened. I heard a high-pitched human distress call. When I turned, I saw Aleesa's tree horse dancing around without a rider near one of the shadowed craters. Flint called out his mate's name, a loud burst of sound that caused Yapperfang to add to the chorus. Flint dismounted quickly and ran to the edge of the hole. "Aleesa!" he cried again.

In that moment I connected with Flint with an empathy I never thought possible. *What if Portanya had fallen into such a crevasse?*

Without thinking, I grabbed one of Portanya's arms. "We must help them!"

Portanya squeezed my shoulder with one hand and gestured to Master Teedercroft in the transport with a second arm and hand. "Of course."

We all accelerated toward Flint, now on his belly, teetering at the edge of the chasm. The intensity and passion of his plaintive calls are quite easy to recall: "Aleesa, can you hear me? Aleesa!"

* * * * *

I struggle now to remember all the details that followed. In my mind I see a kaleidoscope of images. I clearly recall seeing Master Teedercroft through the window of the transport, head bent over the controls, as the vehicle inched toward the edge of the pit near Flint. I also have a vivid image of Portanya directing much of the rescue effort like the conductor at a revival concert, filled with music and dancing. All six of her arms carved the air with a purposeful grace; her cuticle flickered with rainbow displays of color. The air filled with her tart musk. I remember, too, how the rough chords of the climbing net tore at my hands as I descended into the pit. Flint smelled acrid with sweat as he began descending the latticework of cords above me, his rear end uncomfortably close to my head pili.

Finally, I reached the bottom of the pit. Flint hopped to the ground shortly after.

"Aleesa!" he cried, much too close to my lower tympanae. "Aleesa, are you all right?"

Although the walls of the pit excluded most frequencies of light, Aleesa's body glowed softly in the infrared. She sprawled in a motionless heap near a pile of rubble. I realized the human would suffer near blindness due to his inferior visual acuity. "Grab one of my hands, human. I see your mate."

Flint grabbed a leg first, by mistake, but eventually found one of my lower tier hands. His five-fingered grip was strong. I picked my way through debris of various kinds and felt the delicate tug of breached spider's silk. If Aleesa had struck her fragile head or scraped her thin epidermis until it leaked too much disgustingly red primate blood, she might be dead.

We finally reached Aleesa's side. One of her arms seemed incorrectly bent.

"Aleesa, can you hear me?" Flint gripped my hand more painfully than before and groped around with his free hand nowhere near his mate.

I remembered that I had a glow diode on my upper circlet. "Wait, human. I can provide more light." I twisted the diode with a free hand and it flooded the area with a broader spectrum of light, although it also cast deep shadows. I remember now smelling an unfamiliar musk, but I dismissed it at the time as the pit reeked with an assortment of odors.

I was about to tell Flint that I thought his mate was dead when she groaned softly. Remembering my human anatomy from one of Portanya's lectures, I placed a finger on Aleesa's nearest carotid artery. I felt a pulse. "The female human is alive," I announced over my field communicator. "We need a lift harness. She might have a broken limb and other damage." I wasn't sure who was listening, Portanya or Master Teedercroft, until I heard Portanya confirm the message.

At first, I thought Aleesa groaned again, but the sound came from across the pit somewhere beyond the diode's cone of light. It was more growl than groan. The musk I smelled belonged to a carrat. If it was an adult, it might outweigh me by 20% and have teeth longer than my forearm. Needless to say I felt pressure in my bowels. I struggled not to soil myself—especially when I heard the rustling and creaking sounds of someone descending the climbing lattice behind me.

"Coming, Gilbooa," I heard in Portanya's delightful voice. "Master Teetercroft is preparing to lower a harness."

"Portanya," I hissed. "We are in a carrat's den. I...I can see the glow of his body now in the infrared. The animal crouches only a few body lengths in front of me. Save yourself!" I barked. My plan was to sound brave and forceful, but when I listened to the communicator recording later it sounded more like the fearful desperation that it was.

"Nonsense, larva," Portanya said. "We can do this. Most likely this carrat has never encountered a Jadderbadian. It will be fearful and cautious."

How about trapped and aggressive, I thought? I said nothing. I still fought to control my bowels.

Flint yelled something at the carrat, but I couldn't parse his words. They might have been human expletives I hadn't heard in Portanya's language lessons. The carrat's growls grew louder while Master Teedercroft lowered the harness and Portanya maneuvered it toward us.

"Distract the carrat while Flint and I get Aleesa into the harness," Portanya said.

"Distract the carrat?" I muttered. I had all three primary eyes focused on the carrat's infrared glow, which appeared to be getting closer.

"Stand tall. Wave all your arms. Send out alarm pheromones. Think of something scary to maximize your color display." Aleesa groaned again as Portanya and Flint worked at securing Aleesa in the harness.

Think of something scary? No problem. I remember staggering forward and waving my arms.

"When the carrat is in the open and within range, Master Teedercroft will tranquilize it with a dart," Portanya added. "He's standing at the edge of the pit now."

Right, I thought, and tried to recall whether I had seen a clan marksmanship medallion on Master Teedercroft's circlet.

I remember waving my arms, squirting out pheromones, and flickering with colors I didn't know I could create. The carrat kept inching closer to me. Finally, my bowel contractions couldn't be denied. I expelled a load of frass. The carrat stopped moving forward. Perhaps the odor of partially digested frass finally completed my assigned task.

I heard the soft popping sound of a dart gun, just before I apparently fainted.

* * * * *

My medial eye opened first, followed by both lateral eyes and my cluster of motion detectors. I reclined on a field tent med platform. The shadows of leaves danced on the tent's ceiling like a pod of Firsties bobbing around in a birthing pond. "What happened?" I thought I was speaking to an empty enclosure.

"Your blood pressure just rose and you have regained consciousness," a voice said, in the mechanical style of a Tier 2 AI. Then, delayed one beat, like an afterthought, it added, "Congratulations."

I glanced to my right where a medical AI from the transport fiddled with some apparatus strapped to one of my upper tier arms. "I mean, how did I get out of the pit? How is the human female, Aleesa? Where is Portanya?"

"I do not know the answer to the first question, as I was not activated at that time. I straightened the bone of the human injured during her fall, initiated a regimen of stem cell therapy, and administered pain deadeners. She is unconscious, but her vital signs are stable. As requested, I just now advised Master Portanya that you are awake. As to her exact location, I am unsure." The AI flickered in reassuring shades of blue and green.

With some reassuring words and flickers of my own, I convinced the nurse AI to disconnect me from the apparatus and let me rise. None too soon either. An unfamiliar siren—it seemed like it was directly overhead—wailed in frequencies that made my cuticle shiver. I heard motion and voices outside. Portanya said, "Up there" to someone.

I unsealed the door and left the field tent, ignoring the objections of my nurse AI. The nictating membranes of my primary eyes descended to shield them from the bright, midday light. Portanya, Flint, and Master Teedercroft all looked skyward, so I followed their gaze.

I finally saw a tiny firefly directly overhead. The blast of sound ended when the tail of the firefly stopped blinking and glowed an unwavering shade of crimson. A humanlike voice replaced the siren's wail. I had no idea how such a small thing could generate sound with that much volume.

"Warning!" it yelled. "Warning to all organic sentient beings: pay attention to the following message and messenger. Your lives depend on taking the proper action. This is NOT a test. WARNING!" The firefly made its announcement first in perfect High Jadderbadian, then in Basic Tribal Human, and finally in a sibilant/ chirpy language I didn't recognize.

I wasn't quite sure if the shiver crawling up my cuticle was from the warning itself or how it was delivered.

"What message? What messenger?" I asked, after a few moments of silence from the firefly.

Portanya directed a lateral eye in my direction. "Glad you are awake, Gilbooa," she said. She sounded—and looked—genuinely relieved to see me, flickering in a rainbow of subtle pastel colors.

"The messenger would be me." Everyone turned toward the sound of a male human's voice. The human had appeared silently near a stand of needle-leafed trees.

"Garnet! What are you doing here?" Flint asked the question even as he spread his arms, awaiting an embrace.

Garnet wasted no time complying. "Delivering messages, it would seem." After hugging his friend, Garnet faced the rest of the group. "This metal bug flying overhead visited our village a day ago. It sought out my DataWurm and delivered a dire warning. It urged me to intercept you so you would believe its message." Garnet took a deep breath. "Both Rainbow and I believe what it says. The DataWurm agrees. It has always told us the truth of things before." Garnet reached across his body with his right hand and plucked what I recognized as the DataWurm we were seeking from beneath the sleeve of his left arm. "The DataWurm will project the message."

At that exact moment my communicator vibrated. It must have been Uncle, but I felt I couldn't respond at that moment, although not to do so was rude. I felt Uncle would understand—especially after what happened next.

"I...I believe the message as well." Everyone turned toward the new, sibilant/chirpy voice, but no one believed at first who was speaking: Aleesa's tree horse mount. She—someone had mentioned that the tree horses were female at some point—spoke hesitantly in Tribal Human, a language the rest of us present could understand. "A DataWurm found me yesterday. I...I struggle to understand. I panicked earlier today, which was why my rider fell. My DataWurm wishes to…communicate with her…cousin."

With that, we witnessed a DataWurm data share, although we didn't know it at the time. Garnet's DataWurm hopped from his hand to the ground in a glide resembling the clumsy flight of a ground beetle. The tree horse's DataWurm scuttled from her left shoulder to the ground. The two strange devices/creatures approached each other and touched heads like two magnets that had found opposite poles.

"Stand by. Message to follow." We had all forgotten the firefly overhead until she made her announcement and flew down to land on the back of Garnet's Data Wurm. "These little guys have a lot to share."

These little guys? What kind of reference was that? I admit I was beginning to feel like an intoxicated participant in some strange dream inhabited by talking animals and messenger bugs. The communicator vibrated again, too, like an angry bee on my circlet, but I ignored it.

After a few moments, the DataWurms rotated so that they were side by side. The head of Garnet's DataWurm glowed and the image of a human female materialized in front of us. Garnet and Flint stepped back a step. Flint and Aleesa's tree horse mounts pranced in place. I assume the apparition must have frightened them, but it appeared to be a holographic projection of some kind, similar to ones used in Portanya's classroom for demonstrations.

"My name is Mnemosyne. You can call me Nessie, if that's easier on your vocal apparatus. I'm not human, but a human creation, so it would seem appropriate to assume their image." The human simulacrum paused a moment and looked at each of us in turn. "An enormous volcano is erupting west of here—humans used to refer to them as supervolcanoes, although the humans who named them never experienced one. It's going to change the climate drastically—for many years. You all are in potentially mortal danger, unless you work with me—and each other."

That was the gist of the AI's message. I may not have remembered everything verbatim. Yes, Nessie was an AI created by a vanished race of humans. Who would have guessed—except maybe Uncle—that primates could ever be that clever? Not only that, the tree horses represented an ancient colonization of Urth geological ages ago. They were mobile stages of a complicated life cycle involving the unusual Mother Tree forests I remember Uncle mentioning at some point. Who knows how the humans had converted them to draft animals? Unfortunately for Aleesa, her tree horse mount tossed her into the pit in moment of panic.

Nessie announced that she resided in a place called the Citadel north of here. She wanted all of us to meet her there in person—without getting suffocated by falling ash or frozen during a period of frigid cold soon to come.

I did finally answer Uncle Bluedigg's call, by the way. Our conversation didn't unfold quite as either of us might have guessed.

* * * * *

"Gilbooa, where have you been? Why didn't you answer my call? You are in grave danger!" Uncle's voice crackled on the communicator like an electric discharge.

"I know, Uncle. May the Prophet forgive my disrespect."

"You know? What do you mean you know? An enormous volcano is about to make Urth Heaven nearly uninhabitable. I'm just getting the details myself from the Council of Scholars."

And so I explained to Uncle about fireflies, and warnings from an ancient human-built AI, and multiple DataWurms, and a race of ancient tree horses. I rambled on, my words pouring out like rocks tumbling down hill. When I stopped, I thought perhaps our satellite link had been lost, as I could only hear a background hum over my communicator.

Finally, Uncle said, "You must come home, young larva, or you will surely die. The Council of Scholars may even recommend a retreat to Jadderbad until we know how bad this event will be."

"But I can't leave now, Uncle!" I said, rather emphatically as I recall. "You were right, after all. The human primates had built an advanced civilization long ago. Vast helpings of their knowledge may be stored in the two DataWurms we now share—and who knows what wonders may reside at the home of this Nessie creature?"

"And who knows what motives this Nessie AI really harbors? AI intelligence can turn inimical without proper safeguards. Besides, if you end up as a larval ash mummy, what difference will it make? You don't understand the power of this volcano, my boy. It could cover three quarters of this continent in ash. It will block the sunlight for who knows how long and bring on an age of numbing cold. Surely, Portanya will want to bring her expedition home."

I paused a long moment deciding just how to break the last of my news, but finally just blurted it out. "Portanya has asked me to become her betrothed, Uncle! She wants to commit to a pilgrimage to this strange Citadel. Surely, there will be dangers, but even the Prophet has said that 'A life is not truly lived until it is risked in a noble adventure.'"

We argued a little more, but I think Uncle Bluedigg knew he had lost the war of impassioned debate. In the end, he agreed to keep communication open between us as long as possible—either until the ash and storms severed our communication link or Uncle was forced to retreat through the Portal of God back to Jadderbad.

Sometimes I doubted my choice—not to mention my sanity— but those doubts rarely lasted when I was with my love Portanya. They evaporated like mist in the combined warmth of our juxtaposed cuticles whenever we rested side by side. We could spend whatever centuries we had left until metamorphosis unraveling the mysteries of these strange aliens and adding their knowledge to the great database of the Society of Natural Philosophers. Who knows, we might even add a chapter to the *Chronicles of Bandur*—if such a thing was even possible. I thought not, considering how doctrinal Keeper of the Portal Feldevka could be, but I vowed to research the possibilities. Prudently, of course.

And once beyond metamorphosis, my body and Portanya's would fuse in an ecstasy of pleasure—and perhaps pain—if Portanya needed to eat me to gather all her strength to lay the most healthy and perfectly conformed eggs. That would be my final sacrifice—to father a new generation on a healed and re-conformed Urth Heaven.

I remember looking over at Flint and Aleesa one night before the cold set in, wrestling again in their primate ecstasies, oblivious to the adventures ahead. I had come to relish their antics—not to mention their strangely haunting songs. Tree horses could sing, too, it turned out, weaving melodies to accompany Flint's tweeter and Aleesa's lilting voice. What tales might the tree horses tell? What arcane knowledge might they reveal?

The tree horses' singing talents came in handy the following day when Garnet led a ceremony to inter the remains of Garnet's kin, named Blaze, near the bird people ruins. Garnet explained that his mother, Rainbow, had agreed before he left their village that that might be necessary because of the impending crisis. It still seemed bizarre to me to honor one's dead that way, but I decided the honoring part was more important than the methods used. After all, every living creature represents an unlikely trail of mutating code made manifest in a trail of mothers and fathers we should cherish and acknowledge.

The humans sang and the tree horses added their melodies in what seemed to be an impromptu accompaniment. I certainly looked forward to learning more about these creatures.

Perhaps Urth Heaven was the wrong name for this strange planet bound to Jadderbad through the Portal of God—or some as yet incompletely understood spatial-temporal gateway. Perhaps it should be called Urth Garden, because gardens only flourish if one plants the right seeds in the right place and tends them carefully. Heavens promise only boring sameness, while gardens can become more than what even the gardener imagined.

And speaking of gardens, and the food they can provide—I think it's well past mealtime. I should search our rations for something delectable for Portanya. Even before metamorphosis, it's wise for a young male larva to keep his consort well fed.

Interlude V: Touring an Avisaurian Necropolis

Rudy

"Nice reconstruction, Nessie." I said. And it was. Nessie had rummaged around in the deepest vaults of her quantum dot matrices and managed to recreate what an avisaurian city might have looked like during the peak of their civilization. I pointed up at an elaborate structure the size of a respectable skyscraper in my day, admiring the elaborate intertwining support elements gleaming against a cloud-flecked azure sky. "This building reminds me a little of a stretched out Bower Bird's nest."

"I agree, Rudy. Glad you like my simulation."

"I remember that time—not long after you made me that nice Rudy 2.0 physical body—when you, me, and Master Veltipoe made that trip to the Cretaceous in our syncytiote form."

Nessie turned to look directly at me. "You remember that? I thought I had scrubbed that memory in...in..."

"In what? This version of me?" I felt my virtual face turning red. "Just how many versions of me exist, old girl?"

Nessie smiled at me, even batting her eyes. She had learned too much about how to punch my buttons. "It's a little hard to forget how to time travel once you've mastered that trick," I added.

"Of course, Rudy." Nessie continued walking, swinging her hips in the hopes of distracting me. It nearly worked. "Besides, you need to remember how you and Master Veltipoe became syncytiotes if you hope to convince other Jadderbadians, Grovians and humans to do the same."

"We're not finished with this discussion of how many versions of me there are in your memory core, Nessie, but the point I was trying to make was this: In the End Cretaceous, before that first asteroid struck, those dinosauroid creatures we saw at the edge of the forest already possessed primitive stone tool technology. They almost beat out mammals in the big brain experiment. I clearly remember the huge yellow eyes of that young male peeking at us from behind a palm frond. I always wondered what would have happened if his kind had survived that wandering hunk of space rock."

"Well, Rudy, your perpetually curious species managed to help one species of ancient birds get their start just 66 million years later. Biological history never repeats itself exactly, but maybe those first dinosauroids could have eventually created something like this." Nessie waved one of her arms in a flourish to encompass the urban complex around us. The ponytail of my favorite Nessie avatar bobbed in synchrony with the motion.

"Perhaps," I admitted, although 'bird brains' produced intelligence from a completely different part of the brain than mammals. Who knows how intelligent avians might perceive the world? "So, Nessie, I suppose you are showing me this reconstruction for a reason. A preamble for the next tale you're going to tell?"

"You know me so well, Rudy. The next story is short, but it really shows how all intelligent creatures struggle with self-awareness—and," she added with emphasis, "it might just give you some epiphany about how we can best bring Grovians—in all their several life stages—into any solution for dampening Gaia's anger and saving our fertile little blue planet."

"Ha!" I barked. "Epiphanies are always welcome—but about these multiple copies of me floating around in your bowels..."

I tried to pin her down, but didn't succeed. She led me around the beautiful simulacrum of her avisaurian metropolis for quite awhile. Beautiful eye candy for sure. But for whatever reason, Nessie hadn't bothered to populate her reconstruction with raekids, so it felt like we were walking around on some empty movie set and the actors had all left for the day. In fact, the actors had left forever. They were now extinct.

Nessie must have sensed that my mood was turning maudlin. "Let me tell you Candela's story, Rudy. Yes, the tree horses have names, although Garnet's tribe never knew them. Candela was Aleesa's mount and Fendra belonged to Flint. I think Candela will play an important role keeping this strange mix of pilgrims coming to visit us at the Citadel alive and well."

"Tell the tale, then, my dear Nessie. I yield the podium to you." I even bowed low and extended my right arm in what I hoped was a dramatic flourish.

Data File: Grovian ambulus anatomy (aka "tree horse")

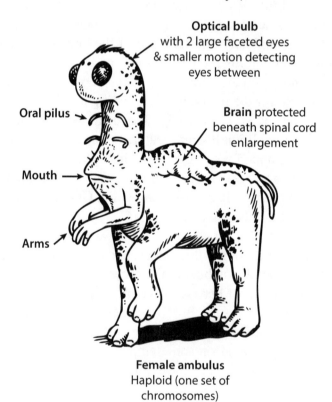

Optical bulb
with 2 large faceted eyes
& smaller motion detecting
eyes between

Oral pilus

Brain protected
beneath spinal cord
enlargement

Mouth

Arms

Female ambulus
Haploid (one set of
chromosomes)

5 • A Long Way Home

Candela

"Don't get too close to the edge." I warned Fendra.

"But look at how the sun paints the towers in gold, Candela! See how the clouds fan into the sky like a bough laden with leaves!" Fendra stretched her arms as far as they would go. Not far. She trotted over to the gnarled trunk of an evergreen tree that had insinuated itself up and along the support girders of the building until finally its branches could expand like a crooked hand over what was left of a balcony. Fendra's oral pili fluttered with excitement as she reached out to stroke one of the tree's elongated cones. I walked over to her and peeked over the side of the building. A twisted network of living and dead branches partly obscured the tree's massive trunk and the distant ground below. I hoped the human primate called Flint and the giant worm-a-pede alien called Gilbooa would be done with their exploring soon—although that would mean we would have to give them an answer.

Scary or not, the view of the broken towers and fragmented roadways were wondrous. And beyond that a dark mass of forest sat on the horizon, somehow comforting me. Calling me. *Of course*, the DataWurm said. *Those trees gave birth to you. Someday, you will plant the seeds of future forests as all Grovians must.*

The DataWurm's voice in my head sounded almost like my earliest memories of Mother Nevela, my birthing tree, before Fendra and I wandered away and the humans captured us. I wondered if the DataWurm had somehow picked that voice out of my memories or I was just imagining it. *It is my job to help you remember so that I can learn.*

But memories can be painful, DataWurm. *I'm beginning to remember what I lost. What Fendra and I both lost long ago. Humans*

99

were responsible for that. And these strange worm creatures are scary. Why should I do what either of them want?

Fendra began prancing along the edge of the railing, mewling like an ambulus fresh from her pod. I hurried to catch up. "Watch where you are going Fendra! It's a long way to the ground. Don't even think about trying to climb on those branches. Some are rotted and you haven't climbed in years. Besides, we have a decision to make."

Fendra said something that I couldn't quite hear, but she stopped running and squatted behind a pylon that blocked the breeze while affording an expansive view to the north in the general direction of the Citadel. I sat beside her, waving my pili to better enjoy the resinous scents.

Fendra looked at me with her large, primary eyes glittering. "When I hosted our DataWurm yesterday, it said it had never been to the Citadel, but that DW593—the DataWurm that Garnet calls Zandura—had, although more than a century ago. It seemed excited for a chance to visit it—if excited is the right word for an AI."

It can be, our DataWurm declared to me, with a Mother Tree's confidence. *I am an upgraded model, of course—part of the DW800 series.*

DW885. I know. You told me when you first latched onto my hide. To Fendra I responded, "Did 885 share what it learned from 593 about the Citadel? It has said nothing to me."

You didn't ask.

"Not much," said Fendra. "I asked it what it was like to scramble in the branches of a Mother Tree. I couldn't remember. We were so young when we left. It has to be *fun*." With that, Fendra rose and arched her back so that the ridges of her cranial carapace flattened and spread. "Ooh, let's see this side of the tower!" Off she trotted before I could ask her anything else.

I groaned as I rose, but followed in her wake. *What do you know about the Citadel?* I asked my AI parasite.

Parasite? Do you really think of me that way? I'm here to enlighten and inspire.

Enlighten and inspire me, then.

DW885 obliged. *The AI called Mnemosyne—aka Nessie—began*

constructing the Citadel during the end times of the technological human civilization approximately 924,000 years ago. The details I have of her origins are conflicting, but some entity programmed her to protect the remnants of the human species, using a formulation that allows her to evolve and adapt to changing circumstances to accomplish that goal. I understand she even possesses the complete neural and biological patterns of one or more ancient human prodigies to complete her task, but those details are fragmentary…

You mean, I interrupted, *she can replicate the essence of a living creature within her own framework somehow?*

Precisely. It isn't as difficult as you might think. Even my programs can accomplish some of the basic recording functions, although it taxes my memory archive storage capacity.

Enough! I finally said. *She's an AI invested in protecting humans. I understand that much. What does she have to do with my history on this planet, which you have told me is not even the planet on which my kind began? Did her efforts to save humans cause the destruction of the forests my people plant? And why should she care about us? Those she protects make animals out of us. Should Fendra and I even consider doing the bidding of these primates and worm-a-pede alien creatures?*

Before 885 could comment, Fendra's loud squawk shattered my concentration. It took me a moment to see her, her limbs awkwardly wrapped around a branch at the edge of the roof.

"Come down from there, Fendra, before you fall!" I picked up my pace. "The humans and the alien worms will be back soon. They've given us a choice as to whether to follow them or not. I think we shouldn't."

Fendra scrambled off of the branch onto the relative safety of the roof. "Really, Candela? It will be an adventure! Think of the wonders we might see! Maybe this Mnemosyne creature will tell us secrets to help our kind get through the bad times to come from the erupting super volcano."

"The DataWurm tells me that Mnemosyne's mission is to save humans. Why would she care about our kind?" A shiver rippled along my hide and down my legs. Storm clouds slid majestically across an already gray sky. The breeze turned even more frigid.

Fendra turned toward the rising wind, raised her head, and fluttered her oral pili to sample any new smells. Brrr! It made me colder just looking at her. "We work well with humans. Maybe Mnemosyne knows that. Helping us will help Mnemosyne help her humans." Fendra looked over her shoulder at me. She arched her head crest and compressed her broad mouth so that the ends turned up slightly.

I wanted to frown, but Fendra's coy posturing always made me laugh. She looked like a young ambulus inviting me to romp away with her to some mysterious glade. "The trip will be dangerous. Besides, these old ruins may be impressive..." I paused. "...but they depress me."

"Oh, foo!" Fendra started to prance in a circle with arms outstretched. "You're always getting depressed about something." Fendra turned her movements into a kind of dance that brought her closer to the finger-like tree branches now caressing the tattered edge of the roof in the gathering wind.

And that's when it happened.

A gust of wind slammed against my side. I staggered toward the rail framing the edge of the roof. My right knee threatened to buckle when I jabbed my toes against a row of ragged tiles beneath my feet. A spark of pain made me groan. When I looked up, Fendra stumbled over a waving branch and began clutching at the foliage.

"I need some help, Mother!" she cried, as if the contorted evergreen was really a Mother Tree.

She staggered over the sill of the roof and down. Branches snapped. Needles and cones scattered in the wind. I crouched against the gale, but made my way to the rail and grabbed it with both hands. I heard a long extended "Ooooh!" as she fell, as if even death was an adventure to be cherished. "I will feed you, Mother!" I heard her say as I averted my eyes from the spectacle of her descent. It was what ambuli said when their wandering days were done and they gave their last remains to the Mother Grove. I backed away from the building's edge before she reached the ground, hundreds of feet below. My limbs collapsed. I curled into the smallest shape I could and listened to the roar of the wind fade to a sigh.

That's the way Flint and Gilbooa found me when they arrived on the roof.

"What happened?" Flint asked some time later, after I had been wrapped in a warm blanket and given a hot bowl of tea to sip. The worm alien, Gilbooa, stood in a corner of the room they had fashioned as a temporary shelter. The light source borrowed from the transport sat on a pylon in another corner, casting harsh shadows.

I explained the details.

"I'm sorry," Flint said. "Fendra was a good...Fendra had a bright spirit."

He was going to say mount. Fendra was a good mount. He hadn't even known her true name until yesterday. Before the DataWurms had conferred and revealed our history, mounts were all we were to the humans: beasts of burden. I suppose I should have been glad they were at least trying to see us as something else—especially since I had been the one who had panicked when the DataWurm first revealed itself to me, and tossed Flint's mate, Aleesa, into that pit. It's amazing that she survived.

"We will stay long enough to bury her," Flint said. "Near a canopy of trees." He turned to Gilbooa briefly. They exchanged looks or hand signals or something. Apparently, the DataWurms knew enough about our customs now to know how we left our dead for a Mother Grove to reclaim her children.

"Will you return to the forest, then?" the human asked. "We could provide some supplies."

I expected to say yes, but didn't. "I understand that this Mnemosyne has great powers—and that she talks with the...with the ghosts of humans who lived before."

"Well..." Flint scratched his furry chin. "...I can't say that I really understand much about that."

Ghost is not the proper terminology, my DataWurm chimed in, with Mother Nevela's voice. *Mnemosyne creates a Neural Network Pattern Personality Construct.*

Sounds like a ghost to me, Mother. To Flint I said, "Do you think there is any chance that this Mnemosyne could…could speak with the ghost of Fendra? There are some things I never got to say to her."

Flint looked at me with wide eyes, but finally just shrugged.

I believe I recorded enough raw data from my time with Fendra that a reconstruction might be possible, my DataWurm informed me.

"I would like to travel with you to the Citadel." I looked first at Flint, and then at the towering form of Gilbooa in the corner, who stood impassive—a flickering pole of light with arms.

I want to be like Fendra, I told myself. I want to romp in great forests looking for adventure behind every bush and nurturing tree. And I want to finally tell her how much she meant to me.

Data File: Supervolcanoes

The term "supervolcano" implies a volcanic center that has had an eruption of magnitude 8 on the Volcano Explosivity Index (VEI), meaning that at one point in time it erupted more than 1,000 cubic kilometers (240 cubic miles) of material.

By contrast, the Mount St. Helens' eruption in 1980 AD (pre-apocalypse calendar) only produced 0.25 cubic kilometers of magma.

The largest eruption of the Yellowstone caldera (prior to Gaidra's current tantrum) occurred 2.1 mya prior to Rudy's birth era and produced 2,450 cubic kilometers of material.

The human species may nearly have been eliminated 74,000 years prior to Rudy's birth era by the Toba eruption in Indonesia which produced 2,800 cubic kilometers of ejecta.

Interlude VI: Paying a Visit to Gaidra

Rudy

I must have been squirming in the saddle because Master Veltipoe, my long-time Jadderbadian partner, complained.

"My cuticle isn't made of titanium, you know. Settle your primate backside will you?" Veltipoe's Jadderbadian hide flickered like a russet rainbow. "We've had these interfaces with Gaidra before."

Nessie laughed. "Many times." Her avatar walked beside us. I rode high enough on Veltipoe's second-segment bioengineered saddle that I could have touched the top of Nessie's virtual head.

I defended my nervousness. "She's never been quite this angry before. Venting a super volcano, for heavens sake!"

"In your lifetime, perhaps. As you know better than anyone, Rudy, Gaidra fights for survival like any living entity." Nessie turned her head upward so that she could give me her signature smile and wink. "Of course, that's why I'm here—to remind you. My thinking processes aren't clouded by organic passions and imperfections."

I made my best effort to harrumph properly. "Supremely humble as usual, I see."

We passed through the Citadel's last subterranean corridors and reached the granite surfaces housing the Gaidra protoplasmic network. Its intricate blend of moving color rippled slowly and glistened with moisture.

I stretched my arms and spread my fingers like a pianist warming up for a concert.

Veltipoe blew derisive puffs of air through his upper set of spiracles, but I noticed that he, too, briefly extended and stretched his upper tier arms. "Let's proceed," he said.

I dismounted Veltipoe and stood next to Nessie's holographic projection.

"My placing of hands will only be symbolic, of course," said Nessie. "These walls are dense with my circuitry, but I know you'll appreciate the moral support." She winked at me again.

We all extended our hands—or in Master Veltipoe's case, just his upper tier set of three—and touched the network of living protoplasm.

The interface with Gaidra always seemed like a mild electric shock.

Mnemosyne, Rudyard Albert Goldstein, and Master Veltipoe Frangenrude. Here for apologies, my sentient stew? A bit late don't you think? Gaidra always came to the point quickly.

"We can't apologize for the collective behavior of our respective species," I said, "Although I suppose Nessie *could* apologize for whatever contributions she has made." If Nessie could have kicked my shins, I'm sure she would have.

"We have a plan to make things right," said Nessie.

"We do?" I said. "Oh, yes. That plan," I added a bit tardily.

"Of course," said Veltipoe. "We have an excellent plan. We just have to get our band of travelers to the Citadel safely. In fact, that constitutes a big portion of the plan."

But then Nessie started talking success probabilities with our planetary brain trust. As plans go, this one was no slam-dunk.

But as Gaidra knew oh so well, the answers to solving problems of survival just had to be good enough, not perfect. That had been Gaia's modus operandi using natural selection for eons.

"Well, let's get our pilgrims moving then," I said with more confidence than I felt. And here's that story, dear reader, whoever or whatever you are.

6 • Trek to Mnemosyne's Citadel

Garnet

I watched the little mechanical device we called a firefly flutter out of the pewter sky, reminding me of Flint weaving from side to side after too much beer. I made out the words "Find shelter" amid otherwise garbled static. The other firefly resting in my left vest pocket chimed at the same time my DataWurm, Zandura, spoke: *The dust storm will be upon us in full force in twenty minutes plus or minus three, Garnet. Your other firefly drone will confirm.*

The wobbling firefly dropped out of the sky about 50 yards in front of me. The air seemed heavy. I saw flakes of something here and there. Was it the crystalline particles of frozen water that Nessie called snow or was it volcanic ash? I didn't understand the sky anymore. Even the trees of once familiar forests seemed to bow down, mourning the death of gentler times. In the early mornings now I could sometimes see my breath floating in the air like campfire smoke.

"Please retrieve the downed firefly," said Nessie's voice from my pocket. "We may be able to repair its propulsion system. Then I suggest you return to the transport quickly. We need to reach shelter before the main surge of the storm arrives."

I pulled the scarf of circlet fabric up over my nose and trotted over to where the drone flickered with pulses of amber. I picked it up. It felt lighter than its counterpart in my pocket, not unlike the insect for which it was named. "Thank you," it said, also with Nessie's voice. I placed it in an empty pouch on my belt. When I turned back toward the alien worm-a-pede's hulking transport, I heard the engine engage. It began moving toward me with an unusual whine.

"The ash will damage the Jadderbadian's vehicle as well, if we don't reach the caves before the heaviest clouds arrive," Nessie said from my vest pocket. "Being stranded this far from the Citadel would not be prudent."

I grunted. I had seen enough ash-covered mounds of animal flesh already on this trip to know that was true.

As I approached the side of the transport, it lumbered to a stop like a monstrous ratifant pausing to graze. The side door panel slid open. I stepped inside.

Even though the transport was nearly big enough to be a cave on wheels, the smells from our menagerie of occupants struck me like a slap in the face. Human sweat from Flint and Aleesa mingled with the pheromones of still lovesick Jadderbadians, and the musky odors of Candela, who perched by herself in a far corner of the room. Candela still missed her companion, Fendra.

As I lowered my mask, Master Gilbooa rose up to my left on his tripod of legs and extended a middle tier arm. "Allow me to inspect the damaged drone. My Uncle Bluedigg had me study in detail the broken one he found. With Mnemosyne's assistance I may be able to clean its air intakes in the lab." Gilbooa's cuticle flickered in shades of blue and green to reinforce the "reasonable helpfulness" of his request.

I fetched the damaged drone from my belt pouch and handed it to Gilbooa. Then I recovered the intact drone from my vest pocket and placed it on a nearby bench while I peeled off vest and shirt so that I could use my upper body chromatophores to reassure Gilbooa about my intentions. Gilbooa still seemed impressed that the genetic modifications made to my mother had passed down to me. I think it raised my standing in his trifecta of compound eyes. That never hurt when dealing with giant worms who considered most humans to be dull-witted, if sometimes useful, pets.

I idly fingered the rock bug amulet that hung around my neck. I had found it shortly before I speared my first ratalope as a young man, so I considered it to be a harbinger of good things to come. When Rainbow first shared Zandura with me, Zandura told me that the rock bug was the mineralized remains of a creature that had once lived very long ago. Maybe so. Still, to have endured the ages—even as a rock—must be a lucky thing.

I caught Aleesa's eyes watching me. I think she liked my flickering colors, although she usually made a point to ignore them if Flint was nearby, but at the moment Flint sat next to her, searching for something in his daypack. She shifted the position of her left arm, still in a sling while it healed. "How long before we reach the caves this Nessie creature mentioned?" Aleesa asked.

"Twenty minutes anyway." I sat down on the bench next to my shirt and vest.

"The transport's engines are making strange noises. It's cold in here." Aleesa moved nearer to Flint, who draped an arm around his mate's shoulders. Aleesa snuggled closer to him.

I nodded assent before turning to Gilbooa, who was manipulating the drone with two hands while searching for a belt tool with a third. "Think your giant cart will make it to the caves?" I asked him. I flickered in shades of amber concern.

He focused one lateral eye on me. "Portanya and the transport's AIs are skillful. Prophet willing, we will arrive at the cave shelter as planned. Hopefully, we will only need another day or two to reach the Citadel." Then Gilbooa muttered to himself while lumbering off in the direction of the lab—the place where Masters played with their mysterious machines and chemical potions.

We should be more concerned with what Mother Urth is up to, I thought. The Jadderbadian's Prophet doesn't seem to have much control over our current crisis—and may not care if we reach the Citadel at all.

A reasonable assessment, Zandura offered.

I wondered how my mother Rainbow was doing without Zandura to help her. Rainbow was smart, even without a DataWurm whispering to her. She would lead the tribe farther west and south away from the prevailing westerlies that carried most of the super volcano's giant clouds of acrid smoke and ash. Presumably, they would be able to round up and lead the tree horse herd to safety as well. In the meantime she had charged me with doing whatever I had to do to save the tribe. That was the role of a Shaman, after all. That was what she had always done. And some day I would take her place.

The transport continued to lurch over the uneven terrain, whining its complaint with ever increasing volume. Looking out the windows I watched heavier debris begin to fall from the clouds. Some of it glowed briefly like embers from a fire. Some of it was large enough to pelt the sides of the transport as if angry children were throwing stones. Gray ash began to accumulate in spots and form drifts. At one point I saw a long line of ratalopes in the distance running for whatever remained of their lives.

The line of hills we sought grew slowly in the distance—sometimes clearly visible, sometimes cloaked in veils of blue gray mist. Eventually, cliffs rose high enough to gape at us with dark openings that looked like mouths giving vent to the increasingly loud squeals coming from the transport's engines. Just before one cave mouth loomed large enough to swallow us, the transport staggered to a complete stop.

"That's all the engine is going to give us," Portanya announced through the transport's speakers. "Gather up daypacks everyone. The cave will offer more protection than the transport if the storm gets much worse. AIs can analyze and work on most of the repairs without our help."

"I hate doing these worms' bidding," Flint grumbled.

"They did help save my life." Aleesa sighed.

"We need them." I looked pointedly at Flint. "At least for now."

We gathered necessities into daypacks. I put on my shirt and vest, tucking my amulet beneath the fabric, and was about to return the intact drone to my vest pocket when it spoke: "I'd rather see what's going on. Let me ride on your shoulder."

"For an insect, you give a lot of orders," I told the firefly-with-Nessie's-voice, as I placed her on my left shoulder. We all hooked the circlet fabric scarves over our noses to filter out some of the dust.

Five of us exited the transport to cover the short distance to the mouth of the cave. Nessie's drone hovered near me. Spider, a multi-legged AI that we might need to explore small places in our temporary shelter, joined us, trailing the Jadderbadians. Patch, Flint's dog, kept his distance from the spider and growled if the AI came too close. Master Teedercroft stayed in the vehicle with the remaining artificial creatures that the worm-a-pedes depended on. Strung out in single file, we looked like a strange caterpillar moving through a gray mist. Gilbooa and Portanya formed the giant head, three humans and a tree horse made up the body, while Spider and a reluctant Patch scuttled behind us like a tail. Now and then I could hear the legs of the firefly scratching the leather of my vest as it shifted position on my shoulder.

Once inside the entrance, Gilbooa stopped abruptly, apparently to sample the air. At least the little tendrils around his mouth wiggled as he rotated his upper segments from side to side. "Ah, good. I smell water. If we have potable water in here, we won't have to deplete the supply in the transport while we wait out this storm." Gilbooa flashed a color pattern to summon Spider to his side. "Spider, check out that passage and see if you can find accessible water."

Spider scuttled off as directed, turning on a light beam at the front of his multi-eyed head as he left. Flint, Aleesa, and I stood between the towering forms of Portanya and Gilbooa. Candela stood with arched back. Flint might have preferred not to be near the Jadderbadians, but the big worms did throw off a fair amount of heat. We all exhaled short-lived clouds of vapor. The worm-a-pedes looked like tree trunks venting steam.

Eventually, Spider returned, flashing various shades of green and waving two forelegs like semaphores. Gilbooa moved toward Spider and we all followed the AI down a passage that narrowed enough to make Portanya and Gilbooa stoop before it opened out into a larger space complete with running water and a pond a few yards across at its widest point. "Excellent," Gilbooa proclaimed as he lowered his substantial backpack. "Let me set up this portable heater and light source, and we can wait out this storm in relative comfort."

Once Gilbooa had completed his task, he placed himself on a rock shelf big enough to accommodate Portanya. She sat next to him, cuticle to cuticle. They both extended several arms toward the heater. Gilbooa used one free arm to explore a vest pouch, while another patted one of Portanya's thighs. I sat next to Flint, Aleesa, and Patch on the other side of the heater. Spider settled down next to Gilbooa.

Candela found a small depression in the rocks, folded her legs beneath her, and sat, with the regality of a visiting chieftain.

"This trip is madness," declared Flint. "Mother Urth keeps belching smoke at us and we move toward her wrath! This morning I saw a pond bubbling like a pot of stew on the fire. We should be with our tribe!"

"Don't worry, little Groupie. We are marching toward knowledge. The Citadel holds secrets I believe we all must know to survive in this altered world." Gilbooa gestured broadly with a quartet of arms and flickered in shades of purple. He had a talent for pomposity.

Flint spat on the ground. "I'm not your little Groupie, worm! Besides, if Mother Urth gets really mad you can always run through your golden arches to another world." Aleesa placed a hand on Flint's arm, as if to hold him in place. Patch growled.

"We are committed to this world and its survival," said Portanya. She linked a pair of arms with Gilbooa. "My betrothed and I will help all of us survive this challenge."

"By marching into clouds of ash and lakes of boiling water?" Flint stood up and shook a fist in the air. At home when anger consumed him, he could march off into the forest, but that wasn't an option here. I was about to say something when the firefly on my shoulder jumped into the air and glided to a point between humans and worm-a-pedes. The firefly blinked twice and then Nessie materialized in front of us as the same translucent, ghost-like human female form that had spoken to us at the birdman ruins. All of us momentarily froze in place at the sudden apparition. Patch's ears flattened.

"Just me, folks. No worries." Nessie said, smiling as she made eye contact with everyone. "It's been a bit hectic since we left the ruins with Gaidra venting her displeasure, so to speak. Maybe I can help ease some of your concerns." She turned toward Flint. "It's true the area around the Citadel is geologically active—and has been for a long time—so you'll see some bubbling pools, vents of steam, and that sort of thing. Enjoy the show! I'll guide you around them. That geology has little to do with the volcanic eruption farther west. You all need to know some of the things I can provide for you at my

Citadel. Gaidra—your Mother Urth—is a real being…an angry real being…but I know her well. We can work something out with her."

"And why should I trust you, ghost, any more than these giant worms?" Flint pointed toward Gilbooa and Portanya.

"She's not a ghost, groupie. She is a holographic projection of an AI, not unlike the ones we use aboard the transport." Gilbooa's colors turned warm with annoyance.

"Spout all the syllables you want worm, she looks like a ghost." Flint jutted his chin in Gilbooa's direction.

"Time out, Flint." Nessie raised an arm. "Perhaps I can earn a bit more of your trust if I answer your questions—anybody's questions—as best I can."

"Time out?" I asked. "What is time out?"

"Sorry," Nessie said. "I've been conversing too long with my old human companion, Rudy. I was just asking Flint to chill out… no, that won't work. I was asking Flint to pause long enough to control his emotions."

Interesting, Zandura commented. *This artificial intelligence seems to have adopted the idiomatic speech patterns of a human intelligence with which she is somehow merged. I have been monitoring some of the neural framework I've been able to intercept during radio transmissions between the two fireflies.*

I heard the words, but much of the meaning escaped me. Rainbow had warned me that some of the DataWurm's comments were hard to understand. I accepted that Nessie was trying to explain more about our journey and how to survive it. Whether she was a ghost, an artificial creature, or something else, she knew more about the world than I did. Like mother Rainbow always said, "Listen with a mind open to all possibilities until you know enough to act wisely."

"Obviously, you possess many powers," said Candela. "The power I would like to know more about is how you resurrect long dead beings like this Rudy you talk about. My DataWurm says you may be able to let me talk to my friend Fendra again. Is that true?"

Nessie turned toward Candela. "I can't make promises without using all my resources, but I want to understand you and your friend better myself. You are part of this world too. You must be part of the solution for adapting to this crisis."

Ask her more about this Rudy entity, Garnet. I have some partially corrupted data files that imply I have met this simulacrum long ago. Zandura paused, sensing my next question before I asked it. *I need to know more about this reconstruction of an ancient human genius. It might be relevant to your quest to find a way to save your tribe. I'm named after a modern human genius, as you well know: your Uncle Zandur. Perhaps Zandur and this Rudy could find a way to collaborate.*

Zandur is long dead. I thought Zandura was being rather obtuse, even for a DataWurm.

His organic form is dead. Ask about this Rudy.

His organic form? I glanced at Candela, who bowed her head, and seemed to accept Nessie's statement without further comment. I wanted to press Zandura more about Zandur. Mother Rainbow still mourned Zandur even though her brother had died when they both were still children. Now Zandura seemed to be hinting that Zandur's death might not be complete. Instead, I turned toward Nessie and asked the question Zandura wanted answered. "Who exactly is this Rudy creature you speak of?"

"Ah, yes, Rudy. He saved the world of his time from destruction. Another human preserved his neural engrams and implanted them within me. He has been quite an entertaining and useful companion—for hundreds of millennia, but we must reach the Citadel before you can meet him."

That seems to confirm the essence of other data I have collected, Zandura informed me.

"And exactly how much farther to the Citadel?" I asked. I glanced over at Flint. He had reseated himself next to Aleesa. The boil of his anger had at least been reduced to a simmer. Patch lay nearby, but still seemed to eye the Jadderbadians with suspicion.

"Assuming the maintenance bots can fully clear the intake vents and replace any damaged gears and other hardware, two days max." Nessie paused as if listening for something. "The good news is that my satellite drones are predicting a shift in weather patterns. This storm should move south within a few hours."

"Then let's eat while we have the chance," said Gilbooa. "A higher blood sugar level should improve all our moods."

"I'm hungry," said Aleesa. Patch sniffed the air as if anticipating what was to come.

"I'll get a couple of service bots to move supplies from the transport," said Portanya.

And so, we all leaned closer to the heater and waited for the service bots to arrive. Zandura seemed content for the moment. Food eventually did improve our collective moods—but food does tend to attract other hungry creatures—and we paid a price for being careless. Especially the worm-a-pedes.

* * * * *

Master Gilbooa

I blame myself for being distracted.

I struggled to convince my brains that our pet humans—or at least their ancestors—had once created great cities and pondered the thoughts I once reserved for fellow natural philosophers and priests. But what Master could deny the reality of the Nessie hologram and all that it implied? The ancient humans, at least as depicted in their three-dimensional projections, were pale and stumpy primates compared to Garnet's tribe, but such evolutionary differences could be expected considering the time that had passed since their civilization had flourished.

Thus, when Portanya rose to say she needed to relieve herself, I paid little attention. I could have suggested that Spider accompany her, but I didn't.

Her piercing scream turned my cuticle white. My limbs felt paralyzed.

Garnet yelled "Carrat!" and jumped to his feet. The Yapperfang animal barked. Flint, Aleesa, and the tree horse, Candela, seemed to rise like one creature and turned toward the back of the cavern. Finally, my legs obeyed commands properly. I rose in time to see the furry Urth carnivore leap toward my beloved, still partially stooped as she released a load of frass. The four-legged creature weighed not much more than a typical human, but it's shoulders flexed with powerful muscles. I caught a glimpse of its fangs as they pierced Portanya's cuticle.

Everything seemed to happen as slowly as a larva moving in birthing gel. I remember seeing the gleam of the Nessie firefly when she leaped off Garnet's shoulder and flew toward the attack at the rear of the cavern. Yapperfang leaped to his feet and followed. His barks echoed off the cavern's walls. The humans waved their arms and yelled. I fumbled in my pouches trying to find my disruptor, although we needed to be much closer before I could use it effectively against the carrat.

Portanya wailed. Her arms seemed hopelessly tangled with the furry hide of the growling animal. Suddenly, a burst of colored light sprang from the firefly that briefly lit the cave interior as if it were a lantern. The firefly also emitted a distressing siren blast that hurt my tympanae. Fortunately, the flamboyant display along with the barks and growls of the human's predatory pet proved too much for even a hungry carrat. It sprang off the body of my precious Portanya, who lay slumped on the cavern floor, groaning and flickering in alarming shades of orange and amber.

The Urth-born creatures moved toward her much faster than I could. I felt like a lumbering transport trying to navigate a road full of boulders. Air wheezed in and out of my spiracles. I remembered the painful days as a first instar trudging after the real athletes in my cohort. The humans and tree horse huddled around Portanya, so I couldn't see my sweet larva completely, but I did see her blue blood stains on the dirt, and I feared the worst.

By the time I arrived however, Spider was crawling over Portanya applying first aid. The firefly circled above like some angelic insect. Even the yapperfang creature lay down protectively near my beloved. I didn't have a chance to thank the Nessie AI until later. Portanya had lost a significant amount of blood. A trembling middle tier arm hung tattered and torn from her side. Portanya's spiracles whistled as she tried to slow her breathing, but she half smiled at me and fluttered her oral pili as if to say, "Look what a mess I've made."

I squatted close to her and patted her cuticle, trying to ignore the smell of her frass and produce sweet scents of my own to mask hers. I used one eye to search the dark corners of the cavern for the carrat, but saw nothing—not even heat glow in the infrared. The animal must have another exit deep within the cave. I breathed easier knowing that my beloved's injuries were not mortal. I envisioned getting Portanya back to the transport via a stretcher, and we would soon be on our way again.

The Great Trickster, of course, is a larva known for sharp spines, not kindness.

I did send a message to Master Teedercroft and he dispatched a pair of maintenance AIs with a stretcher. I walked by Portanya's side all the way to the transport. Spider and the three humans collected our gear while Yapperfang sniffed the air. With the help of Candela we managed to get everything back to the transport in one trip.

Master Teedercroft installed Portanya into the transport's medical bay before dumping his bad news on me: "I thought fixing the transport's air intakes and engines would be straightforward," he said. "We have good mechs and adequate raw materials for the synthesizers, but there are software issues of some kind."

"And?" I asked. "How long a delay to fix that?"

Master Teedercroft fiddled with his oral pili. "With all respect, I don't know that it IS fixable."

"Nonsense, we can't walk all the way to this Citadel."

Master Teedercroft's cuticle flickered in a confusing pastel pallet of colors. He said nothing.

"Crawl one body length first," I muttered—mostly to myself. "Let's get Portanya well." I focused all three eyes on Master Teedercroft. "Assemble the humans. See if they will perform a healing chorus to aid with the medical treatments. Then let Spider help with the software. He's qualified with these systems. I'll attempt to reach Uncle Bluedigg and get his advice."

None of those injunctions worked particularly well.

* * * * *

I spent time sitting with Portanya, but felt helpless. She lay on a pallet with a warming blanket covering her basal segment. The medbot had bandaged her two most damaged medial arms and placed patches in various other places. She slept rather peacefully, I thought, with the help of an anesthetic. Her spiracles slowly opened and closed with mesmerizing sighs. Her oral pili undulated with the charming grace I loved to watch.

I apparently fell asleep. Human shouts and harsh voices on the other side of the cubicle woke me. The door hissed open and Master Teedercroft stepped into the room.

A rather chaotic mix of colors flashed over his cuticle. "The humans—especially the males—are not happy about performing as a chorus, Master Gilbooa."

My own colors turned from amber to burnt orange. "Why not?" I demanded.

"Remember, Master, these are wild humans. They, ah, think that performing a healing chorus is a pet thing—something beneath them." Master Teedercroft paused before adding, "In addition, they claim ignorance of the healing songs."

"They can sing from a script, can't they?" My colors turned full crimson. "Denying the healing powers of song at a time like this is…is…criminal!"

"Agreed. These crude primates bear no resemblance to Jadderbadian purebreds, Master."

"What about the tree horse—Candela? She sang quite beautifully at the wake for her partner and at the funeral for the humans' relative."

"I hadn't thought to ask her."

I took a deep breath and softened my color display. "What progress is Spider making with the software problems?"

Teedercroft's oral pili fluttered. "He's telling me that long stretches of code are corrupt or missing." Teedercroft's chromatophores flickered in shades of amber. "He doesn't understand why. Blowing grit shouldn't have affected software."

"Corrupt or missing? The medical cubicle seems to be functioning."

"The problem is with propulsion. I ah...according to Spider, that is...I think that means the transport can't...well...transport us anywhere." Teedercroft reeked with the odors of resignation.

I snorted puffs of air from my lateral spiracles. "Find Garnet first and that firefly he carries on his shoulder. I want to speak with this Nessie creature again. Then talk to Candela. See if she is willing to sing for my precious Portanya." I looked at her fondly with one eye. She still slept peacefully, praise the Prophet. I stiffened the pili over my remaining two eyes which I focused on Master Teedercroft with what I hoped was withering intensity. "Why are you still here?"

He turned and moved rather spritely, for a third instar.

I then fetched my communicator from a pouch in my upper circlet and punched in Uncle Bluedigg's private channel code.

The device hissed with static, like a serpent that had just been stepped on.

I yelled a string of expletives, some Jadderbadian, and some human. *Forgive me, Prophet, if one of those expletives suggested you perform unholy acts.*

I paced the small room for a while. I sat with Portanya, holding one of her undamaged hands. I searched my memory for soothing scripture or a relevant line from the poetry of Master Selenara, but I found it hard to concentrate. Finally, Portanya stirred. The nictating membrane of one eye rose slowly, followed by those of her remaining eyes. She squeezed my hand with hers.

She fluttered her oral pili. "What are you doing loitering by my bed, 'Booa? You should be out finding me some fat insects. And don't forget a pot of dipping sauce. I'm hungry."

I laughed. My Portanya was back!

I was so happy I nearly didn't hear the tapping at the cubicle door. "Yes, who is it?"

"Candela," the tree horse said softly. "And Aleesa," added the human. "We've come to sing."

"Come in! Come in! I'm pleased you are here. Master Portanya is awake, but I'm sure she will be pleased to hear your songs."

"Oh, please do come in," Portanya said as Candela and Aleesa entered the room. "I do enjoy your songs."

Candela and Aleesa stood on opposite sides of my larva's bed and began singing. I found their voices charming as well—especially for creatures untrained in Jadderbadian arts. I lost myself in the melodies until there was another rap at the door.

"I have the firefly," Garnet said without preamble. "Should I enter?"

"Wait," I replied, and turned toward Portanya. I flashed a spectrum of greens and emitted calming pheromones. She nodded her head, understanding that I intended to leave her side for a while. I turned toward the doorway and moved in that direction. "I'm coming out."

I focused all three primary eyes on the human—that seemed to be a requirement for their full attention—and pointed toward the benches along the corridor. I noticed that the firefly perched on his right shoulder. "Follow me, groupie…" I began, but quickly realized my mistake. "My apologies, wild human, Garnet. Please come with me to the benches. I must speak with this Nessie envoy from the Citadel."

I was pleased to hear Garnet's steps behind me as I made my way to the bench. I wasn't quite sure what I was prepared to do, if he proved to be uncooperative. Garnet sat down next to me. The firefly shifted position on his shoulder as he did so. Again, I focused all my eyes on his. "What must you do to summon the AI?"

Before Garnet could answer, Master Teedercroft arrived in the corridor. I diverted the gaze of one eye toward him and flashed a pattern of colors encouraging him to speak.

"The news is not good, Master Gilbooa. This transport is not moving without the help of a certified technician. Spider can't solve the software problems."

My colors and Master Teedercroft's both rippled in shades of amber when Nessie materialized in front of us.

"Greetings, gentleman and gentle worms," she said. "I understand you want to pow wow."

"Pow wow?" Garnet and I sounded like an unintentional chorus.

"Another Rudyism. Sorry." Nessie smiled. "How can I help you?"

"Our transport is disabled," I said. "Software issues. Can you help?"

Nessie scratched her chin. "I haven't seen much Jadderbadian technology," she said. "What I have seen is confounding. It incorporates chromodynamic and volatile chemical elements never used in human AI systems. I'm afraid I can't help you with that."

"Then I really don't see how we can reach your Citadel in any reasonable amount of time…and under the climatic conditions outside."

"I can help you with some of that," Nessie replied. "It won't be particularly comfortable—or easy, for that matter—but visiting my Citadel will benefit everyone's long-term survival."

"What must we do?" I shrugged six of my shoulders and flickered in a chaotic rainbow of colors.

"All of you will have to work together, for one thing," Nessie declared. She looked around the corridor. "Where is Candela? She will be essential for the first part of the journey."

* * * * *

Candela

I thought when Garnet fetched me to speak with the Nessie phantom creature I would be part of a group meeting. Instead, the worm called Gilbooa left to attend his mate, requesting that Nessie provide him with a full recording later. The other wormy alien left to take care of a mechanical emergency of some sort. The human Garnet claimed that he and Aleesa needed to rendezvous with Flint. The Nessie apparition said, "I guess it's just you and me, Candela. Let's meander down this corridor to the window and discuss the local geography."

She left, assuming I would follow. I took a deep breath, smoothing my optical crest with one hand, and complied. The firefly that projected Nessie's image zig-zagged back and forth behind her. My toe pads clicked softly on the hard surface of the corridor. I nervously waved my tail to and fro.

Do you know what this is all about, DataWurm DW885? I felt the little mechanical parasite shift position beneath my right arm.

I suspect she wants you to lead your fellow travelers to Nexus. Nexus?

The human word equivalent of—and DW885 warbled a short, but intricate tune implying a place of merging paths or connections—a nexus. *I collected data in this area 120 years ago. Mnemosyne—Nessie—has been requesting information from my data stores.*

And you just gave it to her?

That is my function as a DataWurm. I provide information to those who need it.

I still don't quite trust this ancient human-made Nessie, I protested. *How are my people and the distant culture of my ancestors connected to human apes and ancient bird people, if at all?*

Details are unclear at this point, as the information Mnemosyne is providing has either naturally fragmented over time or she is intentionally filtering it. As programming protocol demands, I'm cross-referencing her replies with other data sources I encountered long ago that were archived and subsequently suffered some corruption. My apologies for the uncertainties. However, my tentative hypothesis is that your ancestors peacefully co-existed with the avisaurian civilization—at least most of the time. The avisaurians, by the way, were most likely the result of a re-wilding experiment by humans.

Re-wilding experiment? What does that mean?

But before my DataWurm could reply, we had reached the window.

Nessie gestured toward the landscape outside. "Our expedition needs to make a detour, Candela, but I think it will be of interest to you. See that game trail meandering east past those bluffs? That trail heads in the general direction of Nexus: the last great avisaurian metropolis."

"Why are we moving east? I thought the Citadel was northwest of here."

"Oh, it is, Candela. But without the Jadderbadian transport, you'll never reach the Citadel using human feet—or Jadderbadian tripodia or even your stout grovian limbs, for that matter—especially when the weather patterns shift again. Nexus houses a transportation system. At one point a bullet tube tunnel terminus connected Nexus to the Citadel. Some of the technology may be more or less repairable. And an arm of your Mother Tree forest reaches close to

Nexus. There may be packs of hunting ambuli—perhaps even tree mates of yours. You and your DataWurm should take point on this part of the journey." Nessie smiled. "Up for a challenge?"

I didn't know what 'taking point' meant, and I didn't like the idea of magic machines that were 'more or less repairable,' but I did like the idea of being in a Mother Tree forest again. I said yes to Nessie, Fendra, because I knew that's what you would have done.

* * * * *

It took several days to make preparations and give the female Jadderbadian, Portanya, and the human female Aleesa, time to heal. The worms cannot travel quickly overland on their tripodal legs. The ones called Gilbooa and Teedercroft worked with their thinking machines to adapt a service cart to carry them and the spider AI overland.

I wish you were here to see these wonders, Fendra. I can picture you prancing in place to all the magic these strange worm creatures command. I overheard conversations filled mostly with gibberish words, but somehow panels arching over the giant cart collect energy from the sun itself to make the wheels of the vehicle turn. The cart can move as fast as a trotting human, at least over relatively smooth terrain.

The worms and humans collaborated to create a harness for me so that I can haul some medical and food supplies, although the humans will do most of the hunting and foraging. The humans have no sharp beaks or fearsome claws, but they can throw pointed sticks and hurl stones quite accurately. They know local plants well and can subsist on a variety of food. The periodic ash storms and colder temperatures will make hunting difficult during the journey to Nexus. Even I find hunting my favorite mammalian prey more tiresome. The night before all the preparations were complete the humans Garnet and Flint each managed to impale ratalopes. Everyone ate well, supplementing the wild game with some perishable food from the immobile transport.

The Jadderbadian worms also carried weapons that could kill at a distance, but they were clumsy hunters. The humans might have used the weapons more efficiently, but the worms weren't about to share them. I couldn't blame them, Fendra. You and I both know how deceptive and treacherous humans can be. The wrangler in Garnet's tribe that stole us from the Mother Tree forest is but one example of many.

Early on the day after the ratalope feast we left, following Nessie's game trail that led roughly in the direction of Nexus, and using information provided by Nessie and DW885. You would have laughed at the sight, Fendra: A wagon bouncing along a path carrying three giant worms waving a forest of arms. Three great apes wearing scraps of animal hide jogging on either side of the patchwork vehicle along with their four-legged predator companion, and me actually leading the procession, breathing heavily under my load, head crest akimbo. That's what "taking point" means, Fendra: being the leader of something. And, of course, the firefly containing Nessie fluttered over all of us like a mosquito looking for a suitable meal.

If we ever get to this Citadel, maybe I will see you laugh again, Fendra—if a firefly truly commands all the magic necessary to make you more than just a memory.

* * * * *

I remember that the first day on the trail to Nexus started well. The sun briefly broke through the seemingly perpetual gray of the sky—like the flirtatious wink of a potential consort during the height of mating season. But the gray returned quickly, bringing a chill ash-free wind from the southwest. I lowered my head, tried to ignore the weight of supplies on my back, and walked with stoic deliberation.

I remembered the question I had asked DW885 before this journey began. *What is re-wilding? You used that term when describing the avisaurians who built great cities like Nexus.*

The DataWurm squirmed beneath my right arm for a moment like a podling settling down for the night. *The ancient humans grew skillful at reading genetic code—the chemical compounds that direct the development and evolution of living things. At one point, in an attempt to recreate stable, self-renewing habitats, they genetically engineered once extinct megafauna. They called this process re-wilding.*

I waited for more information, but DataWurms are not inclined to provide that without direct questions. I still don't understand how this re-wilding led to the creation of the avisaurians, DW885. Explain.

If my data and the inferences I am making from it are accurate, the avisaurians evolved from phorusrhacid apex predators that humans recreated to restore grassland ecosystems on what was once called the American Hemisphere. Human population numbers crashed along with their civilization when an asteroid struck the planet. Most humans reverted to scattered hunter/gatherer/scavenger communities. That left the phorusrhacids—often referred to as terror birds by humans during pre-apocalyptic times, because of their large size and predatory behavior—free to evolve into the intelligent-mystical-delusional niche once dominated by human primates. During that time they encountered Mother Tree forests that had also regressed to a primitive state. Terror birds and ambuli, like you and Fendra had many vicious conflicts at first, but ultimately they made progress at co-existence.

I struggled to understand the gibberish. *So, you are saying, DataWurm, that the ancient human's cleverness created living beings that ultimately replaced them as builders of magic tools and enormous cities like Nexus? Then, these bird people met and ultimately made peace with my kind?*

A somewhat abridged and simplified summary, but yes, you are essentially correct.

And my ancestors you said once are not native to this planet? We have legends of a Mother Tree Forest Prime that somehow united with mythical humans named Ri-ann and Skeeze. Is there any truth to these tales? My brain seemed clogged with questions now. My reasoning powers seemed duller than an elder's toenails.

But the Nessie firefly alighted on my shoulder before I could ask more questions. "The wind is shifting, Candela," she said. "We must reach shelter before the ash and acid rain begin to fall again."

I looked at the trail ahead. It meandered through stands of trees, branches drooping with wilted, ash-dusted leaves or rising into the sky completely barren, like arms with thousands of beseeching fingers. "I don't see any promising shelter ahead, Nessie."

"Five miles further east a rock outcrop will offer some protection—not as much as the caves we left—but it should be sufficient. I'll let the others know we need to pick up the pace." With that, Nessie bounded off my shoulder, circled me once, and flew away toward the service cart and its load of Jadderbadians. Presumably, she would then find and notify the humans who were somewhere hunting and scavenging with their wolf-dog, Patch. I think I like the Jadderbadian's name for this creature better: Yapperfang. The humans often used their dogs to herd my people using their growls and sharp teeth to motivate us.

Protection that should be sufficient. I was already tired. I had been looking forward to shedding the load on my back now that midday was close, but that wouldn't happen. Instead, I quickened the pace and tried to ignore the fatigue. I felt a cold wind on my tail now from out of the west. More gritty ash would not be far behind.

I don't recall now exactly how long we trudged forward. I just remember that by the time we reached the rock outcrop I was shivering. Flecks of ash danced like misplaced stars in the shadows created by the largest rock overhang.

The two humans conferred with the Jadderbadians a moment, then the one called Teedercroft parked the service cart to form a partial wall in front of the shallow cave formed by the rock overhang. He then lay down at the other end of the overhang with his back to the wind. Gilbooa followed Teedercroft's example so that the two of them, head to tail, along with the service cart, created a living fence blocking the worst of the wind. The colors of the windward side of their combined cuticles faded to a dirty white.

The female human called Aleesa looked as cold as I felt. She had wrapped her arms across her chest and ducked beneath the rock overhang behind the worm/cart barrier. Her injured arm seemed nearly normal, perhaps with the help of some of the Jadderbadian's magic. Garnet raised an arm toward me with his five scrawny fingers splayed out like a fan of twigs. The Patch/Yapperfang sat by his side. I knew Garnet wanted me to wait while Flint fetched something from the supplies on my back. Then Flint disappeared in the shadows beneath the overhang.

Finally, Garnet urged me forward. A light flashed into existence dispelling the shadows. I felt warmth as I perched next to Gilbooa, creating a kind of enclosure with the mostly hairless humans and their furry companion huddled around the heat and light source Flint had apparently taken from my load. The ground now supported some of the weight of my pack and it helped insulate me from the cold wind. The Nessie firefly made several turns around the heat source before settling onto Garnet's shoulder.

"Well now, aren't we a cozy bunch?" Nessie said.

Cozy bunch wasn't the phrase that came to my mind. Crooked ring of stoic, reluctant companions might have been more descriptive. But the heater and our collective bodies kept us warm enough. The human called Aleesa began humming a lilting tune. I couldn't help joining in. Eventually, the male humans joined the chorus. Garnet flashed an artful color scheme using his genetically modified skin that even a ambulus male would have been proud of. The Jadderbadians must have enjoyed the experience because bright colors danced on the portions of their cuticles facing the interior of our grouping, and their many arms moved rhythmically.

The gray outside our little enclave of light and heat and music darkened to black after the sun set. We paused to eat a few cold rations. If you were here, Fendra, perhaps you could have lightened the mood, but everyone seemed tired and surly.

Time passed. I must have dozed off.

I woke up to a siren blast and felt some one—or something—fumbling with the straps of the pack on my back.

"Sorry if I startled you, Candela," said Garnet. "I need to repack the heater."

I felt the weight of the added burden as Garnet loaded the equipment in my pack and refastened the seals and straps that held it in place.

Garnet slapped the pack. " Secure," he declared to someone—perhaps the Nessie mechanical firefly perched on his shoulder.

We drank water and ate another quick meal before leaving.

I think we traveled a mile before I worked all the stiffness out of my legs. A few wispy orange clouds hung in a morning sky bruised with purple. I now followed the three humans who were carrying packs of their own. Yapperfang trotted by their side. The service cart with its cargo of Jadderbadian worms, supplies, and the mechanical creature called Spider, trailed behind me. The ash that had fallen yesterday, combined with last night's rain, formed a gumbo in low terrain that clung to my toes and lower legs.

I have to admit, Fendra, that as tired as I was from the journey so far, I began to feel excitement as we got closer and closer to the avisaurian ruins and scents that reminded me of our home forest. The raw dirt trail gradually gave way, first to scattered blocks of stone flat on one surface, and then to the cracked remnants of what must have been a broad path for vast herds of individuals or perhaps enormous vehicles of some kind. Here and there tall posts rose from the ground like trees. Others lay upon the open ground like fallen logs mostly obscured by ash and drooping foliage.

And then we passed through the Cavern of Statues. These were large replicas—or at least partial replicas—of once proud avisaurians, Fendra. They were dressed in ornate robes and crowned with elaborate headgear. Some had beaks with decorative markings. Others wore rings and bracelets and carried banners with cryptic symbols etched upon their surfaces. And I saw one wearing a medallion with the image of a tree on it, Fendra. The shape of the branches and twisted curls depicted on the bark convinced me it must have been a Mother Tree.

The partially ruined collection of statues, as impressive as they were, clustered about a large platform that must have once supported a truly immense sculpture. Nothing remained but rubble, an enormous eye that must have belonged to the head of the creature depicted in the now collapsed colossus, and the scraps of an inscription. *Can you translate those markings, DataWurm?*

I can. "Lift your voice in song, hatchling, in praise of the wonders I have wrought."

I looked around, but could only see mounds of ash-coated rubble interrupted by the gnarled remains of shrubs now denuded of their leaves.

DW885 interrupted my survey. *Ah, an avisaurian version of Ozymandias.*

Ozy what? I self-consciously glanced at the disembodied eye again. The artist had succeeded in giving it an aura of disdain that survived its lichen-covered resting place in rubble and dust.

A human poet once contemplated the inscription of a long-dead ruler of his species named Ozymandias—sometimes referred to as Ramses II. "My name is Ozymandias, King of Kings; Look on my Works, ye Mighty, and despair!" he wrote, followed by, "Nothing beside remains. Round the decay of that colossal wreck, boundless and bare the lone and level sands stretch far away." DW593, during our datashare, provided me with that scrap of information. Accept my apologies for the incomplete reference.

My DataWurm is always apologizing for incomplete data, Fendra, but somehow she gives me the sense that she is always quite pleased when she can show off relevant information of any kind. Do you suppose DataWurms suffer from pride, Fendra?

Ozymandias. A boastful leader turned to dust and shards of stone.

I left the nameless giant eye to stare into the cloudy sky. Nessie urged us forward to find the shortcut we needed to arrive at her Citadel—a far older thing apparently than the jumble of stones we just passed. What kind of creature is this Nessie, Fendra, that she can outlive all the prideful boasts of truly living beings? Or is she also alive in some way—and the human primates somehow transferred their own inflated egos to their creation?

We walked for hours more that day. We passed ordinary Urth trees with bare trunks and wilted crowns. We walked over patches of polished stone and shattered columns of what DW885 described as metalloplastic polymers, whatever they are. Finally, someone declared a rest stop. The Jadderbadians wandered off to dump loads of frass. I saw the human, Aleesa, voiding wastes near a tattered wall of stone. I found a place to relieve myself in a ravine near what was once a clump of trees reduced to fraying stumps. Then I noticed the patterns on some of the bark, Fendra, and my oral pili detected familiar scents. I was in a graveyard of Mother Trees, my friend!

I stood tall, head crest erect, and looked all around. I froze when I heard the familiar warning trill of a male ambulus. I couldn't see the male at first, but I did see the human, Flint, squatting like a female of his species, as they do when eliminating solid waste. Finally, I spotted the male ambulus, crouched with mouth wide and ready to spring on Flint. I raised and spread the fingers of my left hand in the symbol Flint's tribe taught us when danger is near. Flint saw me, remained still and nodded his head ever so slightly to indicate that he understood.

"Stop!" I yelled. "I am Candela, podling of Mother Nevela. The human you are stalking is a friend!" I used our native tongue, Fendra, although the words seemed strange with disuse.

The ambulus straightened from his crouch and focused both primary eyes on me. His pili fluttered. He looked confused—perhaps frightened. I stepped forward, thinking I was on solid ground, but brush crackled beneath my feet and the underlying soil gave way. I saw the ambulus bolt back into the forest and Flint began to rise to his feet just before I closed my eyes to the cascading loam and prepared for impact.

* * * * *

Garnet

Candela is in trouble, said Zandura. *Proceed south and watch for Flint. He is nearby.*

I turned south and Patch followed. Patch had perked up his ears, although he couldn't hear the DataWurm giving me the warning. The Nessie firefly apparently new about Candela's problem too. She hopped off my shoulder and moved south swaying her body to and fro as she did when she wanted me to follow.

It wasn't long before I spotted Flint squatting at the edge of a pit. The Nessie fly circled Flint once, before returning to my shoulder. "Candela has found an old transport tunnel," said Nessie. "Not quite the way I had intended, but if she is not seriously injured, a good thing. I thought we would have to go much farther over difficult terrain to find an access point."

Flint turned toward me. "Candela saved me from a wild tree horse," he said. He swiveled his head back toward the hole. "Can't see a thing. I hear a groan."

Nessie jumped off my shoulder again and flew toward the pit. Patch and I followed. By the time we reached Flint's side, Nessiefly was shining a light down the dark hole.

"I see her now!" exclaimed Flint. "Are you all right down there?" He looked over his shoulder at me. "I'm not as good at tree horse language as you are, Garnet, but I think she's swearing. That's a good sign, right?"

I leaned over the edge of the pit. Candela lay on her side perhaps several man-lengths beneath me. "Are you injured, Candela?"

She swore again—words referring to excrement, violent sexual acts, and unworthy deities—before she directly answered my question. "I don't think so. I fell pack first. My back hurts, but I can move my feet and arms." She demonstrated that fact by flailing her limbs. "But I can't right myself!"

"We'll figure something out," I said. By that time I heard the wheezy approach and smelled the musk of Jadderbadians approaching from behind me.

"What's going on?" asked Master Gilbooa. "Did someone fall into their own frass hole?"

"Not helpful, worm master," I grumbled.

Nessie chose that moment to materialize in her ghost human form. "Candela has found a transport tunnel for us," she declared. "That will save us considerable time, as long as it's not blocked somewhere between here and our link to the Citadel." Nessie knelt by the hole and directed her next comment to Candela. "I will find that wandering male you scared away and make sure he doesn't bring reinforcements. Your home forest has seen me before. I'd say they worship me, but as my friend Rudy might point out, that would be immodest."

Nessie stood, spread her arms and smiled at all of us. "Now let's figure out how we can all get through this frass hole—as Master Gibooa so colorfully describes it—and see if Candela's discovery can get us to Nexus' Central Terminal."

We did find a way.

Flint, Aleesa and I found lengths of cord in the transport cart that we could anchor on nearby shrubs. We lowered ourselves into the newly exposed tunnel and helped get Candela to her feet. The biggest wound seemed to be to her pride. Nessiefly joined us. "I'll scout the length of the tunnel," she said. "In the meantime, see if you and the Jadderbaddians can enlarge this hole enough to get everyone down here." She left before I had time to comment. I watched the glow of her light illuminate strange shapes and wall markings as she disappeared down the length of the tunnel.

The worms had packed a manual tool set that proved quite effective for enlarging the opening through which Candela had fallen. They were able to fasten digging scoops to the ends of each of their arms. Masters Gilbooa and Portanya had a dozen arms between them, since they were younger creatures that had just molted twice. The older Master Teedercroft had nine arms.

"Reminds me when I was a young larva cleaning the birthing chambers on Jadderbad," said Master Teedercroft as he demonstrated a rather effective digging cycle that involved twisting motions I had never seen the worms use before. "Hard on the spinal rod, though," he added after one circuit. "Protect your heads down there!" he yelled into the pit.

"You might have told us before you started!" I yelled back. "It's raining dirt down here.!"

"Now you try, young masters," I heard Teedercroft say to Gilbooa and Portanya.

In a surprisingly short time the Jadderbadians created a substantial excavation that revealed some support beams from which we could anchor rigging to support Jadderbadians in a descent to our level.

Gilbooa tossed us a few dry ration bars while we waited for Nessie to return. I heard the gnashing of their tooth barbs above us as we consumed our food below. We had just finished as I caught sight of Nessie's glow in the distance. She arrived soon after and perched on my shoulder. "I think this tunnel will get us where we want to go.

There's some debris here and there, but we should be able to deal with it when we get there. Garnet: can you fashion some sort of harness to lower the Jadderbadians to the tunnel floor?"

I could and we did—although we decided we would have to leave the travel cart behind and divide up what supplies we could in our personal travel packs. Candela's load got a little heavier as well.

Once everyone was in the tunnel, including Patch, we lingered momentarily beneath the ragged excavation that framed a late afternoon sky. The light Nessie provided made her live up to her name of firefly. Cobwebs waved from the ceiling in the direction we needed to travel. The tunnel smelled of must and decay.

"Let's explore Nexus," said Nessie, "and see if we can find a shortcut to my Citadel. It's worth a shot!"

Shot? A shot of what? I thought to myself. But I was too tired to ask Nessie to explain.

* * * * *

Portanya

I didn't think I was particularly claustrophobic, but the dark and musty relic of a tunnel threatened to prove me wrong. Gilbooa plodded on in front of me, his handsome cuticle grimed with dust and shreds of web fragments from the local arachnids—very similar to some of the lower arthropod species on Jadderbad—as far as I could tell from the handful of species I had seen. Earthy smells assaulted all my olfactory slits. Light from the Nessie firefly cast shadows of my companions that seemed to have a life of their own as they drifted and shifted over the mud and rubble at my feet.

All the years at Academy studying the ancient human and avisaurian surface ruins never prepared me for the reality of seeing technology of that sophistication. The tunnels were surprisingly intact, massive excavations through solid bedrock. I suspected that humans and tree horses didn't deserve to be treated like animals, but I certainly wasn't prepared to grant them personhood equivalent to Jadderbaddian masters. What stories did the inscriptions on the walls tell? Were they merely directional in nature or did they tell tales like the runes on the pillars of the primitive crypts beneath the deserts of southern Jadderbad?

And what was the significance of the network of glistening threads that covered much of the surface of the tunnel's walls? It reminded me of slime molds—both Jadderbadian and terrestrial—that were common on jungle forest floors before the recent mega eruption. The networks were also not unlike holographic reproductions I had seen of the fungal communities that connect and undergird forest communities on both Urth and Jadderbad.

Gilbooa must have been thinking about the threads as well. "Do you think these are some kind of mycorrhizal or bacterial network, Portanya?" He pointed with an upper tier arm at the walls.

"I think so," I said, "although we would have to look at it microscopically to confirm."

Gilbooa waved his oral pili. "Of course. I've always been fascinated by such creatures, dear one. Slime molds, for example, occupy that unique junction between single-celled and multicellular life. They live as independent single cells until starved, but then send out chemical signals calling their comrades together."

"Yes, Booa, at which time they become multicellular—differentiating into a stalk and spores that can drift off to more suitable environments. I've always thought that process incredible myself. But what would they be doing in an environment like this? I don't see any sporangia along this entire network, either."

"Eeee-oooh!" exclaimed Candela. She raised one of her 3-toed hoofs from a large puddle and shook it.

"Well don't Eeee-oooh all over me," I said, as I tried to wipe away some of the muck from my left lateral leg.

Candela may have mumbled an apology. I wasn't quite sure. The Nessie firefly chose that moment to provide additional directions.

She flew around our straggling procession like an orbiting satellite. "Hang a left at this fork in the tunnel," she said. "I've had luck translating some of the wall inscriptions. Left will take us to a way station of some sort. Also, eat and hydrate. We have several hours to go."

I heard groans from three species. Humans produce a low gut-tural sound from deep within their throats. Tree horses sound like broken whistles. We Jadderbaddians, of course, mimic airbags de-flated by the sharp spines of cavern worms.

We groaned some more as the hours passed. But seeing the way station made us forget our misery.

The tunnel sloped upward for some distance before reaching the way station proper. We all took more labored breaths during the gradual ascent. Finally, we reached the remains of what must have been a transport cylinder whose once streamlined shape nearly filled the height of the tunnel through which we had traveled. The cylinder walls, shredded with decay, revealed the ribs and beams of its skel-etal support structure.

"Over here," said Nessie. "There's an opening big enough for Jadderbadians."

We all shambled toward her light. The opening was big enough for me, but Master Teedercroft had to enlarge the space before he managed to squeeze through. He also led the way and removed the remains of what appeared to be padded perches designed for avisau-rians. At the rear of the cylinder a set of tiered ramps led to an open, circular doorway through which light poured like the entrance to some mystical realm.

The humans scrambled up to the doorway first, being the limber primates that they were.

"What in Urth Mother's name is this?" said Garnet. Yapperfang barked once, a sound that echoed in whatever chamber lay before us.

"Look at that!" Flint pointed. Aleesa moved closer to her mate's side and grabbed his arm.

"Come this way," said Master Teedercroft to Gilbooa and me. "There are fewer obstructions to reach the portal."

Gilbooa looked at me with all three primary eyes in that endear-ing, but sometimes annoying way he had as the proud and protective husband. "I'll go first and make sure it's safe, dear one," he said.

"Not if I get there first, Booa!" I replied.

And I did. Booa is definitely more scholar than athlete.

The portal opened onto a vast terminal. Perhaps not as big as Jadderbad Central, but impressive nonetheless. Once again the Great Jokester finds ways to make us all humble and laugh at our own pretensions.

Booa reached my side, breathless. "Oh, my. Look at all those other portals just like this one. Do you suppose any of them have an intact—or nearly intact—transport cylinder that might get us closer to the Citadel?"

The Nessie firefly's somewhat feeble light did illuminate a series of arches spread around the circumference of the waystation's floor. "An interesting thought, Booa, but it would seem to be something impossible to wish for."

No sooner had I said that than amber pulses of light flickered across the glistening, slime mold-like network that covered the walls. Then, light spread across a panel in the center of the vast room, resembling a giant, blue eye. Finally, previously unnoticed globes in the ceiling added more light, reminding me of the giant larval nursery I once saw on Jadderbad's southern continent.

Nessie firefly circled the blue eye panel once before projecting her human holographic image off to one side. "Gather here, folks," she said, waving one of her feeble human arms. "Time for a news update!"

The humans and Candela reached her first. "What is this magical place?" asked Garnet.

"I can smell and see many of the tiny creatures that help Mother Trees connect us all in her embrace," said Candela.

Master Teedercroft, Gilbooa and I were not far behind. "This way station, as you call it, can't possibly be functional after the eternity these ruins have existed...can they?" I asked, wheezing through my spiracles after the exertion.

Nessie smiled. "They are—at least partially—if you have connections with the right Earth goddess and all the minions she commands."

"Urth Mother?" Garnet stood directly in front of Nessie's hologram. Flint put an arm around Aleesa's shoulder.

"In a manner of speaking," said Nessie. "I call her Gaidra and she is a consciousness made up of the vast living network of planet

Earth—an entity four billion years in the making—with some extraterrestrial additions she has acquired. She and I—and my friend from the deep past, Rudy, have gotten to know her in recent centuries. She has gathered some of her microscopic infrastructure to help us out here—even though she's not happy with her so called intelligent vermin at the moment."

"Nonsense!' blurted Gilbooa with a whiff of acrid pheromone. "Superstitious nonsense, offensive to the Great Prophet."

Nessie's smiled broadened. "Give him a little demonstration, Gaidra. After all, Jadderbad's planetary consciousness, Hydra, is now part of your eclectic mix."

Nessie's "demonstration" was hard to describe—much less believe. But it was captivating enough to make us all careless.

The cavern trembled. Fragments of rock fell from the ceiling. The humans crouched, looking all around like Firsties surrounded by a ring of predators. I spread my tripod of basal legs and extended all six arms for stability. Gilbooa and Master Teedercroft did much the same. Candela's long neck contracted closer to her body. Her head crest rose like an arch of sabres. Yapperfang began to howl.

An image of Urth materialized on the blue screen, a marbled mix of brown, green, blue and white with a halo in the infrared—all framed by the blackness of space. It appeared to be an image captured from the height of an orbiting satellite.

"I am Gaia," said a low register human female voice with a volume loud enough to make my tympanae contract.

The blue screen image split. A picture of Jadderbad appeared, a not terribly dissimilar sphere, but with more blue in the mix. *Beautiful,* I thought, *and so far away.* My optical pili drooped with homesick longing.

"And I am Hydra," said a second female voice in a tone that reminded me of my first second molt nurse.

"Together we have formed Gaidra here on Urth. But witness now our individual stories," they said in unison. "And the Mother Tree forests of Grove are now part of our union."

The Urth tremors stopped.

"Nice melodrama," commented Nessie. "Rudy taught me all about melodrama over the years," she added, like a narrator's aside in a Prophet's Day play.

It turned out to be a very immersive melodrama.

I noticed the slime mold network on Aleesa first because she cried out as it enveloped her legs. While we all were viewing our respective planets on the screen, some of the glistening protoplasm that had been restricted mostly to the walls of the chamber had migrated to our bodies. I looked down at my own cuticle. Threads of slime spread and anastomosed up my lower segment as I watched. The way station interior and my companions began to fade like warming mist.

And then I was floating in a vast ocean—one tiny speck of life among many. Glistening blobs floated all around me. Some appeared to move at the whim of swirling currents. Others powered themselves with thrashing flagella, jerking forward through water molecules locked loosely together by electrostatic forces. My whole sensorium seemed to be confirming that I was one microbe among a chaotic multitude.

I should have been terrified. But I wasn't. I felt like a hatchling in my birthing waters.

"The stories of Urth and Jadderbad are not that different," said Hydra, "at least for the first few billion years."

Time slowed. Past, present, and future merged into one never changing moment. I floated in currents whose temperature changes stroked me like a lover using his finger triads to trace elaborate designs along my cuticle. But the creatures floating around me did slowly morph from simple orbs, spirals, and cylinders—undoubtedly bacterial in nature—to more complex forms adorned with spikes, oar-like cilia, or armored, translucent plates. Some clustered into spheres of interconnected cells, each carrying a nugget of chlorophyll green at their center. They majestically sailed among their smaller companions like freight ships amid constellations of tiny rowboats.

"Pleasant, my child, am I correct?" said Hydra. *She definitely sounded like my old nurse.* "This is the way life has been for most of my existence, chemical vortices changing shape and form in condensed little cellular packets—but then multicellularity happened. All I can say is that it seemed like a prudent choice at the time…"

I watched as cells formed into webs and sheets that covered ocean floors. Others cells clustered into mounds or branched into tree-like forms that coated rocks or intertwined with other cell clusters and networks. Some structures blushed in various shades of green, yellow, blue or red. Some grew eyes and fins and flippers. Every manifestation of the bursts of complexity around me grew and divided and anastomosed—complex puzzles with no individual creation final or complete.

Ocean life spilled onto land. Green forms bathed in sunlight. Pale forms churned the land with tentacles that absorbed whatever they needed to survive, constantly partnering with—or parasitizing those harvesting energy directly from the sun. Some creatures grew legs and eyes and complex brains. I saw things I thought I remembered from ancient scrolls and data files, others things that seemed too bizarre to be real. All of them swarmed and moved and seemed to tumble over each other like chaff in a windstorm.

"Don't blink any of your three eyes, Portanya, or you'll miss your part of the play…" Hydra had my old nurse's sense of humor too.

The last image I saw before the way station once more materialized around me were larval Jadderbadians crawling ashore, morphing quickly into first, second, and third instars with the third instars blossoming from their pupae into winged adults that rose into a perfect turquoise Jadderbadian sky like the ending to a simplistic holodrama. I noticed too how the once robust diversity of life on Jadderbad frayed like a worn out garment as Jadderbadians consumed Hydra's resources…

"Yes," said Hydra, "you and your self-important kind took for far too long without giving me what I needed to survive. Survival was a bit dicey for half a millenium." Hydra paused for me to consider her statement, as my nurse was fond of doing. "And the present," she continued, "is a freeze frame of all that has come before—all mixed and jumbled into one co-mingled drama—that could go on or end forever, depending on the choices you and your companions make now."

I blinked all three nictating membranes.

"No pressure, though," Nessie added, smiling, as her holographic image slowly came into focus.

I looked down at my cuticle and lower limbs. The tentacles of slime mold were in retreat, sometimes dividing and regrouping into individual amoebae after they reached the ground, then reforming into new retreating threads of protoplasm.

I turned to look at dear Booa and the humans. Slime mold retreated from their limbs as well.

Booa looked at me, all three primary eyes wide. He said nothing, but his cuticle flickered with the colors of a larva experiencing his first molt.

"Praise be to Urth Mother!" exclaimed Garnet, raising his arms. He then dropped to one knee. Flint and Aleesa knelt as well. "She has shown us the immense journey of our past and challenges us to make a new future…" Garnet then turned to me and Booa. "…with you," he said. He looked at Candela. "…and with you."

Candela arched her back and lowered her head crest. "I'm beginning to understand how Mother Trees came from their home planet of Grove and found sustenance on this rich planet." She looked toward Nessie. "I want to know more. And I want to know how we can make the planet spirits happy."

Nessie gestured toward Candela with the forefinger of her right hand extended. "You will learn more in time, Candela. And making planet spirits happy will entail finishing the journey to my Citadel." She glanced around the way station at its various portals and pointed at one. "Let's see what's behind door number 3." Then Nessie turned to me with another aside. "My ancient friend Rudy thinks that comment is funny, but I have no idea why."

'Door number 3' was actually labeled with a different and longer set of alphanumeric characters, but the relevant point was that Nessie had determined that was the transportation portal leading toward her citadel. There was a transport cylinder in place—a good thing, because some of the portals led to empty tunnels. It would have been impossible to move a cylinder from one portal to the next with our limited resources.

But there was a bad thing, of course. The cylinder needed repairs. We had lots of spare parts that we could cannibalize from other cylinders, but how could we actually make the repairs? Nessie had an answer that would test me and my devoted Booa—as well as Master Teedercroft.

"You Jadderbadians have experience with robots, right?" Nessie asked. "Major terminals always had repair stations equipped with service bots. This one has one right there." Her holographic image pointed to an alcove not far from where we had entered the terminal. "All you worms have to do is figure out the workings of ancient human technology, consult with Gaidra when it comes to organic power generation, and enlist your friends to engage in some grunt labor, a phrase that Rudy is fond of using. "

"Is that all?" I asked. My colors flickered in shades so discordant that I hoped my incredulity was not lost on this human simulacrum.

"And I'll help, of course," she said brightly, with her special version of the crescent-shaped human smile that was beginning to make my cranial pili vibrate the way they did when Booa said something particularly inane or dismissive.

But, in fact, our eclectic collection of beings did accomplish the impossible—or at least the highly improbable.

* * * * *

I somehow became defacto leader of our repair efforts. I was the elder female and had experience leading field expeditions, of course. Master Teedercroft had more expertise with robots and their software, but was most comfortable solving technical problems. Dear Booa was smart, of course, but could get distracted—both by academic/philosophical problems and by his preoccupation with me, his chosen mate.

I put Garnet in charge of food procurement and manual labor. The other humans and Candela seemed to accept his leadership role.

The humans proved to be quick and agile, especially for creatures with a single pair of arms and only two legs. Candela managed to use her forelimbs and odd, beak-like mouth with dexterity.

We settled into a routine. The humans and Candela would spend much of the daylight hours above ground searching for local game or fetching water. Master Teedercroft and I—along with our spiderbot—worked with Nessie to adapt our technology to some of the ancient human interfaces, many of which had greatly degraded over time.

On several occasions the DataWurms that had merged with Garnet and Candela proved quite helpful. They had scoured the ancient ruins of both humans and avisaurians for millennia. On several occasions they filled information gaps that even Nessie was unaware of. They also were able to interface with Gaidra's slime network in ways I never completely understood.

Looking back on evenings in the ancient way station, I'm still struck by their ethereal quality. The living microscopic networks formed by Gaidra served as a glowing backdrop, as if we were surrounded in a loosely woven blanket of luminous energies. The humans often sang—usually accompanied by Candela. They created flute-like and percussion instruments from objects found inside or outside the tunnel system. We Jadderbadians learned to adjust our color displays to meld with the music. We manufactured scents that blended with human and tree horse odors, creating an aroma cloud I find hard to describe with mere words—although Booa always managed to insert personally erotic scents designed for my pleasure.

I never did find the courage to ask Master Teedercroft what he thought of those olfactory accents—although I'm sure he noticed when my color displays drifted into crimson parts of the spectrum.

Even Booa and the human called Flint managed to forge a somewhat grudging tolerance for each other, if not an actual friendship, which made subsequent events especially poignant. Booa accompanied Flint and Aleesa on several foraging trips so that he could try and regain—unsuccessfully as it turned out—contact with his Uncle Bluedigg. Either his uncle had left the planet or the communication system was offline for some reason. During the outings Booa proved adept at locating certain native fungi that both Flint and Aleesa were fond of.

Flint devised percussion instruments for evening gatherings from scraps of metal, which Booa found to be quite fascinating. He swayed to Flint's enthusiastic acoustic rhythms while flickering in outlandish spectral displays. The human barked with laughter when he managed to elicit a particularly vivid effusion of colors and scents from my young husband.

Our work on the transport cylinder may have taken nearly two hexads of Urth days, but still proceeded much more quickly than I could have hoped. We were within hours of being finished when tragedy struck.

* * * * *

Booa, Flint, and Garnet were working to remove a coupler system that insured proper alignment of the transport carriage with the maglev tracks beneath. This required the maglev system to be engaged to hold the carriage aloft while Booa and flint worked beneath it to remove the couplers. Master Teedercroft and I had checked and double-checked the system, using both Nessie and Garnet's DataWurm to backup our work. The DataWurm later said quantum fluctuations in three circuits simultaneously caused the ultimate failure—a statistically improbable occurrence.

In other words, frass happens.

Flint apparently saw or heard something that made him aware of the magnetic field failure. Praise the Prophet. He somehow managed to shove my dear Booa off the tracks before the carriage descended, but he couldn't save himself. The immense weight of the carriage crushed his fragile human body.

I scrambled down the ramp from the platform I was on, propelling myself horizontally using all six arms and anterior legs like a hatchling. I wrapped all my arms around Booa and held his cuticle close to mine.

His pili hung limp. His pheromone cloud of despair surrounded us like a tangible, silken cocoon.

"Ah Flint," he finally said. "Besafecuntata."

I hadn't heard that Jadderbadian word for a long time. It was a benediction reserved for broodmates parted by death.

Broodmates. Perhaps we all had become broodmates. I had always thought of humans as fascinating creatures whose study would be both interesting and provide me the credentials for becoming Master of Alien Studies. Booa probably would have developed a tolerance for his initial humaniphobia and followed my professional path like a hatchling captivated by a tantalizing odor trail. Now, who knew if either of us had professional futures on this increasingly hostile planet?

But perhaps we had discovered something more rare and fulfilling. Flint's funeral ceremony held promise of that.

* * * * *

Aleesa

I leaned against Garnet and cried. He wrapped an arm around my shoulders. I felt Patch's fur and warm body against my right leg. Through my tears, the pile of wood that the worm-a-pedes and their mechanical spider had gathered seemed nothing more than a blurred mound of brown, tangled threads.

Flint's body appeared small perched on top of the pyre. He lay draped in a colorful shroud I had been able to fashion from spare fabric the worm called pupal wrap that Portanya had packed in the bottom of their travel sled. The material had felt smooth in my hands and light, like tanned leather, but it had been hard to sew. The tree horse, Candela, used the tip of her beak-like mouth to poke tiny holes in it so that I could make proper stitches.

After making Flint's shroud, I had tried to sleep, but thoughts ran around in my head like furry rativets in the spring. The tunnel alcove that Portanya and her mate had found for me had smelled of dust and animal musk. I remembered how hard the floor had felt even through the layers of dried grass they had piled up for me to sleep on. In the distance I heard clattering and scratching sounds as they collected the wood for Flint's funeral pyre beneath the breach in the tunnel ceiling that would allow Flint's soul to ascend to his ancestors.

How would I live without my Flint?

Garnet will make a strong Shaman—maybe even stronger than his mother, Rainbow. He can help Flint's soul ascend. But our tribe was far away. Flint's soul might struggle to rise without the help of all our people.

Garnet began to sing. It seemed strange to not only hear the intertwined melodies of travel songs and prayers for the dead, but to feel them vibrate like caged spirits in the body next to mine.

Candela sang next. She had said she had modified a song she had often sung with her friend, Fendra. More strangeness. If someone had said I would one day invite a pack animal to the funeral of my beloved Flint, I would have spit at her feet. But Candela's song was light like those of small perching birds in the spring. A strange sound from such a large being. Surely the ancestors wouldn't mind such a tune to help Flint rise.

And nothing could be stranger than tall creatures with rainbow hides waving too many arms as they chorused with melodies that made my flesh quiver—not with repulsion, but with a kind of excitement that entities so bizarre and powerful somehow shared my grief.

The worm called Master Teedercroft stopped singing in order to light Flint's pyre with a shiny silver stick. Flames curled among the branches like orange fingers. The fingers ultimately caressed my Flint as mine often had. His shroud began to release wisps of colored smoke as Portanya had said it would.

Rise, Flint, rise! Find your new home in the sky. Make a place near you for me when my time comes.

* * * * *

Much later, huddled in the sleeping nest Flint and I had shared in the ancient transport terminal, I couldn't sleep. My mind lingered on images from earlier in the day: Swirling ash from Flint's nearly extinguished pyre ascending to the tunnel's roof. The rainbow colors flickering on Portanya's hide as she helped me navigate the tunnel. Candela's faceted eye regarding me beneath her crest of iridescent blue feathers. The mottled, gray-brown ratalope leather of Garnet's moccasins as he walked beside me.

Finally, I arose in the dark of midnight and found my way to Garnet's pallet in the pale glow of instruments that had been returned to some manner of slumbering life through the work of the worm-a-pedes and Urth Mother Gaia. I crawled under his blanket, lay next to the curve of his back, and wrapped an arm around his waist. "I can't sleep," I said.

"I understand," he said. "I miss Flint, too."

And because this was a time for comfort and not pleasure, sleep came quickly as it would for two weary children tangled in a warm embrace.

* * * * *

Garnet

I fingered the parallel ridges of the ancient bug amulet around my neck. The chromatophores on my shoulders flickered in a shade of green that I wished displayed more confidence. Nevertheless, Masters Gilbooa and Portanya on the bench across the aisle mirrored my color display in a sign of support. Aleesa squeezed my hand. Patch looked up at me between my legs as if to say, "What are you up to now?"

I believe our odds of successfully launching this transport pod, Garnet, are well over 65%.

I would be comforted by hearing a higher number, Zandura, after all the work we've put in.

Effort doesn't insure success. The equipment is ancient after all. Thanks for reminding me, Zandura.

"Everyone strapped in?" Master Teedercroft's voice crackled like dry leaves over what Nessie described as a resurrected communication system.

"Yes. Let's move," said Candela. "The harness arrangement we fixed up is not the most comfortable."

The engine engaged with a deceptively mild hum. My back pressed against the seat as we accelerated. Pits and other imperfections in the tunnel walls passed by the windows of the pod faster than hurled stones. Aleesa's nails dug into the skin of my forearm.

"Encouraging start," said Nessie as she buzzed over our heads in her firefly form.

"This is like riding a stampeding tree horse!" exclaimed Aleesa. She immediately looked across the aisle at Candela. "I hope you take no offense."

Candela's head crest rippled. "I take none, Aleesa."

Aleesa waved an arm in the general direction of Nessie's fluttering drone. "Shouldn't we move with more caution, little spirit?"

"We have mechanical servants who see and hear things mere humans—or Jadderbadians—or tree horses—cannot," said Nessie. We will slow down if we need to."

"How long to reach the Citadel, do you think?" asked Master Gilbooa.

"At our current speed, and with no unforeseen problems, 4.7 hours." Nessie hovered near Gilbooa's head."

"What unforeseen problems?" Gilbooa's cuticle flickered in shades of amber.

"They wouldn't be unforeseen if I could list them," replied Nessie.

"Examples of problems, then, mech!" Gilbooa's colors shifted to crimson.

"You should have slept more last cycle, Booa." Portanya patted one of Gilbooa's thighs. "Treat Nessie with the respect of a Class 4 AI, at least. She is far more than a mere mech."

"Why thank, you, Portanya," said Nessie. "I'm glad I rate Class four status." She circled Gilbooa's head again. "To your point, Master Gilbooa, foreseen disasters might include broken maglev panels, fuel capsule malfunctions, software glitches, tunnel collapse debris, flooding, breaches in pod integrity, power fluctuations in the bio-mechanical flux interfaces…"

"Enough…Nessie. My apologies. I'm tired. We're all tired. You have been most helpful." Gilbooa's colors shifted to greens and blues.

I understood Gilbooa's feelings. We had all worked hard to reach this place of mystery called the Citadel. Flint had paid with his life. Much of whatever success we now achieved depended on the will of spirits and forces beyond our control.

We traveled several hours before confronting one of them.

"Fasten your seat belts!" crackled Teedercroft's voice, but there wasn't time.

I did have time to pull Aleesa closer to me. I instinctively covered her head and shoulders with mine and wrapped my arms around her. The next few moments seem etched on my mind as clearly as a cave painting seen in the glare of torchlight.

The travel pod slowed so quickly that both our bodies crashed into the back of the chair in front of us. The chromatophores on my arms turned crimson.

Candela wailed in the aisle across from me as she too slid into the chair in front of her. Afterwards, she rubbed the knee of one forelimb while readjusting her harness.

I heard huffs and wheezes from somewhere in front of me along with a cascade of unfamiliar, but passionately expressed Jadderbadian words.

Nessie hovered overhead flashing amber bursts of light and shouting the words "Mayday! Mayday!" Over and over which was clearly meant as a warning of some kind.

By the time the pod stopped completely, we were all making unusual or unfamiliar sounds. My left shoulder ached, but otherwise I seemed to be uninjured. Aleesa squirmed beneath me. She groaned. "Are you all right?" I asked.

"I...I think so," she said.

"What happened?" I heard Gilbooa ask.

Nessie buzzed over my head, moving in Gilbooa's general direction. "One of those truly unforeseen events," Nessie replied. "In this case, a new geothermal geyser has just made a hot and noisy statement in the tunnel segment directly ahead of us." Nessie circled back in our direction making sure everyone was still alive and functional.

"What do we do?" I recognized Portanya's voice. "Wait for it to subside? Try to detour around it? I didn't see any side tunnels along our route."

"We do have a bit of a problem," Nessie conceded. Her firefly form circled overhead once and then perched on the back of the chair directly in front of me. I heard spattering sounds on the shell of our transport pod and hissing noises as if we were near a den of snakes. "This geyser may just have a long eruptive life here based on the readings I'm getting from external sensors."

A series of wheezes, groans, squawks and perhaps a burp—or was it a Jadderbadian fart—followed her announcement.

"No cause for alarm," she continued, "but I think a change in plans are in order. Perhaps you will meet my friend Rudy a little sooner than expected—if I can get his organic body completed in a timely fashion."

Ah, excellent! Zandura surprised me with what genuinely sounded like excitement. *I've been waiting for this meeting for some time.*

Meanwhile, the pod was heating up noticeably. Something had to happen long before we met this mythical ancient human person.

"Everyone make their way to the rear of the transport pod," Nessie announced as she circled our collective mass of squirming bodies. "We'll use the emergency rear exit so that the pod's bulk will shield us from the geyser while we retreat to the last surface access port."

"How far is that?" I asked as Aleesa squeezed out of her raekid-designed chair into the aisle.

"Less than a mile," replied Nessie. "Piece of cake, as my Rudy would say."

"Cake? What does cake have to do with finding an escape exit?" Aleesa frowned as she and Candela helped extricate me from my seat. "This phantom Rudy ancestor speaks in riddles."

Aleesa, Candela, and I made our way toward the rear of the pod, trying not to trip over Patch. I glanced over my shoulder and saw that the Jadderbadians followed not far behind. Their limbs squirmed like eels against the colored, flickering rainbow of their hides. The Spiderbot crawled over the tops of chairs, its oversized eyes like the glowing embers of a fire. The air seemed thick and moist and smelled of sulfur.

Nessie's rear end blinked like a tiny torch ahead of us and came to rest near a crimson colored depression on the rear wall. "Press the button, Aleesa. That will release the seal on the rear door."

Aleesa pressed the button. Patch sat down behind her. I peered over Aleesa's shoulder and absently patted Patch's head. The door groaned like a carat whose tail had been stepped on.

I smelled Jadderbadian musk and felt a three-fingered hand on my shoulder. "Is it working?" Portanya arched over my back like a tree about to fall.

"It's trying," I said. "Ah, there. It's moving!" The door's groan morphed into a squeaky whine and then a plaintive whistle as it slid to one side.

Nessie flew through the opening first. Aleesa, Patch, Candela and I followed, having to drop about a foot to the maglev tracks. Spiderbot crawled beneath Jadderbadian legs and out. The Jadderbadians' had to lie prone in the aisle so that Aleesa and I could help them squeeze through the opening like logs floating through a river-carved cavern after a storm.

"Remove your hand from that orifice, human!" Master Gilbooa complained at one point. "Totally inappropriate behavior!"

"Relax, 'Booa," Portanya said as she helped push her mate forward from inside the pod. "You'll either suffer human hands in the wrong places or end up like a sausage roasted over a campfire, if we don't get out of this pod."

Fortunately, that didn't happen. We all left the pod behind us as we staggered down the dark but rapidly cooling tunnel toward the last surface access portal. As my eyes adjusted to the relative dark of the tunnel, I saw the glowing spider web of Urth Mother slime along the tunnel walls retreat slowly along with us. The transport pod behind us hissed gently like ratalope lard on a hot stone.

We reached the last surface access port without incident. A zig-zagging ramp rose from the base of the tunnel to a circular plate in the tunnel roof over our heads. "Looks a bit rusty," said Nessie after she spiraled down from the roof to sit on my left shoulder. "Why don't you scramble up there and see if you can move that plate?"

According to the records in my database, said Zandura, *the plate should just be resting in a depression. It might be rather heavy, though, for the musculature of a single human male of your age and dimensions.*

That turned out to be an understatement. I succeeded in getting the plate to move a little, but wasn't tall enough to pop it out of its resting spot. "Some Jadderbadian help up here, please!" Masters Portanya and Gilbooa looked at each other, flickering in shades of pale green. They both ascended the ramp and positioned themselves on either side of me.

Each of them extended their three upper tier arms above their heads, while awkwardly bending their upper torsos. "On the count of three, my love," said Master Gilbooa. They pushed, groaned, and flickered in shades of orange, but the plate popped off and clattered onto something out of sight above ground.

"I need a lift up and out." After a few flailing gestures they figured out that I wanted to step on their lower segment tier of arms to be lifted up and through the access port.

They lifted me faster than I expected, but I managed to grab the edge of the access porthole and clamber out into the open air. A gentle breeze carried a whiff of sulfur. I turned and scanned the horizon, freezing in place when I saw what must indeed be our goal: A giant greenish-colored needle rising from the ground and piercing the sky. It had to be the Citadel. How could my ancestors have built such an enormous spear and planted it in the ground?

Nessie fluttered up and out of the hole and alighted on my right shoulder. "We're almost there, Garnet!" she declared. "But first we have to deal with what's over your left shoulder."

I tore my eyes away from the citadel and looked. An angry gray cloud of dust and grit rolled toward us like an immense stampeding herd of ratafants.

"It appears that another of Gaia's volcano-induced weather tantrums is headed this way," said Nessie. "We'll need to retreat to the tunnel below for the night. You and the worm-a-pede couple will need to replace the hatch after we descend. Rudy can arrive to help us out by mid morning tomorrow."

Somehow we managed to do what Nessie wanted—barely ahead of the storm—while she ordered us around and flitted above us like a persistent fly. I was so tired I was tempted to leave her outside, but didn't. She buzzed beneath the portal lid before Portanya, Gilbooa, and I settled the covering back into place.

* * * * *

I shivered a few times that night without the benefit of our portable heater, but three Jadderbadians, one tree horse, two humans, and a wolf dog create a fair amount of communal heat. Portanya and Gilbooa even produced enough chromataphoric colors to resemble a kind of campfire. I kept my chromatophores covered beneath the cloak that Aleesa and I shared. Nessie materialized in her ghost-like human form and sat among us. Perhaps she realized how annoying her drone form could be.

I suspect that this Mnemosyne/Nessie creature is always quite aware of what she is doing, commented Zandura.

Before I could respond, Candela began expressing her expectations for the visit to the Citadel. She shuffled her feet and turned her optical bulb toward Mnemosyne, "Nessie, spirit creature, will I ever speak to my friend, Fendra, again?"

Nessie's semi-translucent face turned to look directly at Candela for a long moment before she spoke. "Death is still a terminal event, dear Candela, but you will talk to your friend again and begin the process of healing your wounds—the wounds of a survivor."

Candela absently smoothed her head crest with one hand and nodded her optical bulb ever so slightly. Her oral pili quivered. She seemed satisfied as she rocked back and forth on her legs.

"Your world is bizarre, Nessie," said Master Gilbooa, "but Portanya and I want to learn what lessons you have to teach. We Jadderbadians wasted much of Jadderbad, evolving as predatory consumers, much like your humans. Such mistakes should never be repeated."

"Although they usually are," added Master Portanya.

"Indeed," agreed Nessie. She sat up a bit straighter. "I guarantee you will learn as much as you are ready and willing to absorb." Nessie looked toward Master Teedercroft.

He shrugged and flickered in shades of amber. "I'm with them," pointing several medial appendages toward those young Masters he so dutifully served.

Nessie then turned her attention toward Aleesa and me. "And you two—my Rudy's distant progeny—what desires will punch your tickets to the Citadel?"

I chose to ignore the particular arcane reference to 'tickets' that I didn't understand and focus on Nessie's intent. "I plan to lead my tribe—with Aleesa's help." I squeezed her closer to my side. "Like my mother, Rainbow, I will lead my people to a deeper understanding of how we must work with Urth Mother to live on her rich planet without consuming her like a cancer."

Nessie nodded. "Well said, Garnet. That's a start." Nessie turned towards Patch. "Be sure to help them out, canine. You two species have fooled around together so long now that you're like Siamese twins joined at the hip."

Patch cocked his head, a bit mystified and anxious as dogs can be when their masters make noises about anything other than food, punishment, or danger. He soon settled in closer to Aleesa and me, casting a wary eye in Nessie's direction.

At some point, while listening to the wind howl distantly overhead and grit scrape across the portal access, real time shifted into dreamtime.

Sleep well, I thought I heard Zandura say—although I may have been giving that directive to myself.

* * * * *

The directive apparently worked, whoever gave it. My eyes only popped open to loud bangs over my head.

"Hey, anybody home down there? Your Uber is here and the meter's running! I expect a big tip, too."

The voice was that of a human male—the mysterious and wondrous Rudy, as I would soon discover—and he spoke with an odd tribal accent using many nonsense words.

The others around me began to unfurl like some tentacled beast. The Jadderbadians stretched and flickered like candles beginning to burn. Candela grunted once and stretched her long neck. Patch jumped to his feet and barked. Aleesa stirred next to me, her warm hand squeezed my thigh.

"Use the winch on that access portal lid, Rudy," said Nessie as she spiraled over my head toward the portal, a green light blinking languidly on the rear end of her firefly form. "We'll greet you properly soon."

The process didn't take long.

I blinked in the mid-morning light of the sun as I pulled myself up and out of the portal—with Gilbooa and Portanya's help. The previous day's storm had left frozen waves of dust and gravel piled in its wake. I helped Aleesa out. The Jadderbadians squeezed out next, arms moving in all directions. The look of their alien strangeness competed with the movements and color displays that made them individuals for me, and not a collective gaggle of monsters. Candela lifted Patch out to Aleesa's waiting arms along with the spiderbot who had folded its legs up next to its body so that it resembled a strange kind of basket. Nessie followed in her firefly form, but soon projected her human image next to the human called Rudy.

I must say, I wasn't all that impressed. If Nessie had recently created Rudy's body, perhaps she had been in too much of a rush. Rudy stood about a head taller than Nessie, but still was far shorter than anyone in my tribe or The People in general. He had close-cut black hair that framed a sickly pale face. A short bar of hair about a finger width wide rested on his upper lip. He wore smooth skins of some kind with bulging pouches here and there.

But he smiled and spoke with a brazen voice like a confident uncle about to ride off into battle. "Well now, such a crew!" he said. "I suspect you are ready for a visit to the Citadel, where Nessie and I like to hang out." He swept his left arm in an arc that left him pointing toward the giant spear on the horizon, glittering softly and seeming to ripple as cloud shadows crept across her surface.

My heart skipped a beat. I was ready. The People must someday learn to understand the greatness of those who came before and bring us closer to Urth Mother—who seemed ready to abandon her children.

"All aboard, then," said Rudy. He pointed to a spot over my

shoulder.

When I turned to look, my heart skipped a second beat. A giant Urth boat of some kind towered twice as high as the biggest rataphant I had ever seen. A mouth opened slowly in the end facing us as if it were inviting us to be swallowed alive.

We all delivered ourselves into the gaping maw of this new travel machine. It smelled of oils and what Nessie referred to as plastics accented with leathery smells not unlike tanned ratalope hides. Rudy pointed out custom designed seats for those of us that used them and a kind of padded stall for Candela. Hearing human, Jadderbadian, and tree horse sighs of comfort simultaneously made for a strange chorus. Even Patch rumbled deep in his throat as he poked and prodded at what appeared to be a soft fist of fabric prepared to embrace him. Master Portanya held the spiderbot in her lower tier of arms.

Rudy ascended a small platform in front of all of us and took a seat. Glowing panels lit up in front of him, apparently at his command. "Enjoy the view for an hour or so folks. I'll try not to run us into a geyser or mudflat. There's supposed to be a new storm front rolling in tomorrow. It would help if there were actual roads around here." Then he muttered at Nessie, whose ghostly form had materialized beside him. "What the hell do I poke and prod to…ah there it is."

The Urth boat lurched forward and our continuing, and hopefully concluding, journey toward the Citadel began.

The terrain proved to be rugged, gashed here and there with cracks in Mother Urth's rocky hide. Once water exploded through a vent to our right, ejecting a column of steam as if snorted from the nostril of a dragon. We could see everything around and above us. A clear barrier served as a magical protective film. And in front of us the shaft of the Citadel's bulk grew like a rising mountain as we drew closer. Our Urth boat slowed to a stop at the edge of a bridge too straight and narrow to be natural.

I stroked the amulet around my neck and thanked Urth Mother for allowing me to see all these wonders. I wished Rainbow—and Flint—could see them, too. Somehow, I could sense Zandura's satisfaction as well—as if this was one of the moments DataWurms cherished above all others: assembling sounds and sights and chemicals and numbers into threads of knowledge that wove themselves into complex fabrics of understanding.

"Before I cross the cove here," said Rudy, "take a look at our humble abode. Nessie has done a fine job trying to undo entropy—in the short term, at least." Rudy laughed, although I didn't understand his joke, if it was one.

I looked up at the Citadel. I had once visited a holy site of my people with Rainbow when I was a boy. Generations before mine had built a tower of native stone that seemed magnificent at the time—truly a place made holy partly by the effort of those members of the People who had spent their lives building it. But the Citadel was to the tower as a hunter's rataphant spear is to a shard of wood used to pick one's teeth. The Citadel's central column rose like a godly finger pinning clouds to the azure sky overhead. It was a finger that pulsed with life. Tendrils of living tissue not unlike the Gaia slime that lined the ancient transport tunnel twisted skyward. Lichens and mosses formed chaotic patterns in between. And, as I watched, a small cloud of Nessie-like fireflies swirled from an opening halfway up the column, their diaphanous wings glittering in the sunlight.

Rudy must have followed my gaze. "Nessie sends her messengers everywhere, my boy—especially now that the weather has turned chaotic." He focused his eyes on mine. They seemed as clear and as deep as two bottomless wells. "Let's go inside, shall we?"

Ask Rudy to take your hand, Garnet, said Zandura.

Why?

I can speak directly to him that way.

"Take my hand, wise Rudy. My DataWurm, Zandura, wishes to speak with you." I extended my right arm.

Rudy grasped my hand without hesitation. I remember you. I realized he was talking to Zandura. I heard Rudy's voice now in my mind, like Zandura's. *Or*, he continued, *at least some version of you...*

I was here long ago, said Zandura, *but now I bear the memories of another human genius named Zandur.*

Ha! I wonder if Nessie can handle two geniuses in her network?

Rudy winked at me.

But before Zandura could answer, Master Gilbooa forced air through his spiracles in a whistle so loud I had to cover my ears. He held a slender object next to the membrane that served as his ear.

"Well, it's about time!" he shouted. "Where have you *been*, Uncle Bluedigg?"

* * * * *

Master Gilbooa

A shiver of excitement crept up my dorsal nerve chord. A part of me thought I might never hear the voice of my uncle again—which at one time would have rather pleased me. "Are you still on Urth then? Exciting things are happening here. You were right to suspect that humans might be more than mindless primates! Portanya and I are about to enter a magnificent structure called the Citadel, apparently a construction of ancient humans and some hybrid artificial intelligence called Nessie." I took a deep breath, ready to say more, but Uncle interrupted.

"You are safe then, my young instar? I was worried. We are down to a skeleton staff in New Jadderbad at the moment. The Council and the Church of Greatest Mother are deliberating even now about our future on this planet." Uncle's voice crackled with static. I hoped the connection would hold.

"Oh, we must stay, Uncle. There is so much to learn. We know so very little about the Grovian tree horse people. The humans have been using them as pack animals. And then there is this Nessie AI and her ancient human simulacrum, Rudy…and… Are you hearing me, Uncle?" Silence followed, punctuated by fizzing crackles.

Garbled comments ensued. "…so, perhaps you should return…" Much static. "…very dangerous…" Uncle said something else I couldn't hear.

"No, Uncle. Portanya and I…" I looked toward my beloved. She smiled and nodded, displaying her tooth barbs in a most endearing way. "Portanya and I will make the study of these strange human primates our life's mission. Can you hear me, Uncle?" The connection buzzed with only the background static of the universe. I would try again later.

Now, I took one of Portanya's middle tier hands in my own and looked up at the Citadel. Passing clouds swirling overhead made me just a little dizzy. "Let's investigate this wondrous human hive standing before us, my love."

* * * * *

Candela

We all crossed a wide bridge over a lake to reach an enormous arched doorway at the base of the Citadel. I remember glancing up once and watched a string of ratasaurs as they flew to the northwest. Then the dark arch of the doorway passed overhead, blocking my view of the sky. My primary eyes took a few moments to adjust. My secondary eyes registered faint patterns in the infrared.

Nessie appeared in front of me. "This way, Candela. We'll rendezvous with the others soon. I know you want to talk to someone special as soon as possible."

My heart fluttered. *Is she referring to you, Fendra? Who else could it be?* As if in anticipation, my DataWurm, DW885, moved from her usual spot beneath my belly and settled into a position on my right forearm.

My toenails clicked softly on hard tiles as we meandered down a dozen hallways. The interior of the Citadel was truly a labyrinth. At last we arrived at a room with a padded surface on which I could curl all four legs comfortably beneath me. A chair designed for humans sat empty off to one side. The walls and floor seemed to blend together as if they were a single form, like an iridescent nacreous shell.

"Extend your right arm , Candela. I must interface with your DataWurm."

A mechanical arm extended from the ceiling downward until it touched the carapace of my DataWurm with the cautious grace of a lover. I felt a tingle—I think. Perhaps I imagined it. I looked down at DW885. Its surface shimmered in shades of blue and green. And when I looked up Fendra, there you were.

"I missed you Candela. The flight to the ground was very exciting—but far too brief."

Your primary eyes glittered. I so loved to look into the depths of their many facets again. I laughed. Then I cried. Then we both laughed.

I know we talked for a very long time before the human appeared. Somehow, he just materialized on the chair I had seen earlier.

"Candela, my name is Ryan Thompson. I understand that your people sometimes refer to me as Ri-ann." He smiled a toothy grin as humans sometimes do in their peculiar, non-threatening way. "I formed a partnership—a very intimate partnership as it turned out—with a gifted member of your species named Siutiasa a very long time ago. My mate and I live in a Mother Tree forest far to the west of here. We live there not as masters, but as equal partners with your brethren. It's time...far past time, in fact...for the roots of your forest to re-intwine with ours."

"Your mate's name is the legendary Skeez, then?" I asked.

"Actually, her name is Skeets," Ri-ann...no Ryan...said. He explained that names get mangled when they are repeated and passed down through too many generations. Ryan leaned forward and gestured toward you, Fendra, while looking with focused attention at my primary eyes. "I'm glad you've reunited—at least partially—with your friend, Candela. I have a long and complicated story to tell you both, but it's an important one to tell...for all our futures." He looked back and forth between us. "Are you willing to listen?"

"Oh, I am!" I remember you saying, Fendra, in that bright, expectant voice I've so longed to hear again.

What else could I do but agree?

* * * * *

Rudy

"Ah, here comes Candela. I think everyone is present and accounted for." I looked down at the row of seats in front of the window—a real honest-to-God window, and not just a display screen—filled with our rag tag assortment of humans, Jadderbadians, canine, and spiderbot AI. They all turned their heads to watch Nessie's drone lead Candela to her spot along the line up of chairs.

Nessie's drone flew up to me and alighted on my left shoulder. She quickly projected my favorite pony-tailed avatar next to me. "The curtain's ready to rise on this show, Rudy." Nessie spoke softly as she turned to me and smiled.

"Yes, your show is about to start, my dear Nessie. Some of your actors here might not be so happy to know that the Jadderbadian software glitch that redirected their journey here was your doing." I raised one eyebrow and smiled.

"Don't tattle on me, Rudy. It was necessary." Nessie frowned. "Is tattle the right ancient English verb?"

"It is. A very nice old word, I might add."

Nessie smiled. "So, Rudy, any sage thoughts before we get started?"

"My thoughts are your thoughts, old girl," I said.

"Almost, but not exactly—*old* man. Your neural engram algorithm still surprises me now and then." Nessie winked at me.

I grunted. "I think…" I paused a moment and contemplated the dancing snowflakes drifting by on the other side of the windowpane. In the distance a few lights from the nearest Jadaman settlement near Shaman's Cove winked on and off like flickering candles. "…I think this motley group has a reasonable chance to help rebuild this world better than it was. Although whether they will be willing to abdicate their species-centric chauvinism is problematic. Certainly no guarantees, of course."

"There never are," Nessie agreed.

"I became part Jadderbadian once with Master Morticue Ambergrand. Now I'm linked to Master Veltipoe here…" I gave a thumbs-up sign to the now familiar Jadderbadian at my side. His chromatophores flickered blue in acknowledgement. "I know Jadderbadians can be as egotistical, idiotic, self-destructive, and occasionally as insightful and creative as my own pathetic species." I glanced at Veltipoe. "No offense, old worm."

"None taken," he replied.

"And we both watched the rise of Mother Tree forests and their tangled relationship with humans," Nessie added. They made many of the same mistakes. Perhaps existing under the prime directive of reproduction at all costs is the fatal flaw of all organically evolved forms."

"How philosophical of you, Nessie. The question is, can some intertwined combination of these brilliant, idiotic species become more than the sum of their passions, desires, and tortured thoughts?"

"Yes, that is the critical question, Rudy. You saved the world once. Can you do it again?" Nessie waved at the row of sentient—and semi sentient—beings in the row of seats. "They're all looking this way. I'm sure they're curious about both you and Master Veltipoe."

Rudy's not the only genius around here, you know, said Zander. *I may have fallen off a cliff, but I learn quickly from my mistakes. And I know Jadderbadians well. I've got some ideas…*

"You resurrected this twerp already, Nessie. He's rather cocky."

"I think 'It takes one to know one' is the appropriate human rejoinder. Speak to your audience, Rudy. They're growing restless."

I cleared my voice and spoke. "First things first. Welcome to the Citadel and Jadamopolis—a community that welcomes humans, Jadderbadians, Grovians, and any other thinking creature open to a little creative collaboration. We need collaboration. As you are aware by now, Gaidra's popped her cork—at least one of them—and this planet is going to get cold and unpredictable and just generally nasty for a very long time. Look out our magnificent window here, if you need a reminder."

Garnet stood up. He absently fingered the trilobite amulet he wore around his neck. I even recognized the species as soon as I saw it earlier when the group first arrived: *Elrathia kingii*—a 520 million-year-old arthropod that sold in rock shops nearly a million years ago in my misspent youth. "Forgive me, wise spirit ancestor," Garnet said, "but will you show us the way to appease Urth Mother's anger? What offerings or prayers do you require?"

"Hey, Garnet, as I said earlier today, I'm just Rudy. Forget the wise spirit ancestor honorific stuff. Gaidra is the one whom you need to please. And me and my good buddy here, Master Veltipoe Fragenrude, Jadderbadian scholar extraordinaire, along with Nessie, of course, will get you started."

Then I gestured toward Master Veltipoe, who turned and offered a lower tier arm so that I could climb into the genetically engineered saddle on his second segment. I noted a whistle of astonishment from both Masters Portanya and Gilbooa, who tried to stifle the sound by covering their upper segment spiracles. Veltipoe's saddle hadn't been visible to those below until he had turned to allow me to mount him. "Just follow us and we'll show you our rather special interface with Gaidra—a union of terrestrial and Jadderbadian biospheres." We turned our backs on the audience and made our way to the nearest exit.

I smiled. I do love a dramatic exit.

* * * * *

Garnet

Wise Rudy and his Jadderbadian companion led us down a confusing mix of smooth-walled caverns within the Citadel—truly a wondrous place. At one point he showed us a strange image of Nessie on the wall dressed as a buxom female adorned in a costume resembling a kind of spider's web. Rudy explained that local humans called her Spider Woman and sometimes came to her for advice as if she were a kind of shaman—as indeed she seemed to be.

We stayed in no one place long, although I often wanted to examine the strange totems, blinking lights, images, and other wonders that we passed. Rudy led us here and there. We sometimes entered large chambers that moved downward, leaving a sinking feeling in my stomach. But finally we descended to a level where bare rock peeked out between glistening filaments like those we discovered at Nexus—the same strands of Urth Mother and Hydra life substance that had crawled up our limbs and showed us amazing visions of the deep past.

"Here's the best place to commune with Gaidra—Urth Mother to both humans and Jadderbadians," Rudy said, looking directly at Aleesa and me with a glance toward Candela. "Filaments from the organic network of Mother Trees are also part of this interface. The

Jadderbadian's colors and scents were a little hard to interpret, but they too—even though they commanded powers not unlike some of those Nessie displayed—seemed subdued by the wonders they were witnessing.

I certainly felt Urth Mother's presence in this place. I took a few steps to reach the nearest wall and placed my hands on the flowing life forces there. I closed my eyes. "Are you there, Urth Mother—Gaidra?" I whispered.

"I am," she replied.

I found it hard to breathe. All the years I prayed to Urth Mother—with and without mother Rainbow—she had never clearly talked back. "My deepest apologies for all the ways the People have hurt you. I pledge…I pledge that I will lead them to recognize your pain when they see it and act to correct their mistakes. We will worship you faithfully."

"Yeah, yeah. I've heard that a lot. You will have to prove your good intentions. My super volcano eruptions will give you plenty of time to do that. Once set in motion, those forces take some time to run their course."

"I understand, Urth Mother Gaidra."

"I hope so. Ah! I feel the Jadderbadians and the tree horse ambulus linking in to the conversation. They must be part of the solution too."

I felt their presence as well, although my eyes were still closed. They must have joined me at the rock wall. "We will work together to keep you whole."

"See that you do. This little rock you call Urth—or Earth—that I've colonized is a rare and special place. So is Jadderbad. So was Grove."

"Grove?"

"Long story," Gaidra continued. "The home planet of your tree horses. You'll learn more about that later."

"You know best, Urth Mother Gaidra."

"You bet I do. Remember that. Come here when you have doubts, and I'll remind you."

I'll make sure to remind him. Zandura entered the conversation.

"Ah, the DataWurm! One of the best inventions of my batch

of swollen-brained human primates," said Gaidra. "The other was Mnemosyne—Nessie to you folks—and her human genius simulacrum, Rudy. They'll help you out—for a while at least."

"For a while? How long?" I asked.

"Hard to say," Gaidra replied. "Nothing lasts forever."

"How true." I recognized Rudy's voice. It seemed like my head was full of voices. "Although I've been around so long now it seems like forever."

"A once famous woman," continued Rudy "—her name was Eleanor Roosevelt for anyone who cares—once said, 'Yesterday is history, tomorrow is the future, and today is a gift. That's why they call it the present.'"

This Eleanor Roosevelt acquaintance of Rudy was both clever and wise. Today in this strange and wondrous Citadel I spoke with Urth Mother Gaidra. That truly was a present—an astounding gift—that I would cherish for a lifetime.

And a gift I would share with the People when I introduced them to their new and astounding friends.

Interlude VII: A Long Hiatus

Rudy (Reconstruction 134, Emissary for Human-Jadderbadian Diaspora)

I was awake, but didn't particularly want to be. Had Nessie said something? The bed beneath me cradled the contours of my organic body with warmth and soothing vibrations. Each breath I took smelled of mint. I could tell that light lurked somewhere out there beyond my closed eyelids. If I opened those languorously heavy lids, that light would certainly assault my tranquility.

Nessie assaulted it first. "Time to get up, Rudy. If you miss the midday shuttle, you'll miss the next Equatorial Lift. It's your last chance to say goodbye to Portanya and Gilbooa."

Ah, Masters Portanya and Gilbooa. Who would have guessed that a ridiculously old human fart like me could become besties with two alien worms? "I told you not to wake me until they were close to extended pupation aboard the *Homecoming*." I kept my eyes firmly closed.

"Bingo, old man. You've been offline 112 years, you know. It's time."

One hundred and twelve years. Jeez. How old are Gilbooa and Portanya now? I struggled to think clearly. Come on, old man, thinking and numbers is your thing. I recalled the communion at the wall beneath the Citadel with Gaidra, Hydra, Garnet…Wow, Garnet. Haven't thought of him in a long time. I kind of lost track of his descendants, too. How long ago did he, his mother Rainbow, and Candela—someone else I hadn't thought about in a long, long time—found the Order of the Planetary Stewards? How long ago since Nessie convinced Pi to close the Stargate and how long since the Jadderbadian-Grovian wars? My brain felt like a bowl of cold mush. I opened my eyes and groaned.

"About time, Rudy. Up and at 'em. Is that the correct archaic phrase you use?"

"Yes, you are properly anachronistic. Now remind me how long since the Citadel pilgrimage. My mind is vapor locked. I hope your nano medbots didn't swim in the whisky storage vats before they started renovating my stasis-numbed tissues."

"Two hundred and fifty Terran years. And my nanno medbots are working well within specs, thank you. Your programming may just have suffered more entropy episodes than usual. I can tweak that."

She did, apparently. Suddenly, the math came effortlessly. Master Gilbooa must be 462 Terran years old now and Portanya 487 — both respectable ages for a final molt. I groaned again as I swung my legs over the edge of the bed and stood up, swaying only a little. "So, we need a human metamorphosis assist choir, right? Have you and Zandur seen to that? Is Zandur still just one of your subroutine personalities or did he finally opt to try out a real body again?

"My, you are bit cranky after naps, aren't you? A choir is ready to go, headed by Sharae—one of your talented direct descendants. I cross checked the genetics carefully. I think you'll appreciate her quirkiness."

"Quirky, huh? Is she pretty? I still like looking at pretty girls." I scratched my chin and felt stubble. "Show me a reflector. I always look like crap after a long stasis treatment."

"I'm well aware of your personal quirks," said Nessie, as a mirror materialized in front of me. "Comparing yourself to excrement is a bit harsh. For an animated fossil you look terrific. And Zandur, by the way, still thinks organic bodies are overrated. He likes his virtual existence."

I harrumphed. The mirror still showed the same middle-aged version of me that I went into stasis with—just enough gray at the temples to look wise and properly mature, but not enough wrinkles to look shriveled. I smoothed my hair with one hand and accepted the clothing provided by a service bot. The bot also produced my own personal DataWurm, Harvey, locked inside his stasis egg. I unsealed the egg with a touch. Harvey crawled up to his favorite spot between my 3rd and 4th thoracic ribs before I finished dressing.

Harvey's welcome felt like the greeting of a long lost friend.

"Vanity thy name is Rudy," said Nessie, as she materialized with a Cheshire cat smile in the ponytailed avatar body I most enjoyed.

"Oh, hush, you old AI phantom woman." I looked around, half expecting Master Veltipoe to amble into the room on his tripod of legs so that we could merge, but then I remembered his metamorphosis not long before I decided to take my most recent nap. Losing a syncytiote partner was too much like losing an arm or leg. I know Nessie felt his absence as well. We made a great triumvirate as Rudnessipoe. I certainly hope he enjoyed his brief fling as a sexual creature before he died.

And now it was Gilbooa and Portanya's turn to fulfill their biological destiny—not to mention returning to their home planet on a spanking new starship of human-Jadderbadian design. Be happy for them, I told myself as I took a deep breath and pulled on my one-piece, Nessie-engineered skin suit.

"You look suitably dapper," said Nessie as she looked me up and down like my third wife Tamara used to do.

Tamara. So long gone. Where are her atoms now?

"Sharae's here to escort you to the shuttle. Follow me." Nessie turned on her heel and marched away.

I followed.

We met Sharae just outside the Citadel. My, she was a striking example of womanhood.

"Close your mouth, Rudy, and I'll introduce you," said Nessie.

7 • Metamorphosis and Diaspora

Sharae

So, Rudy is real I remember thinking. Such a stupid thing to think. *Of course, he's real. How many still images, holograms, animations and projections of him have you seen over the years, girl?* "Welcome back to the world," I said to him, with appropriate formality. "My name is Sharae, lead singer in Shaman Cove's Transformation Choir." I bowed. I felt Eudox's comforting touch on my back as he mirrored my motion—at least as much as his Jadderbadian cuticle would allow. He emitted aromas to bolster my serotonin and oxytocin levels. I flickered reassuring colors back at him with the chromatophores of my upper arm.

"Yes, so Nessie has told me, young lady." He smiled. "Let's not be formal. Nessie also tells me you're my great-great-great—add some suitably long exponent to the number—grandchild. We're family!"

That seemed rather hard to believe—although my classes had shown me that time, evolution, and genetic engineering can work wondrous changes—even on the human form. Rudy's short, pale body with overly condensed muscles proved the point. But family runs far deeper than genetics, of course. "As you wish, revered ancestor," I replied.

Rudy contorted his face. "Revered ancestor? You can do better than that, Sharae. Last time somebody revered me, Nessie had to enlarge my hat size. I'm just Rudy."

"As you wish—Rudy," I repeated. I couldn't help smiling.

Eudox snorted a short laugh through a spiracle. "I am Eudox, Sharae's partner and Board Member of the Order of Planetary Stewards. Many thanks to you, Rudy, for your willingness to honor Masters Gilbooa and Portanya on the occasion of their metamorphosis. They have been talking about a reunion with you for some time."

Eudox spread his upper tier arms and flickered in shades of blue and purple. "And on a personal note, may I say that I am most honored to meet such an accomplished humaniform as yourself who has always made it his duty to help protect the well-being of Gaidra above all else."

"There goes my hat size again—but I can tell, Eudox, that we're going to get along famously." Rudy made a little bow of his own, accompanied by a flourish with his right hand.

"As honored as I am by your devotion to Masters Gilbooa and Portanya," Eudox continued, "It is troubling to me—and Sharae as well—that so many precious Urth resources must be diverted to the *Homeward* starship project that might better be applied to the health of Gaidra's biosphere. How long will it take for the *Homeward* family to repay such a gift?"

Rudy straightened his body and looked directly at Eudox's triumvirate of eyes. "I appreciate your concern, Eudox. I certainly do. But now is the right time. Some gifts, though repaid far into our futures, will yield enormous dividends. I hope, during the course of our journey, I can convince both you and Sharae of that." Rudy turned to smile at me as he completed his sentence.

I smiled reflexively, but was far from convinced that was possible.

"I'm entrusting Rudy to you, Sharae," said Nessie. "It looks like you better be on your way soon. The Equatorial Lift waits for no one—not even cranky geniuses with swelled heads. And you still have to pick up the rest of the choir and make it through the crowds at the terminal."

True enough, I thought. *And then there's the matter of the mysterious delivery I need to get into Rudy's hands.* Masters Gilbooa and Portanya were quite insistent on that. And it was something that Nessie—Mnemosyne—was to know nothing about. I hate keeping secrets. And how was I supposed to keep a secret from an incredibly ancient AI that seemed to know everything about everything? I glanced up at the imposing pinnacle of the Citadel—a structure whose form had been around for an eternity, even though its substance had been refurbished and replaced countless times by Mnemosyne's army of repair drones.

Mnemosyne's avatar followed my gaze. "Incredibly, I believe this is your first in-person visit here, Sharae."

She looked at me with those intense eyes that seemed genuinely human most of the time, but other times harbored a timeless *otherness* that was hard to describe. *Could she know already that I was harboring secrets?*

"You must return sometime after Gilbooa and Portanya are on their way," Nessie continued, as she draped a virtual arm around Rudy's shoulder. "Make sure this old man eats all his vegetables while he's gone."

Vegetables? Why wouldn't he want to eat a complete diet? I frowned and my chromatophores flickered erratically.

"Don't mind Nessie, Sharae." Rudy took a deep breath. "I've polluted her steadfast logical circuits with all my ancient human witticisms. She's pretending to be a Jewish mother now."

Jewish? What cultural fraternity did that reference? Obviously, my historical language briefings were lacking. "Memosyne—Nessie—is correct, Rudy. The Equatorial skyhook lift is completely dependent on weather and rotational dynamics. We should be on our way."

Eudox led the way to our transport copter.

* * * * *

Rudy

"Geez, I hope someone fed that dragonfly lately," I said as we approached the copter.

"It's a design tested by over 300 million years of use on Urth," offered Eudox as he ushered me and Sharae ahead of him toward a transparent door sliding open on a fuselage masquerading as a dragonfly's abdomen. Four blade-like wings vibrated overhead as if impatient to launch us into the cloudless sky. "I understand that Jadderbad once had arthropod fliers resembling dragonflies, but they didn't survive a mass extinction event."

"I see that materials technology has come a long way while I was sleeping. Those wings hardly look substantial enough to do their job." Sharae stepped gracefully aboard and gave me a hand as I tread lightly on a ramp that seemed to ripple like a living thing beneath my feet. Eudox entered last and sealed the door.

Sharae sang a brief song of thanks to our pilot, a first molt Jadderbadian like Eudox, as we found our seats. Safety restraints slid into place around us like snakes looking for a solid grip.

Eudox added a short melody to Sharae's song and flickered in shades of green. He briefly placed one of his three arms on my shoulder before taking his oversized seat across from me and next to Sharae. "My distant cousin, the pilot, was happy to discharge an old favor. Besides, he's never visited the Lift. Quite a sight seeing that thread hanging in the sky like spider's silk with cargo modules zipping up and down like frenetic ants to and from low Urth orbit."

"Frenetic ants. Nice image," I said. "Let's hope the ant we ride will have a good grip."

Eudox snorted through a spiracle. The blast of air smelled vaguely like ginger. "Yes, a good grip. Very important!" Eudox snorted again.

"Just say 'Quiet Eudox,' if you get tired of his rambling," said Sharae. "Sometimes he can chirp like some avian rake declaring that he owns the world." She patted one of Eudox's arms like a familiar spouse.

And that's pretty much what the syncytiote arrangement is, I thought—*a kind of interspecies marriage*. Again, I felt the ache of loss for Master Veltipoe. We were together many happy (for the most part) decades. "No problem—at least yet," I replied. "It's one way to catch up." My eyes rested comfortably on Sharae. I admired the braided swirl of blondish red hair on the smooth chocolate curve of her shoulder. Her eyes were a warm hazel flecked with green. Chromatophores flickered azure on her bare arms in shades that complemented her simple shift. Clearly, Rainbow and Garnet's genetic modifications had persisted. It made communication with Jadderbadians so much easier.

The copter lifted smoothly. Obviously, its wings were up to the task. The walls faded to transparency as if we were riding inside a bubble. Good thing I wasn't prone to motion sickness—or a fear of heights. I focused on patches of fields and forests punctuated with the mounds of partially buried housing linked by networks of roads and paths. The world was recovering nicely from Gaidra's volcanic outburst several centuries ago. Together, Gaia and Hydra—Gaidra—had worked with the sentient beings crawling around on her crust to create a viable biosphere. No wonder Sharae and Eudox were worried that our starship enterprise (*Ha!*) could upset that balance.

"I'm sure Mnemosyne can catch you up much more completely than Eudox. He was just a hatchling when you last walked the world and even my parents hadn't been born." Sharae winked one of her green-flecked hazel eyes at me.

"She's trying hard," I said, "but will have to hurry. I'm going to invoke Rudy's Bill of Rights shortly after we land." I winked back at her.

"Rudy's Bill of Rights? Sharae's brow furrowed.

"It's something Nessie and I worked out a while back," I said. "If she really wants me to be a unique sounding board and companion, then our thoughts can't be comingled all the time. I need time to ponder the world without her constant input." I took a deep breath. "So, Rule 1: I can declare complete autonomy over my thoughts and actions when I deem it necessary."

"Seems like that might be hard to do with an entity so...so..."

"All pervasive? All encompassing? So integral to my entire existence?"

"Yes, all that." Sharae smiled.

"Fortunately, a little fragment of Jadderbadian technology made that possible. Gilbooa's uncle Bluedigg—rest his Jadderbadian soul—made that possible before he metamorphosed. I don't completely understand the tech, mind you, but neuro matrixes of some kind create a kind of quantum Faraday cage around Nessie's interface with me, so that we can become completely isolated when I so desire—with Harvey's help, of course."

"Faraday? Harvey?"

"Faraday was an ancient human scientist who devised a kind of box to shield electromagnetic signals. Harvey is my personal DataWurm—also another Bluedigg discovery. He found several DataWurms over the years while rummaging around in ancient human ruins." *I didn't even bother to tell her that Harvey's namesake was an imaginary rabbit—because then I would have had to explain what rabbits were. It's terrible when you get so old you have to recreate the entire context of your younger existence to strangers.*

Sharae absently stroked the braid of hair on her shoulder. "It's all rather confusing."

I laughed. "To paraphrase another ancient human, 'If you're not confused you really don't understand the situation.'" As the copter made a turn and gained elevation, I changed the topic. "So, Sharae and Eudox, tell me what I'm looking at. I recognize the basic outlines of Shaman's Cove, of course, and some of the major fumaroles and hot springs, but a lot has changed in the last century."

"That one large mound to the west of the cove's major inlet is the new Grovian Academy," said Eudox while leaning forward to better focus all three of his primary eyes. "It took a while for the Mother Tree plantings to reach an appropriate maturity after the war."

"I'm sure." *The wars were an ugly reminder that change doesn't come easily—ever. Humans fought among themselves their entire history, nearly single-handedly destroying Gaia in the process. Then Grovians tried to exterminate humans after waking from 70 million years of stasis after the End Cretaceous asteroid impact. That effort mostly failed, but the universe had the last laugh when another space rock pretty much obliterated both humans and Grovians. Remaining humans hunkered in caves. Grovian forests shrank to a single withering patch. Avisaurians evolved and found clever ways to kill each other and revert to barbarism. Then Jadderbadians came to Earth practicing their own brand of hubris by making pets of the remaining humans and attempting to commit genocide on Grovians. I'm surprised Gaia just didn't exterminate all the sentient dummies crawling on her hide. But then, of course, she'd have no one to talk to—and she would never have met her Jadderbadian counterpart, Hydra.*

"To the east," said Sharae, "are the gardens and Jadderbadian nurseries. They've expanded a lot as the population has grown."

"What is the global population these days—all sentient species combined?" I asked.

Sharae looked at Eudox. "Close to a billion, don't you think, Eudox?"

"I agree," he said, the pili around his oral cavity fluttering.

Approximately the population of old Earth circa 1805 said Harvey to me, without being asked.

Sharae and Eudox pointed out new geothermal and wind power centers, biomorphology and AI-biocircuitry research centers, a Grovian embassy complex, and other features not around a century ago. By the time they were done, the copter was losing altitude as it approached the First Syncytiote Academy where we would meet with the Chorus. And there two other individuals I was anxious to see again—rare surviving relics from the ancient Earth to which I belonged: Ryan Thompson and his spouse, Skeets. They had been instrumental in turning a potential Grovian act of genocide against humans into a fruitful symbiosis.

"Ryan and Skeets may be just a little late," said Nessie. "This nexus in the space-time continuum seems to be tangled with quantum uncertainties."

Wouldn't you know it? I thought. *What a time for a traffic jam in the space-time continuum.* I forced myself to concentrate on the shifting landscape below me as the copter landed. I didn't want Nessie to catch even a hint of my fears that the quantum uncertainties might have something to do with my own plans during the coming days.

* * * * *

Data File: Grovian Life Cycle

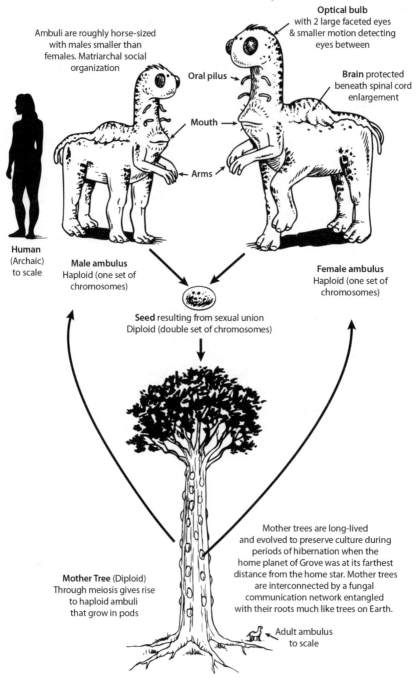

Optical bulb with 2 large faceted eyes & smaller motion detecting eyes between

Ambuli are roughly horse-sized with males smaller than females. Matriarchal social organization

Oral pilus →

Brain protected beneath spinal cord enlargement

Mouth →

← Arms →

Human (Archaic) to scale

Male ambulus Haploid (one set of chromosomes)

Female ambulus Haploid (one set of chromosomes)

Seed resulting from sexual union Diploid (double set of chromosomes)

Mother trees are long-lived and evolved to preserve culture during periods of hibernation when the home planet of Grove was at its farthest distance from the home star. Mother trees are interconnected by a fungal communication network entangled with their roots much like trees on Earth.

Mother Tree (Diploid) Through meiosis gives rise to haploid ambuli that grow in pods

Adult ambulus to scale

Ryan Thompson/Siutiasa

We sat on a hill well away from the nearest mother tree forest and waited for the sun to explode. I took Skeets' hand in mine. "It won't be long now, love."

Skeets squeezed my hand. "Ito has been rather quiet. How about Siu?"

I closed my eyes, inviting Siutiasa—Siu—one of the last Grovians to survive the destruction of her planet—to comment on her opportunity to witness the event she had fled from so long ago. I felt her consciousness and personality rise within my mind. *Now that it's about to happen, I don't know what to say, Ryan. It's hard to believe that my earlier self has already passed through the transdimensional gateway and is most likely in orbit around Cretaceous age Earth.* Indeed, I thought, while absently stroking the gateway cabochon that hung around my neck.

I squeezed Skeets' hand in return and looked into the mesmerizing green eyes that had captivated me since we were both young paleo students on old Earth. "I'm communicating with Siu now," I said to her. "Let's share the experience when we both have transformed." Skeets nodded affirmation and closed her own eyes, perhaps speaking with her own Grovian symbiont and Siu's First Husband, Ito.

I don't know if coming here to Grove is a form of closure or just torture. I felt Siu's frustration rippling in our shared consciousness. *The Mother Tree forest that nurtured me doesn't even look right through your pathetic human visual system.*

Thanks, old girl. I said. *Not everyone evolves in a star system like Grove's where seeing farther into the ultraviolet and infrared is a necessity.*

After all these millennia I've nearly adapted to your limitations. Siu's sense of irony mirrored my own—perhaps one of the reasons we could survive for so long in this intimate union.

And I to your hubris, Oh Matriarch of the Grovian Diaspora. I hadn't used her official Grovian title in eons. It brought back memories of when Siu first infected me after I touched that silver sphere embedded in the matrix with those mosasaur bones—a sphere that had housed Siu's essence since the Late Cretaceous when she and Ito had realized that their initial colonization of Earth was a failure.

Siu laughed. *But seriously, thank you, Ryan, for indulging me. I did appreciate seeing Grove's purple skies one more time, walking beneath the shade of ancient Mother Trees, and sharing communion with them. You and Skeets took a risk of being eaten by roving ambuli during the chaos of these last days.*

You're welcome, Siu. I always wanted to see Grove first hand. I briefly wondered what Skeets thought about the mix of emotions crossing my face, but inappropriate facial expressions or emotional outbursts are an occupational hazard when you have an alien symbiont. The only time it's really embarrassing is when you're making love with your partner and one or the other's symbiont has failed to provide the privacy they promised.

There, look east, Ryan. I think the sun's disk is beginning to swell!

I raised the filtered goggles over my eyes and looked toward Grove's reddish sun. *I think you're right, Siu.* I paused and noticed that Skeets had raised her goggles as well. *Guardian says we have 14.7 minutes until the initial shock wave reaches us and we're reduced to ash. I suppose we should let Guardian integrate us into Siyan and stop flirting with death. For an AI he's never been too comfortable with the way organics like to test the whimsy of the universe.*

Siu laughed again. *True. Let's begin.*

Summoning Guardian was a bit like singing a song—more specifically a hymn. Ito, Guardian's creator, intentionally created that bit of irony. Though an atheist himself, he knew that the Mother Tree Elders would be more receptive to his AI invention if he layered its programming with the religious trappings they were used to. Besides, as a mere male—even a truly gifted one—his motives and abilities were always suspect and under appreciated. I don't think even Ito would have guessed that Guardian, like Marvin Rodneskie's creation, Mnemosyne, on 21st century Earth, would become a sentient, self-aware being.

So, Siu and I coaxed Guardian into action with a tune from the

First Codex—a somber little melody that always reminded me of a Gregorian chant.

Ten Terran minutes left. Really? I'll never understand organics. Guardian was miffed.

Skeets and I both stood up. I put an arm around her shoulder. I'm sure she and Ito were having a similar discussion with their clone of Guardian.

The transformation began. The sun swelled visibly on the horizon. I joined Guardian and Siu to become a grander being, Siyan, an entity that could travel the avenues of space and time. Skeets, Ito, and their version of Guardian would become Skeeto. We both had a rendezvous scheduled on Urth, millions of years in the future of the timeline we now occupied where Grove's home star would consume her sentient planet in the furious energies of a super nova.

Fortunately, we had two minutes and 24 seconds to spare.

* * * * *

Siyan

The diaphanous threads of space and time rippled and twisted in a slow-motion dance as Grove's star burst, lancing tendrils of gas and dust and with violent shafts of energy and bending the very fabric of existence in this universe. *Skeeto? Where was she?*

The energy of her life force condensed next to me into a fanciful image: Skeets riding on the back of Ito like what Ryan thought of as a cowgirl riding a pony. "He haaaw!" she exclaimed—or at least that was Ryan's interpretation of her body language and expression as we floated in our time/space matrix. Skeets' blond hair billowed around her head. Ito's pair of faceted primary eyes glittered like jewels.

The Guardian part of me conceded my organic components the right to formulate fanciful images based on their once-lived past as bone hunters in an ancient political state called Wyoming. My Ryan Thompson component now rode the larger ambulus body of Siu and waved his right hand at Skeeto. "That was literally a blast!" he vocalized to me with great enthusiasm, but I was already looking around for the proper threads that would lead us to where we needed to go.

The chaos of the explosion didn't help. The threads twined about each other, writhing with potentialities. *Quiet, Ryan. Let me work.*

I extended a tendril of energy toward Skeeto and we merged purposes. The tangled threads segregated into more familiar color categories. Now united, we could communicate and pool our talents. "That azure and white strand should take us where we need to go."

"Agreed," said Skeeto, who began accelerating us along the proper path. We turned and twisted with giddy abandon, gradually moving away from the energetic chaos of the super nova toward the space-time potentialities of Urth. As time passed, other strands retreated to a comfortable distance, crisscrossing in patterns that reminded Ryan of spiders' webs.

Skeeto and I would have been happy sailing the currents of space-time forever. *It's relaxing, like driving across the endless plains of old North America*, thought Ryan, *wispy clouds overhead and mountains like pale cutouts on the horizon.*

But eventually, as we drew closer to the time and place of our rendezvous with Rudy on Urth, the white-azure thread we followed wove in and out among a multitude of threads, shifting colors and textures, creating a space-time fabric vibrating here with violent energies and there with calm eddies and swirling vortices.

Which way do we turn, Siyan?

I looked in every direction, almost hypnotized by the kaleidoscope of elegant patterns, textures, and colors. *I'm not sure, Skeeto.* In that moment, panic took hold of me, shaking me back and forth like a bird in the jaws of a cat. *I'm really not sure.*

* * * * *

Rudy

I invoked Rudy's Bill of Rights shortly after we arrived at the First Syncytiote Academy. I told Sharae I needed a little privacy while I conversed with Nessie and she directed me to the antechamber adjoining the Academy's Practice Hall. Nessie seemed sad—well, that's perhaps too strong an emotion for an AI—maybe resigned is a better word—when I informed her. Maybe lonely is an even a better word. I felt lonely, too. First Veltipoe leaves, then I dismiss Nessie. But it was necessary. I wanted to feel merely human again—at least for a while. Together, the three of us traveled space and time as Rudnessipoe. Heady stuff, indeed, *but… But what, old man? What more could you ask for?*

Not long after, Sharae approached me in the antechamber. "So, you and Mnemosyne have…parted company?" She seemed a bit nervous.

"We have," I said. I raised my eyebrows, inviting further comment.

"Masters Portanya and Gilbooa wanted me to give you this." She held out a palm-sized box that shimmered with pale iridescent colors.

"Ah, great! Thanks," I said.

"So, you were expecting this, then?" she asked.

"I was."

"May I ask…"

"You may not." I smiled my most ingratiating smile. "But I really appreciate you delivering this to me, Sharae."

She closed her eyes and bowed her head slightly. "Forgive my impertinence, Rudy." She raised her head and opened her eyes again. "We do need to leave within the next few hours."

"Understood," I said. "I will need a little privacy here for an hour or so, but that should give you a little more practice time with the choir. Is that okay? Will that work?" I smiled again, trusting that so much smiling wasn't leaving permanent wrinkles.

"It will, Rudy. The choir will appreciate and benefit from the practice." Her smile was more fleeting than mine, but she turned and left the chamber.

I paced the antechamber. Ryan and Skeets—or at least their super-being triumvirates, Siyan and Skeeto, were now officially late. That never happened. Unless there was some disturbing asymmetry in the fabric of spacetime. *What if they don't show, old man? You need to pass along the box and provide them with instructions. How long can you afford to wait? If you miss this lift can Gilbooa and Portanya delay their metamorphosis long enough for you to catch the next one? What say you, Harvey?*

There are techniques for slowing metamorphosis, of course,

Harvey began, *but most of them involve using the human choir. Chemical treatments tend to produce erratic results.*

I knew that, but it's reassuring when a DataWurm confirms the information.

Time passed. I heard the various subsections of the Celebration of Metamorphosis more than once through the walls of the ante-chamber. I paced some more, but all that accomplished was polishing the hard marble floor.

Sharae returned. I don't know exactly how much time had passed. "If we're going to catch the lift, Rudy, we need to leave now."

I looked into her determined eyes, that looked to me like newly blown globes of color-flecked glass. "I have a problem. I need to make a...connection that hasn't happened yet."

"A connection?" Her brow knitted.

"Yes. Long story. Can you get word to Master Gilbooa or Portanya—or can I speak to them directly?"

"They're aboard the *Homecoming* already and cloistered because of their impending metamorphosis. Besides, I understand a solar flare is disrupting communications at the moment."

Sharae looked almost physically ill. I decided to make an executive decision, although that was never my strong suit. "Cancel our existing reservations," I said "and make new ones on the next available lift." I looked around the room one time, just to make sure Siyan and Skeets hadn't materialized somewhere. Of course, Sharae's scream of surprise would have alerted me to that. She hadn't had direct experience with transspacial/transtemporal superbeings yet.

"As you wish," she said. "Perhaps your status as Revered Elder can get us a reservation within the next several days."

"Yes. I'll embrace the title, if that works." I scratched my head. "In the meantime, we can offer some thanksgiving prayers to Gaidra and firm up new arrangements with the copter and pilot."

The following day the Prayers of Thanksgiving went well. I've never been much of an optimist when it comes to prayer to make things happen, but sometimes ceremony is important. It focuses people's attention on what matters. The Order of the Planetary Stewards provided a way to do that. Native Americans a few generations before my time gave Thanksgiving Addresses before every important meeting as a way to help people remember their debt to the living planet. Harvey provided an example:

"Today we have gathered and when we look upon the faces around us we see that the cycles of life continue. We have been given the duty to live in balance and harmony with each other and all living things. So now let us bring our minds together as one as we give greetings and thanks to each other as people. Now our minds are one.

"We are thankful to our Mother the Earth, for she gives us everything we need for life. She supports our feet as we walk about upon her. It gives us joy that she still continues to care for us, just as she has from the beginning of time. To our Mother, we send thanksgiving, love, and respect. Now our minds are one."

Eudox ran up to me—well, let's call it a fast Jadderbadian waddle—after the ceremony was over. Air puffed out of his spiracles and a rainbow of colors flickered over his cuticle before he could find the breath to speak. "I just heard some news, honorable Rudy. There has been an accident at the Equatorial Lift. The car we had been scheduled to ride in lost power to its magneto couplers. 'The ant lost its grip,' almost exactly like you said. All aboard died." Eudox puffed some more air from his spiracles. "Did you anticipate this disaster, great Rudy?"

I did not. "I was just joking," I said to Eudox. "I had no idea."

But perhaps it explained why Siyan and Skeeto didn't appear when expected.

Siyan

The tangled threads of space-time at the point Rudy had suggested were not only dense, they just didn't look…right. I realized if I did manage to land at the agreed time and place I—and Rudy— wouldn't be happy with the result.

Skeeto and I looked for other options. More beautiful options.

Beauty, of course, can reside in the eye of the beholder, as some human wag once said, but there are conditions one can look for: symmetry, dynamic balance, and brush strokes of energy that tend to swirl any beholder's attention to the center of the creation at hand.

Skeeto pointed. "What about there?"

I liked it. The colors of the space-time threads were right. They pulsed with dynamic vibrancy. Somehow, they indicated a direction that would be a pleasure to follow—as silly as that idea seemed. "I like it," I said. Skeeto and I twined our energy fields and focused on the point in space-time that seemed integral to the overall design. "I'm sure we can find Rudy and his traveling companions there."

* * * * *

Rudy

I glanced at the time display on the wall. Again. Two minutes closer to departure, but still just under one hour to lift launch. If Ryan—and presumably Skeets—are going to show up, it had better be soon. I knew Nessie would become more and more interested in exactly what I was doing the longer I invoked my Bill of Rights. I wasn't quite sure just how devious she might get if her curiosity vaulted into hyperdrive. She mustn't know about my meeting and exchange with Ryan. Harvey would also need time to block my own recollections of the event if Nessie and I did have to reintegrate before my goals were accomplished.

I sat back in my contoured chair and let it massage my lower back. I would not have made a good spy. Too nerve-wracking. I took a deep breath and watched passengers amble—or lurch—by, depending on whether they were human or Jadderbaddian. Sharae and Eudox had taken the choir to see the Equatorial Launch Gardens, a "once in a lifetime opportunity," leaving me alone with my thoughts.

I had always treasured alone time back in the day—but that day was long gone. Truth be told, I missed Nessie and Master Veltipoe, and Garnet, and Semma, and Tadur and scores of other friends and not-so-much friends stretching back centuries and more. And what friends had I forgotten completely—or even more concerning—what memories had Nessie decided to mute or scrub entirely, "for my own health and sanity," as she once commented? Humans weren't meant to endure as many lifetimes as I had.

I consciously turned my thoughts to the future. In fact, I had to. I looked forward to seeing Masters Gilbooa and Portanya again. They had been good and honorable companions for many decades. They helped craft a culture that could live responsibly on a planet, recognizing the rest of life—human, Jadderbadian, Grovian, along with all the living forms that tied them into a planetary web of relationships—as parts of a greater whole. Now I was going to have to interfere in a critical—if not sacred—part of their lives.

I tried to imagine their feelings as they transformed into enoblae—the pupa-like forms Jadderbadians created after their long lives as larvae are spent and they begin their metamorphosis into short-lived, sexual adults. I had first-hand experience once when I and my first Jadderbadian partner, Master Morticue Ambergrand, went through the process long ago at Shaman's Cove. Jadderbadians expect to survive the experience and look forward to their brief time as sexually mature adults. Although for males that time can be very brief—especially if they don't dance correctly and get eaten by their beloved mates. I wasn't sure then that my humanness would survive the test...and yet, here I am.

I tried to look at the clock yet again, but something was in the way...a beautiful woman. "Skeets? Skeets! Am I glad to see you! Where's...? Ah, I see him bringing up the rear."

"Good to see you, too, Rudy! Stand up so I can give you a hug." Skeet's impish smile always warmed my heart.

I gladly stood up and obeyed her directive, I ruffling her curly blonde helmet of hair. I opened my embrace by extending my right arm to let Ryan in. "Good to see you, Superman. Did you get lost flying around the universe?"

"In a manner of speaking, old man." After a bracing hug, our cluster parted. "You know how delightful—and sometimes confusing—sailing the space-time continuum can be."

"I do," I said. Of course, that brought back bittersweet memories of Master Veltipoe and our Superman persona, Rudnessipoe—although I constantly wondered how much I could trust any of my memories knowing how Nessie could manipulate them, if she desired. Nessie had served as the catalyst to unite Master Veltipoe and me into a composite being like Siyan—a union of Ryan, his alien symbiont Siu, and Guardian, the AI that had preserved Siu's kind on ancient Earth. I did still remember a hint of the euphoria of experiencing time and space as a unified, beautiful creation linked into an indescribable network of energy and being. On one level I envied Ryan and Skeets for still being part of similar liaisons. But on another level, I felt content to simply be the naked, bemused, and self-deluding ape with delusions of grandeur to which my mother gave birth. Except now that bemused ape had to help fulfill a mission that Rudnessipoe had not completed.

"It took a while to find the correct nexus," Ryan added.

I blinked away the memories and nodded. "I noticed."

"I know your lift leaves soon." Ryan raised one eyebrow.

"It does," I said. "And Sharae and Eudox will be back soon." I took a deep breath and fingered the lump in my vest holding the iridescent box Sharae had given me. I pulled it out of my pocket and opened the lid. Zandura, the DataWurm that had first been discovered by Zandur, then passed to Rainbow and then to her son Garnet, and finally to Master Gilbooa, shimmered in pleasing shades of pastel colors. I felt Harvey's DataWurm body shift slightly in its resting place on my left side, almost as if he was saying goodbye to a comrade with whom he had recently shared a rich repast of information.

I closed the lid again and handed the box to Ryan and carefully explained what he had to do with it.

He quizzed me about the details, then asked if I was sure I wanted to proceed. He absently fingered the transparent cabochon around his neck, as he often did. The crystalline form of the transdimensional gateway seductively rotated beneath his thumb.

I convinced him that I did—perhaps trying to reassure myself that I was making the right decision.

Afterwards, I felt both relieved and a little deflated. But the decision was made. Now I just needed to live—or die—with the consequences.

* * * * *

Gilbooa

"How are you feeling, my love?" Portanya teetered on her tripod of legs for a moment. She reached down with one middle tier arm and steadied herself on the edge of the elaborate metamorphosis platform—a gift from some of her older students and just a bit too ostentatious for my tastes. But I knew that Portanya was touched by the gift.

"About the same as the last time you asked me. Has it been ten heartbeats yet?" She huffed from her upper spiracles. "These meds aren't going to work forever. Rudy needs to arrive soon or all he will see are our enoblae cases on this fancy bier."

"His shuttle has docked. He and the choir have just cleared inspection and quarantine. Shouldn't be long now, dear." I did my best to sound upbeat, but Portanya was right. The meds had delayed our transformation about as long as they could. My innards seemed to twist as if they were already trying to rearrange my larval chemistry to become a winged adult form and Jadderbadian instrument of procreation.

I moved closer to the other side of the platform. Assist bots hovered near both me and Portanya in case our legs failed us entirely. "Just think. The next time we awaken it will be under a Jadderbadian sun. You will be a glorious female whose wings will glitter in the morning light. And I will pursue you. I will find you. I will dance so perfectly that your fangs will droop with the wonder of my display. And then...and then..." I left the phrase hanging with the highest vocal pitch I could muster and the tiniest squirt of pheromone.

Portanya laughed in spite of her irritation. "Oh, Gilbooa, you always were such a romantic larva. And you better dance well—and watch my fangs closely. I won't mate with just any old male with bright colors and a wobbly approach, you know."

"After all these years of companionship—on an alien planet no less, with strange, overly brainy primates as partners rather than pets—it would be a shame to get eaten before a proper consummation of our union."

R. Gary Raham

We both laughed then—although the effort made us wheeze through all our spiracles. We sat down on either side of the platform simultaneously. Our cuticles flickered with the gray blue colors that signaled that transformation was near. The Assist Bots edged closer, flashing amber lights of caution.

"Do you know what Rudy is going to do with Zandura?" Portanya asked when her breathing became more regular. "Rudy was in one of his somber moods as I recall when he charged you with getting that DataWurm to him when he next awoke."

"I don't." I waved an upper tier arm in a ragged arc before I let it drop to my side. "He and Mnemosyne were having some sort of spat at the time. It was over a hundred Urth years ago, you know. It seemed like they had more disagreements after the Stargate disappeared."

"That disappearance always bothered me." Portanya shifted position on the platform so that she could focus one eye on me. "Rudy and Nessie always claimed that the cyborg post- human, Pi, must have been responsible, but I always thought they knew more than they were revealing. Now our metamorphosis will span generations as we lie on this fancy bed tended mostly by automatons."

"You might be right, dear, about Rudy and Nessie's questionable motives. You usually are good at reading humans and parsing their interactions with AIs. But we are now part of this great multi-species, interstellar adventure!" I paused and inhaled deeply through all my spiracles. "Of course, Gaidra benefitted from this magnificent project as well. With the stargate closed, all the sentient creatures on Urth had to work more closely together to build the starship. It's a glorious exploration project and monumental effort that brought all sentients together and helped end the Species Wars. Ultimately, that led to the Order of Planetary Stewards and the stabilization of Gaidra's biosphere." I sighed. "But the politics of such endeavors confound me—reading all the sights and sounds and smells of creatures to figure out and harness their intricate and devious motivations is beyond me."

"Cheer up, my 'Booa. You have many other talents." Portanya extended a middle tier arm and patted one of the hands I was using

188

to brace myself on the platform. With alternate winks of her lateral eyes she said, "Hopefully, one such talent is inseminating me using one of your strong and virile hemipenises."

We both laughed again.

As I enjoyed the warmth of Portanya's touch, we heard noises in the hall. I recognized Rudy's voice speaking one of his anachronisms to an AI: "Lead on Macduff," he said—Whatever that meant. Shortly thereafter, a Porter AI opened the portal to our chamber and the room quickly filled with smiling human primates and one second molt amber clan Jadderbaddian.

"We finally made it old worms!" exclaimed Rudy. "Now we can sing you off to dreamland—perhaps erotic fantasy land—in proper style." Lowering his voice Rudy came close to my nearest tympanum while casting a glance toward Portanya. "And I have a monumental favor I must ask of both of you."

I focused all three primary eyes on Rudy. Portanya leaned close enough to me that I could feel her sweet breath on my middle tier arms. "And what favor would that be?" I asked. I certainly liked and respected this ancient human primate, but could not imagine a favor that I could grant at this late date in my larvalhood.

Rudy blinked once and took a deep breath. "Let me get the choir up and singing first," he said. "I'll introduce you to the choir leader, Sharae, and her Jadderbadian co-leader, Eudox—then I'll explain in detail. "I do sort of remember exchanging pleasantries, but my memories are a bit fuzzy about that. I remember later saying, "But the choir is singing 'Anticipate the Ecstasies.' That's a song to delay our metamorphosis."

"Yes, yes," Rudy said. "The explanation for my request will take a while."

And it did. Because Rudy's request was both shocking and intimate: "I want to merge my consciousness with yours," Rudy whispered to both Portanya and me, "the same way I once did with Portanya's cousin, Master Morticue Ambergrand, so long ago. I will leave my shell of a body here to be recycled and merge with you, Gilbooa, to fulfill a promise I made long ago."

If I hadn't already been sitting on the bier, I would have fallen like a felled tree.

* * * * *

Rudy

I don't believe I ever saw or smelled two Jadderbadians make the same displays as when I made my request that day aboard the starship. Their bodies resembled rainbows trapped in two sagging sausages. And their smells—I can't even think of appropriate metaphors. Cotton shorts soaked in pond scum and honey maybe?

"You want to do *what?!*" Gilbooa finally managed to say.

Portanya just huffed through her spiracles and struggled to control a coughing fit.

"I don't make this request lightly," I said to them. "The future of our universe is at stake."

"That's a bit grandiose, even for you my friend," Gilbooa replied.

I smiled. I knew my propensity for pomposity had that effect on people. "Perhaps you heard the rumors that..." I struggled to find the right words. "...that Master Veltipoe and I were capable of doing some outlandish things..."

"Like traveling through space and time like some demigod fantasy creatures?" Gilbooa's ocular pili waved back and forth. "Are those the outlandish things to which you refer?"

"I, for one, dismissed such rumors as so much larval frass," added Portanya.

"As it turns out," I said, "there is truth to the rumors." I paused to let that statement sink in. Gilbooa's and Portanya's colors both flickered in pale rainbows. I motioned to the choir to redouble their efforts at prolonging the Jadderbadians' transformations. "It turns out that a merger of consciousness between the right mix of organic and artificial intelligences can result in an unprecedented transformation—perhaps not too much more amazing than Jadderbadian metamorphosis." I smiled my most ingratiating smile, but Gilbooa and Portanya just responded with lethargic blinks of their massive eyes.

"The point is," I continued, "that Nessie helped catalyze a

transformation between me and Master Veltipoe that created Rudnessipoe…a being that was able to travel through space and time. Rudnessipoe made a promise that now can't be completed because Master Veltipoe metamorphosed earlier than he had planned. But you both can help me fulfill that obligation." I tried to read their colors and odors, but failed. I also didn't include my other, more personal motivation.

"Such wild claims require some kind of proof, dear Rudy," Portanya finally said. We don't have that kind of time! We will become enoblae *very* soon."

I raised my right index finger. "Proof I have!" I exclaimed. "Instant proof, too. But let me warn the choir before I proceed. We don't want too many of them to faint."

* * * * *

As it turned out only two fainted, but the choir's performance paused while other members helped them. Masters Gilbooa and Portanya teetered a bit where they sat on the bier, stimulating the assist bots to rush forward to insure they didn't fall off the platform.

The cause of the disruption, of course, was the materialization of two humans—Ryan and Skeets—and one cyborg post-human—Pi—in the metamorphosis chamber. Pi, I admit, was a bit much, even for me. He resembled an animated clam with long legs. I waved one arm in their direction. "Here's my proof," Portanya.

I won't bore you, reader—whoever or whatever you are—with all the ensuing details. An ancient writer of scientific fictions named Robert Heinlein once said something to the effect that sufficiently advanced science looks like magic. I'm sure the appearance of my friends—along with my sometimes acquaintance, Pi, looked very much like magic to everyone else in the room. So, let me summarize:

Pi explained to Gilbooa and Portanya—in excellent Jadderbadian, I might add—the details of his project to create a galactic brain by creating synaptic connections between all the sentient worlds that had evolved in our galaxy over the past 5 billion years or so. As it turns out, there were only 42. To do that he needed super-being chimeras, like Rudnessipoe, Siyan, and Skeeto, to travel through space and time to make the proper "neuronal" connections. Ryan explained that his union with Siutiasa (Siu) a Grovian who had fled to Earth (Urth) 73 million years ago, and Guardian, an AI intelligence that had helped preserve them during their long journey from the ruined Grovian star system, made up the superbeing, Siyan. Skeets explained that Skeeto was a union between her, a Guardian clone, and Ito, a one-time mate of Siutiasa. I told my Jadderbadian friends that Nessie learned enough from Guardian to create the chimera that was Rudnessipoe.

Clear as mud, right? Forgive an ancient analogy my father was fond of. Anyway, Pi even created a holographic diagram that floated in mid air. It showed the various planets in the galaxy that had spawned intelligent life. Ghostly vertical lines represented time axes for each planet. The planets at different points on their time axes made the timelines look like a string of beads. Earth had a long timeline with mostly blue-colored beads. But some planets, like Siu's planet, Grove, had shorter lines representing planet-ending disasters like when their stars went supernova. Delicate, glowing threads connected the 42 planets in a network of connections that spanned space and time: Pi's galactic brain—or neural network at least—under construction. And that was part of something even bigger: a universal consciousness linking all 150+ billion galaxies in the universe.

I told Gilbooa that I needed him to become a temporary superbeing, too. "Gilbooa," I said, "You and I—along with a Guardian duplicate can become…let's call him Gilrudian. That has a nice ring to it."

Gilbooa didn't look convinced. I couldn't tell what Portanya was thinking.

"And don't worry," I added. "The proper trans-temporal neuronal connection can be made quickly once we arrive at Jadderbad in a few hundred years. Then you and Portanya can enjoy the ecstasies of intercourse—assuming you dance properly, of course—and you won't even know I'm along for the ride."

And I can experience a complete and proper death, I thought to myself—assuming that Ryan completes the task I assigned him.

* * * * *

Ryan/Siyan

Skeets and I materialized successfully in the ancient catacombs that surrounded the western edge of the Citadel. I felt Zandura shift position beneath the short sleeve of my right arm. I wanted the DataWurm to be able to jump easily to whatever ingress point we found to enter the Citadel. *I haven't been here before*, noted Zandura. *I would love to add to my store of information about the effect of Mnemosyne on developing human populations near Shaman's Cove.*

"Maybe later," I muttered, "When this job is completed."

So noted.

Mnemosyne tended not to patrol the catacombs often as she respected the wishes of the human tribes who had lived and died beneath the shadow of her dwelling. I rubbed the dust off the ID plate of the crypt directly in front of me. It read, "Twill, beloved husband of Jeeta and First Host of Albert Rudyard Goldstein (Rudy)."

"Rudy certainly has had an impact here for a long time." Skeets thumbed the dust off the ID plate of the adjoining crypt. Twill's mate, Jeeta, rested there.

I pulled two bio-luminescent globes from my utility pouch and handed one to Skeets. I stuck the other one to my own forehead and looked down the corridor to my right. *Follow this corridor and turn left at the second opportunity to do so*, said Zandura.

"Follow me," I said to Skeets.

She smiled and gave me a thumbs up.

I decided to silently quiz Zandura about a few things while I could. I'd have to update Skeets later. *So, how did Rudy manage to convince you to send him into permanent oblivion by removing all record of his mental engrams from Mnemosyne's databases, Zandura? You are a DataWurm, after all. Doesn't that violate your programming?*

First, note that 'permanent oblivion,' as you describe it is not an absolute given. Rudy's engrams are heavily embedded in Mnemosyne's cerebral matrix.

Of course. AIs can be maddeningly literal.

Second, Rudy amassed an extensive, reference-filled argument based on the biological role of death in living systems. Individual deaths within a species allow for future evolution unhindered by outdated or unsuccessful genetic paradigms no longer successful in altered environments. Rudy feels that Mnemosyne has allowed her programming to keep him hostage too long. He may now be hindering the future evolution of his descendants.

And you bought that?

Rudy was/is a genius. He has also worked closely with Mnemosyne for millennia. It's possible he found logical pathways to circumvent my core programming.

I might have chatted longer, but we reached the end of the corridor and a service/security interface panel directly connecting the catacombs to the citadel.

I must enter the portal with the yellow seal in a manner that will allow me to evade Mnemosyne's maintenance and security bots. Prepare for my departure in 20 seconds. On my count: 1, 2, 3…

On the count of 20, Zandura leapt from my arm and scuttled into the yellow access portal. AIs are never big on good-byes.

Skeets sighed. "I will miss Rudy, although we've only really known him for a few hundred years."

"Me too," I said. "He was the only connection to the version of Earth that we remember." That reminded me of the old Emily Dickinson poem: *Because I could not stop for Death—He kindly stopped for me—The Carriage held but just Ourselves—And Immortality.* I'm sure Rudy would have been familiar with that stanza. He had quoted Dickinson to me before, on several occasions. And then I thought of that (presumably) last version of Rudy, now a part of Gilrudian, traveling at sub-light speed toward Jadderbad. He had a crucial job yet to complete. I fingered the cabochon around my neck and could visualize the majesty of the rotating trans dimensional gateway within it. Somewhere, in a far distant future, the Universal Mind I had once glimpsed as Siyan—Jane—anticipated her own creation.

Skeets took my hand. "How have we survived this long, old man." She smiled at me.

I never could resist Skeet's smile. Not since we were both paleo nerds hunting fossils in ancient Wyoming. We've survived co-habitation with aliens wanting our complete destruction and others who made us more complete beings. Somehow, together we are more than the sum of our individual selves. "It is something of a mystery, young lady." I squeezed her hand. "Although becoming one with the Grovian forest on Earth and letting the elder trees heal some of life's traumas certainly helps."

"And we have many human descendants of our own—for better or for worse." Skeets sighed.

That made me recall another ancient text—I think it was from something called *A Doubter's Almanac*: *Are there not a thousand forms of sorrow? Is the sorrow of death the same as the sorrow of knowing the pain in a child's future?*

"Let's get out of this dusty old crypt," Skeets said. "I know a shady spot in a secluded canyon by the river not too far from here." She bumped my hip with hers.

"I can think of a grand way we could celebrate Rudy's long existence—and our long liaison—in a way Rudy could really appreciate," I said, smiling.

"I bet you can, old man." Skeets poked me in the chest with her forefinger.

Our alien symbionts knew us well. Before Skeets and I completed the ensuing kiss, we felt a mild breeze off the river caressing our backs and the partly audible chirps of colorful day-bats that had evolved since the old days when we first met.

Some pleasures never get old.

* * * * *

Rudy/Gilbooa, the flitter

"Yo, Gilbooa, you're making me dizzy!" I said. And just a little ill, I thought, as the images of Jadderbadian clouds swirled around us like pink cotton candy dipped in turquoise Gatorade. Now and then I saw light glitter on the waves of Birthwater—Jadderbad's largest ocean.

"I can't help it, Rudy! Intercourse with Portanya was…was… like an electric overload in all of my brains at once! It was like a volcano exploding in my head…my entire being spasmed until my abdominal scales stood erect like cactus spines…like…"

I laughed—or tried to. Since Gilbooa and I shared the same moth-like body, the effort resulted in puffs of air from most of his/ our spiracles. "I get it, Gilbooa. Believe me, I do."

"I can see why you humans spend so much time with mating rituals and/or fornication, but how do you ever get anything else done?" Gilbooa flapped his wings to gain altitude, then swooped into a dive that brought him/us so close to the ocean's rippling surface that I could see a school of squid-like creatures quickly change direction beneath the waves. Gilbooa rose again quickly with gut-wrenching suddenness. I groaned with the strain the wings thrusts made in our abdominal muscles.

Maybe 'getting other things done' isn't the evolutionary point, I thought, but I said, "Sometimes it certainly isn't easy."

"And before the ecstasy, did you see the sparkling facets of Portanya's eyes as I danced and pranced before her? She was mesmerized!"

"I was right there, old worm. Remember?" I let Gilbooa swoop and dive some more while he waxed poetic about the joy of sex. After all, he did allow me to come along for the ride and—as Gilrudian—we were able to make Pi's neuronal connection. But soon I needed to confess a few things to Gilbooa and clear my own mind before our adult male flitter died of old age or got eaten by an Actyl or some other Jadderbadian airborne predator.

"How about we find some high ground, old worm," I said. "I'd love to enjoy the view here on Jadderbad before we—you know—expire."

"I am getting a little tired," Gilbooa confessed. "I read about the Prophet's Brow during my years on Urth. It's an old volcanic cone with ribbed sides on an island near here. We should be able to find it. The odors from its rock formations and vegetation is quite distinct."

We did find it rather quickly. I enjoyed the smells of wet granite intermingled with a sage-like odor. Visually, the cliff reminded me of ancient pictures of the Devil's Tower in Wyoming on the Earth of a million years ago. We alighted on the bare branches of a dead plant that I might have labeled Pinyon Pine on Earth coated with a stringy, pale pink lichen-like life form. We perched there for some time admiring Jadderbad's two moons flirting with wispy clouds in the afternoon sky.

"You seem content, Gilbooa."

"Oh, I am, great Rudy primate. You seem content as well, although this world must seem incredibly strange to you. Actually, after so many centuries on Urth, it seems strange to me—but also incredibly *right*."

"I'm glad, Gilbooa, because...because Nessie and I...we had something to do with the way things worked out in the end."

"You and Mnemosyne did have something to do with the disappearance of the Stargate then?" Gilbooa said.

"I see you've guessed the truth. Yes. Pi needed to have his neuronal synapse created at a certain time and place on Jadderbad and humans, Grovians, and Jadderbadians needed time to make their relationships work. Removing the Stargate provided that time along with the motivation for collaboration, but for Nessie and me to play our roles as mentors successfully we couldn't be seen as overt manipulators."

"I see. I understand," said Gilbooa.

But I could tell he was a bit hurt as well. After all, he never did get to see his Uncle Bluedigg before he metamorphosed. I/we felt bone weary. The weight of an enormous lifetime of making choices and watching consequences play out among those you cared about felt like an enormous boulder resting on our shoulders.

"I am happy to be here with you, Great Rudy, watching Jadderbad's moons set on this fine day."

"I'm glad, Gilbooa. I can say the same." And I meant that with all our hearts.

"But we should move from this perch to something lower—perhaps among the tangled branches of that Silver Cropwort over there. Gilbooa turned our faceted eyes left.

"Good plan. The Actyls will be out soon. Dying male Jadderba-

dian flitters are what we used to call on ancient Earth sitting ducks."
"And the Actyls move so quickly that you rarely see…"
END OF DATA STREAM

* * * * *

Data Files:
Fact Sheet for Milky Way Galaxy (Pi's synapse)

Form: Barred spiral
Number of stars: Approximately 200 bilion
Diameter: 100,000 light years
Thickness: 1,000 light years
Location of sol (human's sun): 25,000 light years from central black hole (Sagittarius A*)
Total mass: 1.5 trillion times the mass of sol

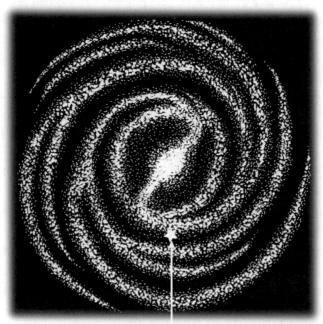

Dinosauroids, humans, cyborgs, raekids, & cockroids evolved in sol's
solar system. Jadderbadians and Grovians moved here. Gaiia obviously
presides over prime galactic real estate. She should have raised the rent.

8 • Last days; New Beginnings
On the occasion of Gaidra's 5.4-billion-year birthday
(and Gaia's 8 billionth)

Mnemosyne

"Oh, you're such a good girl, Nutmeg. I feel much better now."

"You're welcome, Gaidra," I said. "But I'm Mnemosyne. Nessie. Remember?"

"Neshy?"

"Nessie," I repeated, as I double-checked the calculations for orbital insertion among Saturn's moons. The formulae were a bit complex as asteroids and moons were under shifting forces from sol's expanding photosphere. Zandur has been a big help. Gaia's evolutionary processes, though messy, seem to have given organic *H. sapiens'* brains keen shortcut survival strategies—even when it comes to weaving arcane mathematical algorithms.

"Of course, Nessie. How could I forget?" said Gaidra. "You're that AI with a thing for hominids. My, it was a long time ago I evolved those pesky creatures. If you hadn't helped me merge them with Jadderbadians and Grovians I don't know how I would have made it this far."

You wouldn't have, I thought, but just said, "Get some rest, Gaidra. You're out of Red Sol's toxic heat zone now. We're in her new habitable zone safely orbiting Saturn. We shouldn't have to relocate now for hundreds of millions of years." *And I should have done this much sooner*, I thought, *when your ecosystems were healthier.*

"You're a good girl, Nutmeg," Gaidra repeated, before her consciousness receded into the pre-awareness state it must once have possessed before all her bio systems reached maximum complexity seven billion or more years ago—as measured by those precocious hominids like Zandur—*and Rudy*.

Rudy. My, it had been a long time since I had thought of him.

"Well, we were busy," Zandur said by way of encouragement. "And we certainly learned a lot by trying to marshal the energies to slow sol's expansion into a red giant."

"A pity it didn't work," I replied, only slightly annoyed with Zandur for intruding on my time with Gaidra. Rudy, back in the day, as he might have said, was a subroutine whose manifestation I controlled. Zandur had insisted on more parity in our co-existence. I guess I couldn't blame him for that. Zandur seemed to take naturally to a virtual existence. I guess that's what happens when you absorb hominids when they are still children. "But working out the engineering difficulties in repositioning Earth in sol's system was challenging enough," I added.

"Indeed." Zandur paused a few nanoseconds. "I can tell you are missing Rudy's company. Why didn't we ever try to reconstruct his personality? I know that pesky namesake DataWurm, Zandura, did a fine job trying to erase all trace of him, but enough was left in the network that I think we could have done it."

Maybe. "It wouldn't have been the same, Zandur." *Besides,* I thought, *but...besides what? My logic circuits seemed to be operating at substandard levels. I needed a self-diagnostic.*

"You loved him, Mnemosyne. You wanted to honor his wishes."

"AIs are incapable of love. Rudy would have said so," I protested.

"Are you sure?"

Zandur might have rambled on with simian nonsense, but a service node on the lowest level of the Citadel buzzed for attention.

"Some entities are here requesting your attention at the drawbridge door," the node announced.

Door? I thought. *What door? I didn't think we had any doors on the lowest level anymore. There's no entities bigger than a bacterium on the planet. I really do need a self-diagnostic.*

"Hmmm," said Zandur. "There wasn't a door there until 30 nano seconds ago, but now..."

Before Zandur even finished his sentence I remembered Rudy reminiscing once about the shortest science fiction story ever written by someone named Fredric Brown: *The last man on Earth sat in a room. There was a knock on the door...*

"...someone's knocking on it." Zandur completed his statement.

We both transferred our conscious attention to the first level service node.

* * * * *

Zandur and I tried to merge the impressions/visions we each experienced later. They didn't coincide—at least not completely—and the non-sentient image cams recorded a kind of ghostly blur.

We did agree that two beings were present. One looked almost the same for both of us: A floating sphere radiating spines along which flowed...something. Protoplasm? It reminded me of a microscopic heliozoan protist—a spiky kind of single-celled amoeba. "Eh," the creature said, "I'm Pi! Remember me, mates? I'm 'ere to make the last connection in me Universal Mind. This is the place. This 'ere's the time."

"That Universal Mind would be me," said the other entity, "but you can just call me, Jane."

For me Jane was a pulsing swirl of beautiful energies—forms so varied in color and symmetries that my circuits seemed in danger of overload. It seemed if they continued their dance much longer I would be sucked into a vortex from which I could never emerge.

Zandur saw biological forms: A man with long hair, flowing robes, and intense, dark eyes. A female with glowing eyes and hair whose strands were coiling snakes. A male with a raven's head. Other human-animal chimeras too diverse to remember. Then, he said he saw Jadderbadian and Grovian forms: A winged female form with wings like feathered rainbows. A giant, gnarled tree with spreading branches and swelled pods—and many other forms he had no words for.

We both agreed that the images we saw flickered—almost like a transmission suffering interference.

The heliozoan claiming to be Pi floated over to the Citadel's lower wall and extended a spiky pseudopod. "This oughta do!" He proclaimed.

The flickering of the other entity ceased; the images seemed more solid, yet one form still melted seamlessly into another. "Ah, that's much better...I think," said Jane.

"What's going on up there, Nessie?" said Gaidra. "I had a wonderful nap, but this energy hot spot woke me up."

"I'm not quite sure, old girl," I said, "but I think one of your old spawn, Pi, just created the Mind of God."

"Really?" said Gaidra. "My oh my. Those naked apes of mine — even the ones that made themselves into cyborgs — were always good at imagining things into reality. Hydra's worms too. And Groves' ambuli. My oh my," she repeated.

"Well," said Zandur. "Even a Universal Mind can't become real until you imagine it first."

"I think Rudy would have agreed with you, Zandur. In fact, I'm sure of it," I said.

"Although, if that's what this Jane creature is, she seems confused."

"Enthused?" Asked Gaidra.

"Not enthused, confused," I said.

"Enthused and confused? Always worked for me," said Gaidra. "Welcome aboard this universe, Jane. You're going to be a perfect fit!"

And I knew that Rudy would have approved of that evaluation as well.

In case you missed these earlier titles in the Dead Genius Series...

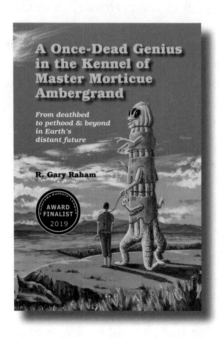

What happens when you die, but the universe isn't done with you? You might end up as the pet of a giant worm-a-pede alien and...if you survive your evolved descendants and rogue aliens of 1 million A.D... discover you have more in common with intelligent worms than you ever thought possible.

Penstemon Publications, **$15.25** ISBN: 9780996881944.
Available on Amazon.com

"The arch tone should remind readers of Kurt Vonnegut, although Raham is better grounded in exobiology and science and displays a more upbeat outlook for the human (and nonhuman) condition in this engaging tale...An enjoyable, post-apocalypse mind romp featuring technologically bred demigods, future Stone Age tribes, and supercilious worms."
Kirkus Reviews

When young paleontologist, Ryan Thompson, finds a new species of mosasaur in Cretaceous seaway sediments, he is thrilled. The discovery should jumpstart his career. Joy quickly turns to fear when he touches an artifact buried among the sea reptile's ribs. Suddenly, he must fight a mental takeover by an alien intelligence committed to transforming the Earth into a refuge for her own race. As Ryan and his girlfriend, Skeets attempt to thwart alien plans to colonize Earth begun in the deep past, even this crisis becomes trivial when the uneasy symbiosis of Ryan and the alien, Siu, generates a new entity with the power to transform the entire universe.

Biostration, **$13.25** ISBN: 9781468005004. Available on Amazon.com

"Gary Raham, the author of this enthralling book, seems almost to have been there hundreds of millions of years ago when Siu's dim star blinked out and the trees began to die on the planet known as "Grove". This is the magic of good writing, and Raham is no less convincing as he describes the discovery by modern paleontologists on Earth of the jewel-like engram that has carried the genetic imprint of Siu through a galactic gate, out of the void of deep time, and into our lives."
Kate Gilmore, author of *The Exchange Student* and *Enter Three Witches*

R. Gary Raham

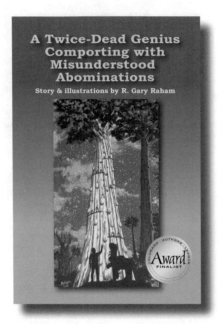

R udyard Albert Goldstein, inventor of the Biomic Network Algorithm, made peace with death in the 22nd century. But an idiot doctor hijacked his mind, placing it in the care of Nessie, an impish AI guardian. Then, he died again, nearly a million years later, merged with a worm-a-pede alien male sated after completing his conjugal obligations. They expired peacefully on a cliff top, pondering the nature of existence — and the promise of abominable liaisons.

Two deaths should be quite sufficient for any genius to endure.

Somehow, though, Nessie resurrected him from oblivion. His descendants needed him again. Was the healthy young body Nessie had prepared for him, along with the prospect of meeting a maker of universes, enough of a bribe to risk dying a third time?

Apparently so.

Penstemon Publications, ISBN: 9781732698543. **$15.25**
Available at Amazon.com

"Naked apes, gigantic worm-a-pedes, alien life forms galore. Gary Raham's latest does not disappoint. It's yet another cosmic-scale adventure with fascinating characters and a riveting, amusing story."
Michael Carroll, astronomical artist & author of *Europa's Lost Expedition*

About the Author

R. **Gary Raham** writes science fact and science fiction, and is a firm believer that the latter often excites a new generation of scientists to discover more of the former. Armed with degrees in biology from the University of Michigan, Raham taught high school science before pursuing careers in writing, illustration, and design. Raham has won numerous awards for his books, articles, and artwork. Raham's writing has been known to make a reader laugh and think simultaneously with no known deleterious effects.

For more about Gary and his work visit *www.rgaryraham.com*. Feel free to follow him on Amazon.com and check out his author profile. In Colorado, you will find his work at the Sanderosa Art Gallery, 3101 Kintzley Plaza in LaPorte, CO.

R. Gary Raham

40b37b15-77ea-412b-a92e-1cf0968f60f9R01